Lionel Hudson was born in Manly, NSW, in ... career in journalism with the Sydney *Sun*. Durin... War he flew with the RAF in the Middle East and Burma until he was captured by the Japanese in 1944 and imprisoned in Rangoon for five months. After his release he resumed his career in journalism, working as a war correspondent in Japan and South-East Asia and then as a foreign correspondent based in Singapore for AAP-Reuter; he later became AAP's desk editor in New York. He has been a television news executive and a producer of wildlife documentaries for television, and has written two books, *Dingoes Don't Bark* and *The Rats of Rangoon*. He now lives with his wife Audrey at Newport Beach. Lionel was a close friend of Mary Marlowe for thirty years.

Books by the same author

Kangaroos in King's Land
The Ghost Girl
The Women Who Wait
Gypsy Royal, Adventuress
An Unofficial Rose
Said the Spider
A Child by Proxy
Psalmist of the Dawn
Island Calm
Gaiety Blue

That Fragile Hour

An Autobiography

Mary Marlowe

Foreword by
Lionel Hudson

ANGUS
& ROBERTSON
PUBLISHERS

The publishers thank the Mitchell Library, State Library of New South Wales, for their permission to use the bulk of the material in this book. They would also like to thank the following: the John Fairfax Group for their permission to use extracts from the *Sun*'s 'Dorothy Dix' column; Paul Brickhill for providing the photograph of himself; and Mrs Alan Reid for providing the photograph of her late husband.

Every effort has been made to trace and acknowledge the owners of copyright material in this book. The publishers would be pleased to hear from anyone who can provide them with further information on this material.

ANGUS & ROBERTSON PUBLISHERS

First published in 1990 by Angus & Robertson Publishers
Unit 4, Eden Park, 31 Waterloo Road, North Ryde, NSW, Australia 2113,
and 16 Golden Square, London W1R 4BN, United Kingdom

Copyright © The State Library of New South Wales and
Lionel Hudson 1990

National Library of Australia
Cataloguing-in-Publication data:

Marlowe, Mary, 1884-1962.
That fragile hour.

ISBN 0 207 16593 9.

1. Marlowe, Mary, 1884-1962. 2. Actors —
Australia — Biography. 3. Actresses —
Australia — Biography. 4. Authors,
Australian — 20th century — Biography.
I. Title

792.0924

Typeset in Baskerville by Midland Typesetters, Maryborough, Victoria
Printed by Griffin Press, South Australia

Contents

Mary Marlowe when she returned to Sydney in 1912.

'So live, so love, so use that fragile hour . . .'

ROBERT LOUIS STEVENSON

Foreword by Lionel Hudson

'Enigmatic Mary', I often called her on those occasions when she retreated into silence but her quiet brown eyes invariably smiled away my taunt. We were close for thirty years. She was my constant confidante but it was a one-way affair. When she died in 1962 there was much I did not know about her absorbing past.

Twenty-five years later, this surprising autobiography turned up out of the blue and tells all. Well, not quite all.

I had the general picture of how this Aussie battler of the first half of the century had filled her 'fragile hour': leading lady on the stages of three continents playing farce, comedy and drama, including Shakespeare; author of ten romantic novels and many short stories, all published; a nurse in England during the First World War; a working journalist in Australia, interviewing for her newspaper and for newfangled radio most of the theatrical personalities of her time.

Many old troupers like to live in the past where they can still hear the applause. Not Mary. She was more than just coy about her stage career. She was tantalizingly tight-lipped. 'I had more tenacity than talent,' was her throwaway line. Mary Marlowe was her stage name. Not until I ferreted out her death certificate a few months ago did I discover that she was christened Marguerite Mary Shanahan and that her maternal grandfather had been a premier of Victoria three times.

Now, there is nothing surprising about a stage-struck teenager from a middle-class Roman Catholic family feeling obliged to take a stage name in Melbourne at the turn of the century. What will always intrigue me is that she persisted in burying completely for fifty years, even from her intimate friends, the name of the family she had loved so much.

Her age—another secret. It was her prerogative, of course, if she wanted to keep it to herself. I fully accepted that until I was faced with editing this book and needed to know how old she was at different points in the narrative. Her writing was bare of clues on the question of her age. It would seem that by the time she had decided to tell her life story it had become second nature for her to hold back every possible clue which would enable anybody to calculate her age. This made it difficult for me to work out when things happened. (Sorry, Mary, but your secret is out. You were born in 1884.) For the sake of the story, I have included some of the pertinent dates (in square brackets). The footnotes are also mine.

Also, I have dug out the first article she ever wrote for a newspaper. It was a few years after she had gone on the stage at the age of sixteen in defiance of her shocked family. Her piece in the Melbourne *Argus* opened with: 'Little girl who would go on the stage! Are you sensitive and shy? Then you have much to endure before you can break open the magic gates of stageland.'

She mentions in her autobiography how she sold up the family dining room furniture in the station homestead near Albury to raise her passage money to London in 1910 to try her luck on the stage there. 'Both of my parents had died,' she told me once. 'I ripped up the large oil portraits of members of my family, relics of more prosperous days, and sold the gold frames. The ancestors didn't mind, being dead, but I was very much alive and determined to see the world.'

No wonder she grew up to be a tough lady—gentle, but tough. As a brash youth I once asked Miss Marlowe why she had never married. She just brushed me off with her usual smile and looked through and beyond me. I never asked again.

In this autobiography Mary tells how she poured out her love story to the Russian ballerina, Anna Pavlova, as they talked in her dressing room in a Sydney theatre after a rehearsal. 'She was the first and only one I ever told until I began these reminiscences,' she writes. A sepia photograph of Pavlova on her toes always hung in Mary's bedroom at Newport.

It was from this book, too, that I learned her heart ached for six sons. What I did know was that she settled for a bunch of striving copyboys—the lowest, but liveliest, form of life in the swarm that is a newspaper office. Among them were eager youngsters named Peter Finch, Alan Reid, Paul Brickhill, Charles Nicol and D'Arcy Niland.

Somehow I, too, caught Miss Marlowe's eye as a copyboy on the *Sun*, Sydney's afternoon newspaper. I was a wide-eyed fourteen year-old, having left school impulsively halfway through the year and taken the first job I could get to be independent of my stepfather. The year was 1930 and the Big Depression was tightening its grip. Copyboys were paid a pound a week to race back to the *Sun*'s splendid new pink-faced building in Elizabeth Street with news reports written in longhand by jaunty journalists covering State Parliament, the courts, the wool sales, the stock exchange and the waterfront. We had no union but we had dreams and Mary Marlowe.

The glittering prize that egged us on, however, was to become a cadet reporter. Vacancies were rare. Competition among us for recognition was fierce. The trouble was that we lacked a window in which to show our wares. Naturally, we took our problem to the motherly Miss Marlowe. What transpired is described in her story. It is enough to say here that she became the power behind the *Sun Junior*, in which a long list of scribes won their first by-lines. Alan Reid would become Canberra's most powerful political journalist, publishing books such as *The Power Struggle*, *The Gorton Experiment* and *The Whitlam Venture*; Paul Brickhill would write a number of bestsellers, the most famous being *Reach for the Sky* and *The Dam Busters*; D'Arcy Niland would become a prolific writer, his most popular publications being *The Shiralee*, *The Ballad of the Fat Bushranger and Other Stories* and *Call Me When the Cross Turns Over*; Charles Nicol would be the army's director of public relations for twenty-three years; and I also wrote a couple of books— *Dingoes Don't Bark* and *The Rats of Rangoon*.

Before long Miss Marlowe had shepherded me into the pictorial library which was her domain. From that day I had a caring mother at the office as well as at home. She fed me good books—Joseph Conrad, Robert Louis Stevenson, H. V. Morton, Axel Munthe and O. Henry. She gently coaxed me into using words just for the fun of it. She lent me my tram fare home on occasions after I had been cleaned out at the penny tossing game of odd-man-takes-it.

Her telephone was always available to her boys for important calls. Alan Reid raced upstairs to use it to tell his mother that he had a cadetship. I was on the same instrument a few months later to announce mine. Peter Finch missed out. He was full of envy towards us. The intuitive former actress, however, was steering him in another direction.

Once we became cadet journalists we, naturally, were too important to borrow meat pie and tram fare money from Miss Marlowe. Yet Mary was still sought out. She always found time to listen to our stories of how some subeditor had 'butchered' our immaculate copy and about our reporting triumphs, however minor. She was not one to volunteer advice. Mostly she just cocked her head and registered reaction. Now and again she would sail down to the office of the editor, Frank Ashton, and have a few quiet words to say in defence, or praise, of one of her boys. She was never one to back away from a fight.

'My plea is for youth,' she once wrote when there was despair on the economic front. 'For the young men and boys who are being crowded out of industry because women are crowding in. We hear a lot about women's rights. What about men's rights?'

In the theatre she was the friend of the indefatigable stagehands while in the newspaper world she revered the unpretentious printers as well as being surrogate mother to the copyboys. Her heroes were people like the low-key leader, Ben Chifley, and modest Arthur Mailey, whom she met and adored after he had finished bowling googlies and turned full time to sporting cartoons. (Mary religiously checked the spelling in the 'balloons' for him before he inked them in.)

Even among the hard-nosed inhabitants of a newspaper office the old actress could still turn heads. The Three Musketeers would have fought over some of her flamboyant hats and there was real panache in the way she tossed her feather boa around her neck as she bustled along the corridor.

It has always astonished me how much we shared. We were an odd couple. Being ten years older than my own mother she was ancient in my young eyes from the day we met. Yet she was so spirited. She was always urging her boys to 'give it a go'.

Once she took me to *The Mikado* at the Theatre Royal, resplendent in her long, black velvet cape, amethyst earrings and aquamarine necklet. We went backstage after the performance and chatted with the cast. Her eyes shone. Her heart had never left the theatre. The older stagehands knew her. She had stayed at the same hotels and eaten at the same tables with some of them. The theatre was her real stamping ground.

Mary once told me that the excitement of being part of a great newspaper, helping to fill a public need every day, riding a rocking horse on the giant calliope of the news, was like being at the circus. The whip was always cracking. The band was always playing. The lights were always flaring. Actors and journalists, she would say, live and work on their nerves. The power to rise instantly to an emergency is peculiar to both—if they are good actors and good journalists. That image never left me.

We were hard newsmen, trained to extract stories from reluctant victims, but not one of my generation of journalists knew that in 1912 our Mary was brought back from England to play Kate Rudd in the original stage production of Steele Rudd's *On Our Selection* with Bert Bailey as Dad. Her past was a closed book.

What the critics said about her performance is not in her autobiography, but her scrapbook, which I have just opened for the first time, reveals she certainly had as much talent as tenacity. The *Sydney Morning Herald* critic thought 'Miss Mary Marlowe gave an excellent rendering of Kate Rudd'. The Brisbane critic 'Kildare' said: 'In Mary Marlowe playgoers have made a charming and accomplished acquaintance. As Kate Rudd she showed what is possible to a true artist.' Only the *Bulletin* critic found fault. He thought the leading lady's reading of the part threw her right out of the atmosphere of the piece.

She was applauded by critics overseas too, but there is not a mention of this in her book. In 1913 she played the lead in *The Glad Eye*, billed as 'the greatest farcical success ever known'. The tour took her across Canada from coast to coast. Said the Montreal *Gazette*: 'Of the four women, Mary Marlowe as Lucienne Bocard, the clever wife who revenges herself by ordering expensive clothing, is probably the best and this success may to some extent be due to the wonderful garments she wears.' The *Ottawa Evening Journal* wrote: 'Mary Marlowe was the pick of the cast and looks fascinating in her wonderful dresses.'

Mary was a modest woman.

All of Mary's ten books have a strong stage flavour. The first three were written and published in London and New York but in the 1920s and 1930s she was a phenomenon in Australia: a woman writing about contemporary life in Sydney, the Blue Mountains, the South Pacific and Lord Howe Island.

One well-kept secret about Mary is that she was Australia's Dorothy Dix for many years in the *Sun* churning out thousands of caring replies to letters from the lovelorn.

Forty years ago, Enigmatic Mary broke her silence. She quietly wrote her own true life story, calling it *That Fragile Hour*. Then she did an astonishing thing. Without a word to a soul she buried the autobiography under a pile of published manuscripts, theatre programmes, photographic albums, newspaper clipping books and personal papers in a large wicker theatre trunk stored in the laundry of her house in Newport Beach, Sydney.

Before she died in 1962 she asked me to be sure that all the material in the trunk was handed over to the Mitchell Library. There was no mention of the hidden life story, by far her most important work. It lay there in the library archives for another twenty-five years until, thank goodness, a perceptive researcher recognized its literary merit. I have just read it for the first time.

Mary describes *That Fragile Hour* as the 'escapades of an actress-journalist who wanted to be a heroine, embracing encounters with the famous and the infamous'. She must have finished it in 1947 and then immediately embarked on another manuscript, *Not For Sale*, which deals with the next stage of her life when she built her cottage overlooking the Pacific at Newport. 'Romance is incurable,' she wrote in the introduction to *Not For Sale*. 'This is a sentimental jaunt through the private lives of pleasant people and strange creatures. It embraces the adventures of a young airman in search of his love story.' The young airman was me.

This manuscript I knew about. Not long before she died she gave me the original. 'You or Jane, when she grows up,' she said, 'may feel like finishing this one day.' Jane is my daughter.

I confess I merely flicked through the pages before stowing it away and getting on with my life. What I read embarrassed me.

When *That Fragile Hour* came to light I dug out *Not For Sale* and really read it for the first time. Now, with the permission of the State Library of New South Wales, to whom Mary left all copyrights in her will, I have taken the liberty of welding the two books together.

Part One

The magnificent adventure

My mother made the vulgar blunder of bringing me into the world in a hotel, thereby dedicating me to a life of vagabondage. It is a well known legend that the child born in a hotel will never have a home. My mother had only herself to blame for what followed.

While she was committing this physical solecism on a hot morning at St Kilda in Melbourne, to the sound of the languorous waves of Port Phillip Bay, a bearded man paced the beach in front of the hotel. He was in the act of becoming my father and nervous about it. Could he have lived to see me grow up he would have been even more mentally disturbed.

On the eighteenth day of February the future was fluid. Would his Maggie pull through? It had been hot up on the station, Warbreccan. Had he allowed her to stay up there too long? With the first baby coming a woman could not be too careful. His lovely Maggie, plump and practical, healthy and gay and courageous! But you never knew with women.

The clock over the hotel porch struck seven. In a tone of higher pitch I gave my first cry. At that moment the Bearded Man's foot struck against a shell. He picked it up. It was a lustrous double shell, delicately fluted and perfect in spite of the fierce scouring of the ocean, a small nautilus. It had served its turn and was vacant. The builder had gone back to the great wash.

The Bearded Man slipped the shell into his pocket and went back to the hotel. There might be news.

My Unmarried and Emotional Aunt, flying down the staircase like the Winged Victory suddenly shocked into life, met him at the door.

'She is born!' she cried.

The Bearded Man rushed past her, bounded up the stairs and into the bridal chamber where his young wife, wan and wondering on the double bed, held me in the crook of her arm. He knelt down close to her. If there is a time in a man's life when he acknowledges God it is the moment when he sees his first child.

'Our daughter, Maggie!'

They told me afterwards that his voice broke. I was too occupied with my own affairs at the moment to notice him. I was hungry.

The nurse came and took me away. I cried because it was cosy in the crook of my mother's arm and the world beyond the bed was too big and there was too much sunshine in my eyes. The doctor said: 'Bandage them, nurse. I think we're going to have trouble with her eyes.'

When they were not looking I dragged down the bandage because I wanted to explore that yellow world, that sunshine. So they had trouble with my eyes. After that they were never quite normal. I grew up with the eyes of a visionary.

The Bearded Man was partly to blame. He was a romantic. When my mother died I read his love letters. My mother made me a vagabond but my father made me a visionary.

As he knelt by his wife's bed that sunshiny morning he drew the shell from his pocket.

'I found this on the beach the exact moment little daughter was born. Shall we tell her she was born in a shell?'

My mother smiled. 'A better story than the one about the stork, John.'

So my absurd father had the shell mounted in silver and, in his neat handwriting, he inscribed my name and the date inside. He stayed beside his Maggie to watch me grow a little but the station wanted his attention and at last he had to go back.

When I was eleven months old—it was too hot for me on the station in January—my father drove one day to the nearest township, which was Albury. It was twenty miles from the homestead. On the way home, the heat being oppressive, the sun like molten lead, he threw his hat on the seat of the buggy. In a little while he was unconscious. The horse found its own way home.

My father had suffered a sunstroke. In three days he was dead.

Once a year until I was twelve, each birthday my mother took the nautilus shell out of its wrappings of violet velvet and cotton-wool and showed it to me. She told me my father had found me on the beach in the shell.

A little girl who lived at the end of our street always came to our place to spend my birthday with me and make a party of it. One day I showed her the shell and told her the story.

'Don't be silly,' she said. 'My mother has a book in her chest of drawers with pictures in it and they show you how you are born. I know where she hides the key. Some day when she's out I'll show it to you.'

'No thank you,' I replied coldly. 'You might have been born like the book shows but I was born in a shell. My father wouldn't have had it mounted in silver—real silver—and put the date inside if that wasn't true.'

The other day, from the rail of a ship mid-Pacific, between the dressing bell and the dinner gong, decks deserted, sun slipping over the horizon, I threw the shell into the ocean. Perhaps some other child might have the chance to be born with the eyes of a visionary.

In this world of jazz and jangle my father's gift is the only thing that has helped me through.

A silver spoon and a scandal

They said I was born with a silver spoon in my mouth. My grandparents had acquired so much of my native soil before I turned up it was reported I was the richest baby in Australia. The silver spoon turned out to be electroplated. The land was devastated with droughts and bushfires. Bank smashes did the rest.

My grandparents were pioneers. On my father's side they were plain pastoralists; on my mother's they were also pastoralists but with political ambitions. They arrived in Australia, sturdy young people with a country to conquer. They bought land and more land when land was a nominal price. When bad times came one tract of land was mortgaged to save the other. Grandfather John O'Shanassy went into Parliament and was three times premier of Victoria [in 1857, 1858–59 and 1861–63]. He fought for Federation, immigration, free trade, and for breaking up large holdings. When a schoolmaster secured the nomination for his seat, after he had given thirty-two years of selfless devotion to his adopted country, Grandfather John curled up and died. He had been knighted for his efforts but that did not cut much ice with him.

Grandmother, more tenacious and less temperamental, survived him for years, queening it in the family mansion, Tara Hall in Camberwell, which had by this time grown into an estate with all the ingredients of ancestral halls. It stood in grounds so vast that you would never guess there were neighbours. The nearest lived a mile away across the paddocks. Today it is a boarding house, surrounded by other smaller boarding houses and nobody remembers whose dreams materialized it.

While Grandfather John was making a nuisance of himself in Parliament or standing under a tree* in the Botanical Gardens,

* The Separation Tree, under which a large gathering celebrated the break from New South Wales in 1850 when Port Phillip district became Victoria, a separate colony. The tree has a plaque marking the event.

holding meetings of the populace and to celebrate the separating of Victoria from New South Wales (New South Wales had been playing up), Grandmother Margaret kept a draper's shop in the city of Melbourne. She sold tapes and stay-laces across the counter in Elizabeth Street and cut and sewed fine gowns for the prosperous wives of the early grocers and hotel keepers. She took time off to bear fourteen children and rear six of them. One set of twins died at birth. A second set brought my mother into the picture.

Though I was not born until long after Grandfather was dead, we were brought up in our family to regard his memory as just a little less glorious than that of Jesus Christ. Every branch of our family accepted the theory that Australia could not have been developed without Grandfather John. Now I know it was Grandmother Margaret and her kind who laid its firm foundations. In her day there were no feminists. There were merely women who helped their men and didn't brag about it.

When Grandmother Margaret died [in 1887] our family commenced to crack up. I am her only granddaughter. I am rather proud of Lady Margaret O'Shanassy . . .

My mother, a young and pretty widow with a flirtatious manner and not much money—things were not panning out quite as had been expected—left the ancestral halls when I was three. She took a cottage in a quiet suburb. It had an enchanted garden. You could lock the side gate and keep the fairies in and the tramps out.

The fairies lived in the belladonna lilies, also called deadly nightshade. I wanted to squeeze the juice of the flowers into my eyes to make the pupils large and lustrous. Our cook said that everybody on the stage did that to make their eyes look beautiful. It was a dreadful temptation, except that you went blind after using it for a while.

One side of our garden had a fence covered with creepers. This was the place to sit and watch the Flemington races. When mother put on her best frock—elephant's breath cashmere embroidered with steel daisies—and set off for the races, she had a devil of a journey before she reached the Members' Enclosure. I merely had to climb the fence. Mother sat in state because my Only Surviving Uncle, Matthew O'Shanassy, was a Victoria Racing Club steward.

When I was six we let the cottage to an actress. She was the loveliest of the fairies grown to life size. She was a pantomime boy. The Pantomime Boy was in possession of our home for three months. Sometimes we went to call on her and I played chasings with her son in the garden. It was difficult to accept her as a mother when

I had seen her in tights with a spangled top, but she was wholly adorable in either role. The afternoon that I saw her being Dick Whittington I made up my mind to be an actress.

When we returned to our home every drawer in my mother's dressing table was spattered with a strange green powder. Our cook knew what that was: arsenic. She said all actresses had to use it for their complexions. I rubbed a little on my cheeks when nobody was looking but it had no noticeable effect on mine.

Two important creatures came into my life soon after the Pantomime Boy left us: the Governess and the Dog.

The Governess, Sarah Blessing, was a young thing, fresh from Ireland with a voice like a harp. They told her I was a fair terror but she conquered me in six minutes. The voice did it. She did not strap me when I was bad. She locked me in the bedroom which we shared. Left to myself on these occasions, I took out all the drawers and shelves I could reach and tipped the contents into a heap in the middle of the room. I never cried or hammered on the door— I was a silent worker. When the Governess came back we would both be satisfied that we had done our worst. Sitting on the edge of the bed I would watch her put things in order, a sorrowful expression in her Irish eyes. Soon she thought up the mean trick of putting me on my honour. An Irishwoman would!

I loved her better than my mother after a while and for a strange reason. A fat, elderly woman used to visit our house regularly. She was poorish and my mother was soft-hearted. She was jealous of the Governess and she told lies about her to my mother. That was the first tragedy of my life. If, at the age of seven, I had known how to murder, the fat, elderly woman would have been done for. Through her I learned to hate.

My Only Surviving Uncle, the racing steward, was not the sort of steward I had first imagined him to be. He didn't wear a white coat, nor did he serve drinks like the steward on the *Edina*, which took me and my mother to Portarlington for our summer holiday each year. No, indeed! My uncle wore a top hat and pale grey clothes and he swung a pair of field-glasses across his shoulders on race days, and he called bookmakers by their first names. Once I was taken to see the Melbourne Cup and one of his horses won a race; after that I knew my uncle was a most important person.

I was fond of my Only Surviving Uncle. He looked a lot better than the dead ones we had on the walls and better, to my thinking, than the life-size of Sir John that Her Ladyship had insisted on having painted when she took him abroad on a world tour.

When he was happy my Only Surviving Uncle was a merry man.

He had a waxed moustache and a twinkle in his blue eyes. That was when he wasn't walking round the table after his Sunday dinners with us. He did this, so my mother said, because he had something on his mind. She was patient but the habit irritated me because I liked to lie on my tummy on the dining room floor on Sunday afternoons, reading Shakespeare from the two large green and red volumes which had belonged to my father and had his name on the flyleaf. Mother preferred *How To Tell Your Fortune By Cards*.

She used the knowledge derived from this work on a jocular middle-aged gentleman in the evenings. I remember him best for his large gold watch-chain, his large gold signet ring, and the black cigar which he smoked all the time I was present. Perhaps he put it out when I went to bed. When he came it was early-to-bed for me.

I used to get out of bed and stand, a-shiver, in the dark doorway of the bedroom and listen while Mother read his fortune. A dark woman was to marry him and he would live happily ever after. He must beware of a fair woman.

Our cook said he was going to be my father. Mother called him 'Your Uncle Bob'. He brought me chocolates with coconut. I disliked coconut. He didn't go down well with me.

He did not become my father. He forgot to beware of the fair woman. One day my mother heard that he had married her.

A month later Mother dressed me in my best frock and made herself elegant too, and we went to call on the fair woman. Your Uncle Bob had come into three stepdaughters as well as a wife. They played with me in the field at the back while Mother took tea and cracknels in the drawing room. I loved them at sight and would have gone back to more play had I had my way, but I did not see them again. Ours was a visit paid to prove how pleased we were that Your Uncle Bob had married the pretty lady with the ripe corn hair and the ripe cherry cheeks. Your Uncle Bob presented me with one volume from an expensive set of Byron's poetical works at parting. He evidently considered me a smart child for seven.

When we were out of earshot Mother said to herself or to me (I couldn't make out which): 'Her father keeps a low hotel in Bourke Street. I don't know if she served in the bar, but she looks like it.'

The following Sunday my Only Surviving Uncle talked seriously to Mother. He explained in language even I could understand that he had thought she was going to marry a rich man. Now he could no longer keep the truth from her. She was broke. The cottage was mortgaged. My mother cried and I lost my place in *As You Like It*. There was a ghastly gap in the conversation and then my Only Surviving Uncle launched his bolt.

'I will make you an allowance and keep this home going if you will consent to share it with your sister, Grace. She will arrive next month. Remember your child. She must be educated.'

My mother cried a little longer and then she consented.

Grace, my Unmarried and Emotional Aunt, arrived from abroad. She had expected to be installed in Tara Hall and our cottage seemed to her a bit cramped after the Continent. She and my mother did not get on. My memory of Aunt Grace was that she always put in an hour at the piano after breakfast—always Beethoven. After a while Mother lost the pretty uptilt of her mouth. Her gay and independent spirit was quenched. The joy went out of her life. She did not thrive under charity and she gave up flirting because she no longer had the heart for it.

My Only Surviving Uncle walked round the table in silence for a few more Sundays and then he turned up to dinner with the Dog. He was a collie pup and a beauty. Lad was his name.

'I want a good home for him,' he explained. 'His folks are going to the country and already they have more dogs than they can manage.'

That night from my darkened room with the door open I heard the sisters talk in tragic voices of the family scandal. My Only Surviving Uncle had taken a wife. He could not introduce her to his sisters because, the voices trailed into a whisper, because she had been an actress!

'I suppose he *is* married to her,' said my mother, 'but it does seem queer that he has never said a word to us about it.'

'Not at all,' retorted Aunt Grace. 'He must be ashamed of himself. Fancy marrying an actress!'

'He's not too ashamed to bring us one of her dogs.'

Aunt Grace had a quaver in her voice: 'He must be taking her and the dogs up to the station. Now we shall never see him.'

'Let us write and ask him to bring her here to tea before they go.' My mother was the radical of her family.

'Don't be absurd, Maggie! Whatever would Marianne say?' Marianne was my Married Aunt. Her husband was a Member of Parliament, Nicholas FitzGerald, MLC, who with his brother Edward had established Castlemaine Breweries.

My mother remembered herself. She thought of Grandfather. There had not been anything like an actress in the family before.

In the days that followed I learned to love the Dog so much that I could not be sure whether I loved him or my mother or the Governess most. Lad was everybody's friend and invariably jolly. He knew nothing of the rancour that had entered our home.

Make-believe

Gladys, my little playmate at the other end of the street, had a garden with a mulberry tree, and a glassed-in back verandah which made the best of all possible theatres on a wet Saturday. We always played pantomimes there. Sunshine or hail, every Saturday morning at 7.30 Gladys came to my place or I went to hers. A play a day was our routine. There were breaks for meals that absurd grown-ups insisted upon but otherwise the play went on from around nine in the morning until eight at night, when Gladys was called for by their cook-general or the Governess came for me.

If weather permitted we played in the garden at my place and finished up in Mother's bedroom, taking turns—not altogether impartial and just ones—at watching the effect we were creating on a mythical audience by playing in front of the wardrobe mirror.

We had a stage wardrobe. Gladys's star piece was a yellow and red gypsy skirt which she had worn at a school break-up, and a little black velvet cap jingling with coins. She always wore them, even if I had to be the gypsy. Possession is nine points . . . ah, but I had a pink corded evening dress which had been my mother's trailing glory in the days of her prosperity, and a cotton-backed satin train the colour of sovereigns set on fire.

Gladys had a devilish knack of making me the villainess. She liked the part of the cheeky but honest girl of the village and though I might start out as a perfectly legitimate heroine she always managed to find some flaw in my character or reputation before the day was half over and I had to spend the rest of it trying to justify myself in the eyes of the world. We made it up as we went along, so anything was liable to happen at any moment.

Gladys's young uncle went on the stage unexpectedly. It made her very superior with me. I heard at second-hand of his triumphs, and once he took her to call on an actor and his wife. It didn't seem fair that she could brag about all this to me when we had an actress in our family and I wasn't supposed to know and daren't mention it.

As we grew older we decided to be actresses all the time, not just on Saturdays. I chose to be Hilda Spong and Irene Vanbrugh and was married to Lewis Waller. Sometimes as Hilda Spong I was very delicate but I always got myself back to health by twenty-mile walks in the country.

Now and again, instead of acting, we played Christmas parties. This meant that we gathered up the toiletries and other treasures of our families, laid them out on the bed and solemnly gave them to all our friends and relations. The best were kept for ourselves, and these were received with effusive expressions of delight and kisses.

Normally, even at that age, I never kissed anybody. I particularly hated kissing women. It was like bumping into a piece of cold pudding. But I knew that actresses did kiss, so I sacrificed my own feelings to be in character. I still hate kissing women. It gives me the cold shivers, and I usually go straight to the running water and wash my face afterwards.

One day Sarah Blessing told me bits of *The Prisoner of Zenda* when she was brushing my hair. I begged her to let me read it, but she was shaken with doubts. There was that Antoinette de Mauban—she did some dreadful things. 'But maybe you wouldn't understand the bad bits, Precious.' I promised I wouldn't. I read it one wet Sunday afternoon, lying on my tummy on my mother's hard box sofa. When I had finished, I slipped to my knees beside the sofa, clasped my hands and shut my eyes and prayed.

'Dear God,' I pleaded, 'let me be an authoress. That's what I really want to be in life.'

Mary Anderson's memoirs came into our house one day. The Blessing had brought it from the Book Lovers' Library. I declared lessons off until I had consumed it twice. By now the Blessing was entirely under my thumb. She had started by ruling me through love and I took a leaf out of her own book.

The next Christmas, when the Member of Parliament gave me ten shillings as his annual gift to a good girl, I lodged an order with the bookshop to send to England for the Mary Anderson book. From then onwards I became a sore trial to my family. Little did the beautiful American actress, whose life had been above suspicion until now, know on what paths she set my youthful feet by her fascinating tale of her stage experiences.

To emulate Mary Anderson first I abandoned corsets. Then I

practised the Delsarte system of physical culture until all the chairs in our house had wobbly backs and scratched rungs. I did voice culture in the bathroom where one could get the best resonance. I memorized fourteen Shakespearean heroines and haunted the cheap book arcades until I found ancient copies of *Evadne* and Bulwer Lytton's *The Lady of Lyons*. I moved with the statuesque solemnity of Galatea-come-to-life for at least one month, and for three Sundays in succession Sarah Blessing was forced to come with me to our local cemetery and help in the search for a tomb with a grating through which I could speak to get the proper sepulchral tones of the entombed Juliet. Mary Anderson had found such a tomb useful in Sacramento, but we could not find one in our cemetery.

By now I was obsessed with Shakespeare. When the original plays were too abstruse for me I resorted to Lamb's *Tales*. I memorized the parts of the easier heroines. Just about that time Sarah Blessing came to the painful conclusion that I was too much for her.

Sending me to school might keep me out of mischief. They tried it, a private school called 'L'Avenir'. The first day I linked up with Stella, one of the older girls, and we found we had mutual interests. We both wanted to go on the stage.

We were well matched. She was practical, I was inspirational. She liked playing the men and only asked for Beatrice in *Much Ado* on account of a natural vanity about her spun gold hair. We spent our holidays in each other's homes and we had *The Prisoner of Zenda* and *The Sign of the Cross* ready by midwinter. For a season of two consecutive nights we performed them in our dining room without an audience.

One year my mother decided to take me to Geelong for the holidays. There I wrote a melodrama. In it the villain strangled the villainess and then tried to make her stand on her feet. He made love to her corpse and cried in a hoarse voice: 'Women like you do not love. You fawn, you flatter, you fascinate. It is your trade. Stand on your feet, Lotus Manners, and take my kisses on your lips like a woman.' The play was not produced. Stella shied at it.

We added *The Devil's Disciple* to our repertoire in the final year at school. Stella was a marvellous Dick Dudgeon—so dashing. I fancy I was suitably demure as Judith Anderson.

One day I met an actor. The wheel was turning. I could scarcely muster the courage to raise my eyes to his. He was shining with glory, wreathed in luminous fame. He said what we all say to the outsider: 'The stage is very hard work.'

Then—oh miracle!—all of a sudden we had our very own actress with us. One day we were supposed never to have heard of her, the next a letter went to my Only Surviving Uncle inviting him to bring her to our home to stay. Two days after that she arrived with him.

My Only Surviving Uncle was in danger of not surviving much longer. The family doctor had warned him against worry and, knowing about the actress, had written to each of his three sisters advising them of the danger. Plainly, he thought something had better be done with the family pride.

She came. She had wheat-coloured hair and eyes like the sea, quiet in sunlight. Her skin was like rose petals. She was tall and built buoyantly. Her maiden name was Blanche Bray. She was a niece of the great actor G. V. Brooke. The moment I set eyes on her I adored her. So did the Dog.

'What are you going to do when you grow up?' she asked politely, patting the Dog.

'I'm going to be an actress.'

'Are you?' Her voice rose on a note of dreamy surprise. 'I'll help you,' she added impulsively and stopped patting the Dog to put her arm around my shoulder. The family was listening and, catching her breath, she said no more.

From that moment she felt at home with me as well as with the Dog. We shared her caresses. Once I heard her say under her breath but as though the thought had been surprised into words: 'How did you ever come to belong to them?'

She did not know about the Bearded Man.

The ancestral halls were reopened to receive my Only Surviving Uncle and his actress wife after they had been with us for a month. She asked me to stay with them and I had a glorious time, hearing about actors and actresses, meeting some who had retired, poring over portraits of Nellie Stewart, who, it turned out, had been a girlhood friend of our actress and was still her good comrade.

When I returned to my own drab home my mother said, 'For God's sake put your hat on straight. You look like a common larrikin when you wear it at that angle. I won't stand any nonsense like that.' My Actress Aunt, of course, had worn hers at 'that angle'.

Every Sunday we went to Tara Hall. My Actress Aunt fed us, cooking all meals herself as she disliked servants, and put up with us. We seldom left before dusk. The family felt the fascination of being back in the grand old home that had been in shrouds for years.

The centre of attention in this 1906 photograph is Mary Marlowe's 'Actress Aunt', Blanche
O'Shanassy, who smoothed the way for the stage-struck sixteen-year-old to get her first role in
Melbourne. Aunt Blanche was a close friend of the star of the show, Nellie Stewart.

By the following Christmas my Only Surviving Uncle was out of his mind. Hiding his actress from his family had been too much for him. At first he was gently puerile, then violent. He attacked his wife, being the person he best loved, as is the way with maniacs. The end was not long in coming. A clot of blood on the brain and it was soon over.

The ancestral halls were closed again. My Actress Aunt moved to a quiet suburb by the sea. The family paid her half-yearly visits but I went to see her every second Sunday. After supper we would clear the furniture from the centre of the sitting room and I would act Shakespeare to a limited audience, sometimes adorned by a retired circus manager or the sister of an actress.

The day came when I met Nellie Stewart. I was dizzy with the ecstasy of it. Nothing could keep me from the stage now.

My mother refused to believe that her ewe lamb was growing up. She loved me dearly but regarded me as a complete fool. I was not even trusted to buy a yard of tape. She bought me a sewing machine on time-payment so I should learn to make my own clothes and at this I certainly proved hopelessly incompetent. We had a maid and I was not encouraged to interfere with her duties but might, at my pleasure, indulge in a little light dusting. I preferred cleaning the windows and grates but I was not congratulated on the result. It was considered very humorous of me to try.

Straitened finances caused me to be taken away from school before it was desirable, but my singing lessons went on as they cost nothing but the fares to town twice a week. The Viennese singing teacher, in direct contrast to my own people, considered me intelligent and gave me all her business commissions to execute, including banking, buying, and general research. Several times she prised me from the bosom of my family to stay with her in her country home at Mitcham. We had singing orgies every evening.

My pigtail goes up

An American star came to our city with his own company and a repertoire of dramatic plays. This was the actor-manager Julius Knight, making his second visit to Australia.* Unknown to my mother, I wrote to him, asking for an interview and mentioning that I had an infinite capacity for taking pains. If he didn't know that meant I was a genius then he was a fool. Maybe he had doubts, but he replied and named a time for the interview.

When I showed the letter to my mother she almost swooned. Her child was growing up indeed! She said she would come with me. That, on the face of it, was desirable.

Stella let down a frock for me and showed me how to turn up my hair in a plait to look grown-up. She rehearsed me in the most suitable scenes from Shakespeare where I could give myself cues. All that night before the appointment I lay in bed shivering under the eiderdown.

We were in good time for the interview at the theatre. My mother sent in her card and a letter with it. In a few minutes the star's personal manager came out to the vestibule where we were waiting. He had the letter in his hand. He regretted that the star could not see me and, as the company was already so large, there would not be the slightest hope of my joining it in any capacity. The stage was a heartbreaking life, he said, and he advised me to give up the idea of it.

I did not argue. It was plain that my mother's letter had done it. Later I found out she had written to Julius Knight asking him not to encourage her daughter, who was much too young to go on the stage. I left the theatre in silence and my mother said she

---

* Julius Knight (1863–1941) first came to Australia in 1891. Mary was thirteen when he made his second visit in 1897. For the next twenty years he was the most popular leading man on the Australian stage.

would have no more nonsense. Tears streamed down my cheeks all the way home in the tram but I couldn't be bothered doing anything about it.

I tried to forgive my mother but I couldn't. I couldn't sleep and food made me sick. I had lost hope. Only the Dog understood me. Then I knew I loved the Dog better than my mother.

Night after night I prayed on my knees that we would lose all the money in our family so that I could go on the stage and earn a living for all of us. I prayed to my father who had left me his Shakespeare and the nautilus shell to show he knew I was no ordinary child. I asked him to fix things for me since there was no living being that understood me except the Dog.

My father played trumps. He fixed it. We lost our money and we had to live from quarter-day to quarter-day on the charity of my uncle by marriage, the Member of Parliament. Father was so quick about it I was afraid the family would find out what I had done.

One day, things being muddled in the housekeeping, my mother actually said: 'Well, I suppose you will have it your own way and go on the stage now.'

My Actress Aunt wrote to Nellie Stewart. She was due back in Australia for a season of costume drama and announcements were appearing in the newspapers that she would revive 'Sweet Nell of Old Drury'. Nellie's reply, in a sprawly personal letter, was an instruction to send me to her stage manager and tell him she wanted me put on with the extra ladies. My Actress Aunt cut out that piece and I took it to the stage manager. He wasn't impressed; there was no signature. He handed back the scrap.

'Sorry. We have everyone we require for our plays.'

Quarter-day came and the cheque from the Member of Parliament. Generous as a gift, it was meagre for three people to live on (we still had my Unmarried and Emotional Aunt living with us). There was a wide gap between the cheque and the monthly bills.

'Can't we take a grocer's shop?' I pleaded. 'Anything is better than charity. Look what Grandmother did. Let us try.'

My mother's spirit was broken and so was her health. We still kept the servant but we had only one real meal a day, and that was mainly rice and cold meat. I was rationed to asking Gladys from the end of the street to tea only once a week now and when she came there was so little to offer I was ashamed.

When Nellie Stewart reached our city my Actress Aunt made a personal effort.

'Of course the child can walk on,' said Nellie emphatically.

Some friends had taken my mother to the country for a month. For that whole month I earned seventeen and sixpence a week. With the first salary I bought a much-needed pair of shoes for twelve and six and squandered half-a-crown on an autograph book. It was to be a lasting souvenir of my stage career. (The autograph book was burned under the copper a while ago when I was getting rid of the evidence of two or three of my past lives.)

I become an actress

The Member of Parliament sat on one side of our dining room table and I sat on the other. In agitation I plaited the fringe of the oriental table cloth. My mother and my Emotional Aunt listened while we battled—an inflexible old man faced an obstinate child. This stage business had got to stop. Where did it lead, anyway?

'I will pay for a course of typewriting and shorthand,' said the Member of Parliament. 'You must understand that you have no money of your own at all now and never will have. You must earn your own living.'

There was only my determination to help me win over the three people set against me. But like grandfather, the former premier, I knew my own mind and steered on an even keel to get my own way.

'That wouldn't be any use,' I said, as quietly as my emotions would allow. 'I am going to be an actress.'

The Member of Parliament did things with his tongue and his teeth that sounded awful.

'If you want to help me, why not pay for a course of ballet lessons? I need them.'

The Member of Parliament talked for an hour. He was the head of the family now and our mainstay, and the two women listened in horror to my replies. By the end of the hour he had told me everything bad about the stage, true or legendary. We didn't argue; he had a clear run. When he was through I said: 'A quarter's ballet lessons would be a great help, but I can manage alone.'

With a fine dramatic gesture the Member of Parliament threw up his hands: 'You'll be sorry.'

He walked out in a rage. Next day his cheque came for a quarter's ballet lessons. From then on he changed his method of attack. Until the day before he died, he seldom saw me without saying in a half-teasing, half-serious way: 'Everybody getting married but me!'

His three guineas went to Jennie Brennan, who was later to become one of Melbourne's foremost dancing teachers. I sprained my ankle at the first lesson but she walked me up and down until something happened that made it possible for me to go on practising. For three agonizing months I tried to learn how to be a ballet dancer. Had I started at five instead of fifteen the results might have been better.

When my mother was a schoolgirl the teacher locked her in a second storey room for disobedience. Mother jumped out of the window. Maybe she was thinking of that before I was born. I have been jumping out of windows all my life.

Jennie Brennan did not recommend me for the pantomime as I had hoped she might. The Member of Parliament didn't come good with another quarter's lessons as I had thought he might. Once more I was at a dead end.

An old actor lived in our street. He had been with Sir Henry Irving in his youth. He taught for a living. My mother won a small sweep—in Tattersalls, I think—and to make up for her past severity she took me to him for a quarter's lessons.

His name was James Cathcart. He had been out of things for years and must have been nigh to eighty when he started on me.

He taught me to tear a passion to tatters on his coconut matting as mad Constance, to make the rafters ring with Portia's denunciation, and to shriek and shudder over the mandrakes torn out of the earth in Juliet's potion scene. The dictionary says they shriek when plucked. Under Mr Cathcart's tuition I think I could out-shriek them comfortably. I had sobbed my way through Juliet's death agonies when he lifted me from the frayed matting. He told me I was the legitimate successor to Ellen Terry and he kissed me gently on the cheek.

I did not ask my mother for a second quarter because I thought at the next lesson he might kiss me on the mouth and then I would be sure to have a baby. With flaming cheeks I reached home and locked myself into my bedroom. I read *The Rape of Lucrece* from beginning to end. Stella had said it left nothing to the imagination. It left everything to mine.

That old actor, close on eighty, put the fear of God—and worse, of man—into me. I said to myself, 'It's going to be difficult with men.'

Suddenly I found myself on the stage.

I had answered every advertisement for extra ladies and interviewed every manager who would see me, all with the same arid result. Julius Grant was the very last. His gentle disposition prompted him to let me down lightly, seeing that he had no possible, probable or potential use for me. Little did he know that some day I would return to Australia as his leading lady!

A friend—Norah Delaney—decided she would like to be an actress. Her family was not horrified. She used to recite in public and was teaching elocution in a small way. Her father had once been able to do John Gunn a good turn. John—of Meynell and Gunn—said to him one day: 'Let Norah start with us. We'll look after her. If she has a girlfriend she can bring her along for companionship.'

Norah had a girlfriend. One day I was without hope, the next I was rehearsing.

In the first play, *A Royal Divorce*, I walked on in a short, royal blue, satin dress with a bit of string lace round the neck, and a peasant's rustic hat. They told me to be merry in the revel scene and the stage manager said: 'Sing up. Don't be frightened of the sound of your voice. I expect we can stand it.'

For my partner in merrymaking I had an old actor, too decrepit to secure engagements except as utility man. When the time came for us to make conversation (not to be heard by the audience) in the Tuileries Gardens he would say: 'Jolly life, this play acting!'

Every single night and twice on Saturdays.

I was too young and enthusiastic to see the pathos. He was past seventy, I was not yet seventeen. His round, histrionic face remained in my memory.

Because I could keep on the note, and partly because of Norah, the management took me to Sydney. From penury and despair I was exalted to two pounds ten a week and my name on the programme. Norah and I took a double room in Hunter Street in a most respectable boarding house.

Between our first matinee and the evening show, the stage manager told me I could go on as the Lady Passenger in *The Silver King*, a melodrama by Henry Arthur Jones and Henry Herman. I was to think of things to say and do that would keep the audience laughing for two and a half minutes, while they changed the scene at the back.

For this great chance I was practising putting on comic make-up in our bedroom when screams started in the room below—awful screams. Smothered in comic greasepaint, hair screwed into a comic knot, a false nose just beginning to 'take' on my own inconspicuous one, dressed in a comic dressing-gown, a very comic shawl and a desperately comic hat, back-to-front on my comic knob, I rushed downstairs and into the room where the screams came from.

A woman was squirming on the floor. She was in terrible agony. When she saw me she uttered the same sort of anguished cry I had used for an early Christian being fed to the lions in our dining-room version of *The Sign of the Cross*.

'Get a doctor!' screamed the woman. 'Send for my husband! Oh, get a doctor! For God's sake! Quick!'

'I'll be as quick as I can,' I said, and ran downstairs to the dining room beneath, where the boarding house keeper and a woman friend were standing, gazing up at the ceiling, listening to the screams.

'I won't go to her,' said the boarding house keeper. 'She had no right to let it go so far. She ought to have gone to hospital days ago. She knew the child might be born any minute.'

'A child!' I was thunderstruck. 'Is she having a child? And you won't go to her? Then I must.'

I ran to the door. The woman realized the absurdity of it—me, tackling a birth in my comic make-up. She came after me, pushed me from the door and went up to the screaming woman. I went back to my struggles with the Lady Passenger.

It was a nice child when it was born, no worse for its mother having seen the Lady Passenger immediately before its birth. What effect I may have had on its after-life we shall never know but the prenatal shock was borne stoically.

At our second matinee Norah and I missed our entrance. We were making underclothing by hand in the green room of the Palace Theatre beneath the stalls and we did not hear the call. We were sure we would be dismissed and sent back to Melbourne. We went down to the theatre early that evening to apologize to John Gunn, but when we saw him we could scarcely speak. John Gunn heard our halting story and smiled wryly. He said what was meant to be kind but it was worse than being sent back to Melbourne. He said: 'I don't suppose you were missed.'

It was true. Amongst twenty extra ladies in the Court of the Empress Josephine two absentees would scarcely make a gap.

We had a shrewd and weatherbeaten set of chorus girls. When Norah was given parts to understudy they determined to take the conceit out of us—I had no parts to understudy but I was Norah's friend.

Norah had talent, some amateur experience and a beautiful speaking voice. She was a friend of the management and she was headed for parts. It became known that she was to join a second and smaller company under the same managers in a few weeks, so the chorus girls decided that she had better learn a few things about life in the chorus before she left us for ever.

Our boarding house rang with the dramatic lines of Norah's first understudy role, Marie Louise, in *A Royal Divorce*. Setting high value on tone, she reached an effective climax with the line: 'I have his infant son and for him you were childless!'

Norah had just reached this peak of royal insolence when her private rehearsal was brought to an abrupt close by the boarder in the next room complaining to the landlady that she could not stay in a house where two women brazenly discussed their relations with the same man.

The management decided to take me to Adelaide. Perth and New Zealand were to follow. We had a half day in Melbourne passing through.

My mother met me. We had lunch at the Hopetoun Tea Rooms in the Block. She came to the wharf to see the ship away. It was impossible for her to believe that her only child was really launched on the open sea of life in a craft of her own. Such a rocky craft! Finances demanded it now. I had to go.

Youth is cruel. I was glad to go. I saw my dreams unfolding. My nautilus was opening. Inside was Fairy Hope. My mother could only see Gnome Despair.

With my eyes closed, I can still see her white strained face, looking up at me as the ship drew away from the wharf. You who would be kind to me, don't ever come to see my ship sail away.

The tide took me.

On tour

Norah and I spent our first night in Adelaide in a cheap hotel. We had small salaries and little practice in managing them.

We were seated at the proprietress's table. The black-faced end man of the vaudeville show at the rival theatre sat on her right hand and the fat soubrette from the same troupe on her left. We were further down. The comedian was Harry Shine, once a pantomime star but then on his last legs. He made lewd jokes. I froze. He lifted his forefinger and wagged it at me, saying, 'She don't like me!'

Our bedroom was over the bar. Traffic went past until the small hours. At seven we rose and went out into the city to find another lodging. Then we returned to pay our bill and collect our luggage.

The proprietress sent for us. She sat up in bed in a red velvet tea-gown and blinked. 'What's the matter, girls? Too noisy?'

We owned up.

She asked where we were going and laughed hoarsely when we told her. 'My brother-in-law keeps that place. You won't be any better off. That'll be half a crown each for the night and I'll throw in the dinner.'

As we arranged our toilet things in the new hotel Norah startled me by saying: 'I wouldn't like to marry Julius Knight, would you?'

He was the star of our company and a matinée idol. A bachelor, as far as we knew. I did not think of marrying heroes at any time.

'Rubbish!' said Norah. 'A woman never meets a man without speculating whether or not she'd like to marry him.'

At the close of the Adelaide season Norah went to her new company. With the Julius Knight Company I went to the West.

On the ship I did not lift my head from the pillow except to ask the third officer whether he intended to stay *all* night in the cabin talking to the chorus girls. 'Because,' I said acidly between vomits, 'if you do, I shall have to make other arrangements.' He tiptoed into the night.

Just as we berthed at Fremantle the ballet mistress decided I had straight legs and could dance the boy in the ballet in the Tuileries Gardens that night. She was too sick to do it herself. The men of the company came upon me in the scene-dock an hour later, practising the steps. I asked one to bend down so I could swing my leg over his head as the boy in the ballet had to. He obliged.

The wardrobe mistress tossed me a pair of sky-blue breeches, a satin Directoire coat and a three-cornered hat and told me to make the best of them. I had a leg up that night—I was in the ballet.

Now I was thrown to the wolves—no mate to exchange confidences with, no one to share things. The woman star asked her dresser to keep an eye on me. She was a kind, timid Englishwoman. We stayed at the same boarding house but she was devoted to her work at the theatre and I saw little of her.

I began to understand the chorus girls. Their sense of values, their code, their ethics were not mine, mainly because of our different upbringing, but their hearts were all right. We had narrowed to a chorus of twelve. We were the chronics and in the big towns we took on extras.

One of the girls was called Alice. She was the Madonna type, a gentle creature with a weak mouth, brooding brown eyes, soft red lips, a serene brow, deep bosom and slumber in her voice. She suggested the mother with her foot upon the cradle. Alice was engaged to a stage electrician who had gone to England to make money and improve his position so that the home he could offer might be desirable. He adored his Alice. She read to us pieces from his weekly letters from London. Amiable to everyone, incapable of saying no, Alice, the Madonna, entertained us all in our spare hours as we gathered round the croupy pianos in our cheap boarding houses to join in the chorus of her songs.

Crissie was the ballet mistress, dark and poignant as an Italian, blade-sharp in wits as an Irishwoman. In her youth men had gone mad over her. By this time she was a trifle ragged, with an Irish nose for trouble. She had married the worst of her suitors and had three beautiful children. Her mother had the children and when Crissie had money she sent it home for their maintenance. It was not always that she could find enough new friends to keep her supplied with the red wine she required to be happy; then she bought it for herself and there was no money to send home. She had a great heart but no head for wine.

Crissie has passed on to the Eternal Vineyards. My head was stronger than hers but I wish I had the same all-enduring kindness.

Red-haired Vivienne was the conventional, the smug member of the troupe. Her husband travelled with us. He had a fine bass voice for the stage and a better one for the bathroom.

Magda, an English dancer 'from the Gaiety', had come to us to dance and die. She was a chocolate-box blonde with the courage of the tuberculosis sufferer. Crissie shared her bed with Magda because the sick girl could not bear to be alone. 'Poor lonely kid,' said Crissie. 'I suppose it's dangerous but I can't hurt her feelings. She won't be with us long.' She was right. In a year Magda was dead. She jested until she lost consciousness. She took friendship, and deeper devotion, where it offered. She took a man from his drab wife. The wife had a tight mouth; the ghostlike Magda was always laughing. Perhaps he went back to his duty when Magda died. There was no open break.

Blanche, plump and passé, had played parts once and could not forget it. On the stage she smiled, in the dressing room she sighed. When somebody in the stage crowd had to say, 'Here comes the prince!' they gave the line to Blanche and she made a part of it. She was happy if she had her name on the programme.

Coralie, a stage door keeper's daughter, was seeking somebody to finance her in a hotel. She believed there was more money in beer than ballet, more satisfaction.

Among such flamboyant beauties I was inconspicuous but I could make a musical noise when I opened my mouth.

Alone

Our company had been in Perth ten days when I returned, a little late, to my boarding house after visiting friends at Cottesloe. I rushed through tea and took the tram to the theatre. As soon as I arrived the young treasurer told me there was a telegram for me at the boarding house. He told me to go back for it. Intuitively I knew what it contained.

The ingenue's mother came with me. Until then we had not been much more than bowing acquaintances but she and her daughter were staying at the same boarding house. It was a theatrical house and had been recommended to me by my Actress Aunt.

We went back by tram. A little boy watched me with absorbing interest while tears rolled down my cheeks. I did wish he would not watch.

'There's a telegram for you,' said the landlady. 'It came after you left for the theatre.'

It had been delivered long before, long enough for the whole company to know about it, but the landlady was a coward.

'Give it to me,' I said.

'I haven't got it. A minister of your church has it and he wants to see you.'

The ingenue's mother led me to the minister's house, two blocks away. She had her arm through mine but I was not conscious of anything near me. The minister said he had sad news. I said: 'Give me the telegram, please.'

All of which seems a roundabout way to tell a girl—a girl who knew the moment she had heard the word 'telegram' at the theatre— that her mother was dead.

Her heart had failed suddenly. Perhaps it failed because it broke. Mothers' hearts are like that. Her only child was out in the world, unafraid of the world because she was unaware of the world.

A strong swimmer and a lover of the sea, she had gone down

to the sea one hot summer afternoon to bathe. A heart attack came upon her. She fell in the water close to the shore and knocked her temple upon a rock. The sinister blue bruise was visible in the morning when they found her, face downwards in the water two feet from the shore. The seizure had taken her at the very moment she went in to bathe. Consciousness never returning, she was drowned.

Next night I played a peasant in a pink frock and a sunbonnet and as I was coming from the stage where we had all been so gay, oh, so gay . . . the leading lady, Maud Jeffries, called me into her dressing room and gave me a small pot of her own special make-up. She said: 'How sweet you look, my child.'

When I had gone she told her dresser, who eventually told me, it was the most she could say; words of sympathy had frozen on her lips. 'They came but I could not speak them,' she said. In those days I worshipped leading ladies so it meant a good deal to me for her to say just what she did.

A girl in the company who was playing parts asked me to share her dressing room that I might be quiet. The chorus girls were so noisy.

'Better to have the gaiety about me,' I argued. 'And the girls would be hurt if I left them.'

The girls went on being gay but kind. Had I gone into that other dressing room they would have hated me.

When I returned to Melbourne my home had to be broken up. The Member of Parliament offered to keep a roof over me if I would consent to look after my Unmarried and Emotional Aunt for the remainder of her life. He was not a great psychologist. They made him Speaker so that he wouldn't speak, but I was always too much for him. I had learned the lesson that the bread of charity is indigestible. There was the hideous example of my mother's broken spirit.

Everything had to go—even the Dog. The night before he went my Emotional Aunt tied a rope round his neck and led him through the front gate and a little way down the road for a rehearsal. In the morning she was to take him to the train. A home had been found for him in the country with some friends of my Actress Aunt.

When I saw the rope round Laddie's neck I threw myself on the bed and bit into the pillows. That night I had hysterics. My Emotional Aunt heard me from her bedroom. She made me a cup of tea and persuaded me to spend an hour or two in her bed. She told me that anyone who had borne up through the trial of losing a mother was completely idiotic to go on like that about a dog. She had never heard about the camel and the ultimate straw.

When the Dog came in in the morning he knew what was in the wind. I took his quivering head in my hands and looked long into his questioning eyes. So nobody should hear, I whispered: 'You've got to understand. I can't help this. It isn't my fault. You've got to understand.'

He understood. You don't need to tell a dog what is in your mind. Through the feverish struggles for freedom, through all the ardent hopes of my extreme youth he had been my confidant and friend. It was he that had comforted me in moments of despair. No more poignant agony has come to me, before or after, than that I went through in giving him up. I needed him so much.

When he walked out of my room, tail down and white ruffle close to the floor, walked out to meet the rope and the train and the strangers in his new home, he left a gap in my life that I have never dared to fill with another dog.

Three months later Lad was dead. They told me it was a bone in his throat. He went wild and chased sheep. Perhaps it was the bone. I would not dare to probe deeper.

If I had to part with a dog again I would poison him, in mortal fear that in the parting he might have to suffer one hundredth part of the misery that was mine in giving up my Lad.

The secret child

At the magnificent salary of two pound ten a week I was re-engaged to go to New Zealand.

We started in the south, which was unusual, and worked up north to Auckland. In Dunedin, the Madonna-like Alice was taken to hospital and her small parts were given to me. My first speaking role on the real stage was the governess in *A Royal Divorce* and I had some original ideas. I raised some laughs where laughs had never been known before and the stage manager had an argument with me about it.

'Even a governess in the court of Napoleon might have a sense of humour,' I suggested.

'Perhaps she was only an understudy,' he replied witheringly. But he allowed me to go my way.

There were some more small parts, all of which I attacked with enthusiasm and tried to make original. Everybody was amused, and Julius Knight, the star, would sometimes watch me from the wings. When I came off he'd say, 'You're doing fine, Mary.'

I would have been completely happy if the Dog had not died while we were in Auckland.

In our second week there Alice rejoined us and took back her parts. She came to stay at the same boarding house where Crissie, Vivie and her husband, Magda, Alec Wilson the young treasurer, a flautist we called Bio and I were entrenched.

Alec was my special friend. He had no woman to care for him and I sewed his buttons on. One day he came to me with his pants held out in his hands. 'For God's sake, Mary, don't use girls' buttons on my drawers,' he said.

In Auckland he bought a pair of dress trousers second-hand. He needed to present an elegant appearance in the foyer each evening while he counted the house in. They were many inches too long but I would tackle anything so I turned them up. Alec was young and poor and couldn't afford to be fussy. I was dying to be of service to the world.

The opportunity came in Auckland.

We played there for a month. Sydney was to follow. Three nights before our season closed Crissie came to my room at two in the morning and woke me up. She sat on the edge of the bed. She was trembling as though in rigor.

'I can't stand it another minute, Mary. I don't know what to do. I've been in the next room with Alice for the last three· hours. It can't be long now. She's moaning and writhing all the time. I went for the landlady but she won't come. I shall go mad if I stay there another moment alone.'

Sleepy and dazed, I sat up in bed. 'What's the matter?'

'Don't you know? Alice is having a baby. Any minute. Nothing ready. Just listen to her!'

Through the wall I now could hear moans. Dreadful moans. Alice. And only a few hours ago I had been on the stage with her.

'How can she be having a baby? She isn't married. Cris, you must be making a mistake.'

Crissie didn't waste words. 'A married man in Sydney is the father. Alice wrote to him, and he didn't answer. She thought she'd have time to get into a hospital in Sydney. Just listen to her!'

'I'll get up.' I felt I was choking. Things like this didn't happen. Not in the next room, surely? In books, perhaps. At home we didn't have books like that.

'Have you anything warm? And soft? There's nothing to wrap round the baby when it's born.'

The Member's wife had given me a frilly flannel dressing-jacket. I told Crissie I would rip the frills off and bring it in.

'All right.' She gave a troubled sigh. 'It's broken the tension coming in here for a few minutes. I'll get back. Just listen! Isn't it awful?'

The rising sound was like the howl of a wolf. Some animal in a trap.

'Wish we could get a doctor.'

'We must.' My limbs were shaking. 'If the men won't go out and find one, I will. Have you asked Arthur? Vivie is her friend.'

'I asked him first. He pulled Vivie back into their bedroom and said they weren't going to be mixed up in this. He locked the door. Magda doesn't want to be in it either. She feels too ill.'

'Alex will go.' He was a good sort, anyhow. 'Would some tea be any good?'

This awakened Crissie to my immaturity. 'You get the jacket ready,

Mary. Then, if you feel brave enough, go down to the kitchen and get the fire alight. It would help. We'll need hot water soon.' She went out and left me in the dark. My teeth were chattering with shock. My body was a-shiver.

I handed the jacket through the door of the next room to Crissie and then went down to the kitchen. On my way I passed the flautist going for the doctor. He had children of his own. When it came to the point he could not listen to the cries of the Madonna and not do something to help her.

The kitchen range was difficult. I had never tried to light a range before. After a struggle it consented to blaze but it seemed an eternity before the kettle boiled. I had just made the tea when the cook came on duty for the day. He was a foreigner. He had evidently heard what was happening upstairs because he looked at me as though I were dirt.

Crissie answered my timid knock when I arrived with the old japanned tray as dawn was breaking. She nodded towards the bed. 'The baby's born. Alice is all right now. You can come in. A girl.'

The red scrap of a thing was being bound round the middle and through the legs with a length of old sheeting by an elderly woman who was staying in the house. She was kinder than the landlady, who had resolutely refused to come to Crissie's assistance.

I turned to the young mother in the bed. Her Madonna eyes had a pleading look. In her sweet drone she said, 'Oh, Mary, what must you think of me!'

What I managed to say softened the agony in her eyes. For nine months this girl had carried her secret in her body, haunted by the fear of being found out and dismissed. I told her she had been brave, oh, so brave, Alice!

The strange woman called me to take a cup of sugared water and moisten the baby's lips. She taught me to dip my forefinger in the cup and brush it lightly across the baby's mouth. It was the child's first meal.

Trying to say to the little creature the things she might under-stand—in the reassuring tone one uses for puppies and frightened birds—I put my sugared finger to her mouth. I told Alice she was a wonderful baby, making light of the fact that her eyes were running sores like an old neglected dog.

In the crook of her arm at last, wrapped up in the Speaker's wife's dressing-jacket, Alice turned her brooding eyes on her child and told her she was a wonderful baby.

Crissie and I cleaned up the room. We burned horrible things under the laundry copper. It was a gruesome business.

The doctor was late. He said we had all done splendidly. Mother and child were doing well. We had left him nothing to do but feel the pulse.

Alice spent that first day worshipping her baby and planning how to dispose of her. She had ten pounds saved and a week's salary due—another three pounds. If she could get rid of the child she could still go to England and marry her electrician. He was sending money for her fare and this might reach her mother's home in Melbourne any day now. She told us her mother and father did not speak though they lived in the same house. It would not be fair to her mother, she argued, to arrive home with an unwanted child. Somebody must adopt her. She sketched out an advertisement for the local paper and Cris put it in for her.

The day we left for Sydney the doctor called for the third time. He asked Alice how much money she had. She told him thirteen pounds and her ticket to Sydney. He took six as his fee. If he heard of anybody who wanted to adopt a baby—a baby with sore eyes— he'd let her know.

Before we sailed there were two answers to her advertisement. Both were offers to adopt the child with a premium of twenty pounds. None of us had the money to help Alice dispose of her baby. We left her, still hoping a better proposition might turn up.

On that voyage, watching the waves, I made a promise to myself. 'One day I shall write a book and tell the truth about this. I will tell as many people as can be reached through a novel all those things my family were too cowardly to warn me about. It shall be as vivid as I can make the truth.'

Some years afterwards, I wrote the book, *An Unofficial Rose.* My family was shocked.

'There is something sinister in this,' said the Speaker's wife. Dear, dear! had she but known to what purpose her cosy dressing-jacket had been put! 'It's too bad of Mary to write about things she can't possibly understand.'

Not understand? It needs no imagination to hear the moans of that woman in her hour of labour or to brush again with my fingers the lips of her unwanted child.

We rehearsed for a new crop of plays in Sydney and then played Perth and Broken Hill. When we reached Melbourne the company was disbanded and I was out of work.

My first press notice

Friends put me up for a month. After that, nothing for it but to creep back into the Member of Parliament's home and be the poor relation. At breakfast each morning came the old jibe: 'Everybody getting married but me.'

There was no job in sight. The hoped-for envelope was never on the hall table. The miracle would not happen. By Christmas I had given in.

'We'll make a home for you if you'll look after your Aunt Grace.' The alternative? I chose it. St Vincent's Hospital—to be trained for nursing.

The Member of Parliament gave me ten pounds at Christmas. No restrictions. Maybe he meant it to pay for uniforms, but it was used to escape for a fortnight from being the poor relation. It stood for two weeks board and train fares to the mountains. At Healesville I would get country courage.

From tree ferns, from tall eucalypts—lie on your back if you would see the tops of them—I tried to draw resignation. Every day I walked the bush until exhausted. Once I lost my way, too hot to walk further. A man hailed me, an Englishman. He had a hut among the trees. It was papered with copies of the *Illustrated London News*. All was neat. He wore a thin white silk shirt and a grey hat, peppered with holes and the scars of bush brambles. I spent the afternoon in the hut. He made me tea. He did not want me to hurry away but the last bus left at six.

In his pipe-dreams this man saw London, and he told me what to look for if I had the luck to get there. His purpose in the dense bush was mysterious. I cannot forget the queer twist in his voice, nor his deep blue eyes with the lost expression of the recluse as he said: 'When we miss our way in the bush we follow the stars. Keep your eyes on the stars, little missie. Don't let the bush bother you. Look up and the sky will answer. Always look up.'

He came to the road with me. Stood, hat in hand, the ragged jags in his shirt showing his tanned skin beneath. He watched me climb up beside the bus driver. I waved until we turned the corner of that winding, red road.

The bus driver said then: 'He's batty, that fellow. Lives by himself up there in the scrub. You took a chance. When a chap lives alone you never know when he'll go off the handle.'

'He was kind, made me tea. Talked about his London. He isn't mad.'

The busman gave me an oblique glance. 'Oh, well, you know . . . Sometimes the bush sends them cuckoo.'

It was dark when we swung into Healesville. Thick gum forests grew up to the outskirts of the little timber village. Except for the cicadas the night was quiet. I went through the wicket gate of the small cottage where I had room and board. I looked up at the stars and they seemed brighter, bigger, nearer than ever before. There was a tearing ache in my side. Tomorrow I must go back to the city.

'If only something would save me from sick people,' I cried in my heart.

The evening meal was over. The landlady gave me strawberries and cream instead. Maybe she knew I was on a flying visit to fairyland.

In the morning two telegrams came for me. One was from my old stage manager: 'Come at once. Two weeks work. Join train in Melbourne for Bendigo and Ballarat. Wire if accept for train time.' The other was from Norah, urging me to rush this chance. She had supplied my mountain address and was going with the company to these places. Maybe the company would take us on again in Sydney.

Had the stars heard?

Nursing was off. It was only a laconic wire from the stage manager, but it was a spiritual message from the skies! Courage was up. I knew what I wanted. Life was jolly well going to give it to me. I had eleven pounds. One isn't a visionary for nothing.

In Ballarat I had my first press notice. Some brute of a critic said: 'Mary Marlowe was adequate in her part.' It looked good to me in print at the time. I knew I must be an actress since I had my name in the paper.

It was not even a speaking part but just one of those little super-extra parts that often stand out because of some special 'business' attached to them or because of some entrance or work with the star. Disguised as an aristocrat aged eighty, I walked down a long staircase with Julius Knight, while the whole company applauded us. I shook vigorously to indicate my age and my face was a mask of chalk and crimson lake.

When I saw that press notice I determined to risk my entire capital of eleven pounds and go to Sydney with the company. The fare was arranged on concession rates; it cost about two pounds. This left me nine to face the world. Then, as now, faith in my star sustained me more than food. Then I ate sausages; now I know the superior value of onions and boiled rice and the energy to be squeezed out of an orange.

In Sydney, my old governess, Sarah Blessing, met me at the railway station. She whisked me off to the YWCA. 'I'll feel safe about you if you stay here, childie,' she said.

The lady in charge explained that morning prayers must be attended at eight o'clock in the morning and that everybody was expected to be in by ten at night. Even as she spoke the atmosphere of the place ate like acid into my spirit. This was not for me.

'It couldn't be before midnight once I start work.'

Then the lady in charge knew it was not for me. She looked shocked and this expression deepened to horror when it was explained that the stage was the work indicated. We mutually agreed the sanctuary of the house would be lost on a vagrant like myself.

I guided Sarah Blessing to Garrett's Hotel—or was Wally Weeks the proprietor then? It smelt of beer and suggested friendship. Sarah had grave doubts. It would be all right, I assured her, because four of the married men of the company were staying there. There wasn't a wife between them but Sarah didn't know that. If you said 'a married man' to Sarah she took it for granted that meant a man complete with spouse. These men were safe. They were affectionate but manageable. Once I heard one say to the others, 'You mustn't say anything rotten before that girl. She's true blue.' Men are like that.

The proprietor gave me a back bedroom with a well window for thirty shillings a week. If funds had not run low, the atmosphere of Bohemia would have been splendid, but at the end of a fortnight I had to move on. Small casts, many imported members in the company, meant there was nothing for me.

A humble boarding house in a Paddington back street was the next place. Seventeen and six a week paid for a big bedroom with a lumpy bed and three pseudo-meals a day. There was much bread and some tomatoes. The grocer's boy who shared this frugal fare wanted me to be his girlfriend. He was polite but importunate. He offered humbugs but I feared to compromise myself by accepting gifts. In a fortnight it was time to move again.

A slip-bedroom in Phillip Street came after. Eight shillings a week for an oblong of space in the city's heart, and the economic problem to be faced of whether it was better to buy a pound of butter at a go for one shilling or two half pounds for sixpence-halfpenny. On a spirit stove you could cook eggs and sausages and these became my staple diet.

At the end of the first week a girl from Melbourne joined me and took another slip-bedroom. We pooled for food but she had an actor-uncle in a job and he took her to dinner in a basement of the Strand Arcade three times a week where you were served with a three-course meal for a shilling. Things were not equal. Her butter didn't need to cover so much bread. She could afford two eggs on Sundays.

Norah arrived in Sydney while we were still in Phillip Street on the sausage diet. She had a real part in a real company and three meals a day. I managed half a pound of mixed biscuits the day she came to tea. The grocer at the corner was kind; he put in four with twisted bits of pink icing on the top. They made a decent showing. Not much of the initial eleven pounds was left by now.

'Why don't you write and make money that way?' asked Norah.

I replied despondently: 'What's the good? Everything has been written before. You must know about things before you can write about them.'

"Well, the stage, for example?'

'I wrote an article about the stage. What it felt like to be an extra lady after a job . . . sitting in theatre passages . . . waiting to be picked up. It was a real heart article and it was true. I sent it to the *Argus* in Melbourne. Nothing happened.'

'Did you use a pen name?'

'Yes. "Silver Arrow".'

'It appeared in the *Argus* two weeks ago. I read it before I came to Sydney.'

I didn't believe it until the cheque for thirty shillings came at the end of the month. I bought a sixpenny pineapple to celebrate and paid the rent for a few more weeks.

Panic possessed me the night the landlady's brother took my young friend out to supper at Paris House. He gave her cheap champagne. It was nearly midnight when she came home. Did I give her what for! 'You'll have a baby if you go on like this.' The Horrible Warning was still heavy on my spirit. I couldn't forget Alice and her child.

We were both rescued from Phillip Street by a lovely lady with a spacious home up the Lane Cove River. She was a Swiss who

"EXTRA LADIES"

BY SILVER ARROW

Little girl, who would go on the stage! Are you sensitive and shy? Then you have much to endure before you can break open the magic gates to stageland.

Sometimes a girl, through great influence or rare good looks, is "placed" in the theatre, which means she is given a part at once, and is thus spared the drudgery and heart-breaks of working up from the ranks. But this is exceptional, and most of us begin as "extras".

A new company is about to open a season in your city, so you set out to offer yourself as a possible extra-lady, hoping, of course, and believing too, that once you are "on" it will be smooth sailing. The stage manager will note your interest and conscientious work. You will be given [a role to] understudy, taken on tour, and the rest will be easy and merely a matter of time.

You go to the theatre a day or two after the company arrives in town, and present your name to the doorkeeper to be taken in. He looks at you rather scornfully, perhaps a little amused, and tells you to wait in the passage, that the stage manager will be out presently.

Here and now, let me say a word for the doorkeeper. He is an ogre that can put impassable barriers between you and the stage precincts, that can make or mar your chances of interviewing the all-mighty managers. He can be very grumpy and disagreeable, but for the most part he is "an old dear", and will go out of his way to do a kind turn for a friend. My first move on coming to a new theatre is to cultivate him.

Well, you find yourself in a dark, narrow passage, containing one long bench, already fully occupied by a dozen other girls, bent on the same business as yourself. So you stand against the wall, and try to look uncon-cerned. Maybe, some kind soul about the theatre brings a chair for you, but this is rare. One does not look for polite-ness amongst stage people. You wait an hour, perhaps two. At first you feel a little nervous, thinking of what you will say. The girls eye you up and down, and you begin to be painfully conscious that your gloves do not quite fit or that something is wrong with your hair. You pat it surreptitiously, and pretend to take an interest in the call-board.

The girls chat amongst themselves, of past plays and companies, for they are mostly old-stagers. This makes you feel more out in the cold than ever. Often have I been grateful for the com-radeship of the theatre cat at times like these. By degrees your hands become moist with nervousness, your lips feel dry, your throat parched. If you ask a chance question or are spoken to, you find your voice has almost deserted you. Your eyes are half-closed with weari-ness, your hair has become disarranged, and you know that all trace of colour has left your cheeks; in fact, you feel a wreck.

I am not exaggerating. I have felt all this—not once, but many times, and vainly have I tried to analyse the fascination of the stage that makes such torture bearable. At last a door is banged. Somebody says, "Rehearsal over", and the members of the company stream out, talking merrily amongst themselves. They glance at you care-lessly as they pass, and you feel small; or they brush past, without noticing you in your corner, and you feel smaller still. You try to pick out the stage manager. My friend, the doorkeeper, sees your anxiety, and good-naturedly points him out to you. Rising quickly, you push forward, grateful, oh, so grateful, for the wave of colour that nervousness has sent flooding over your cheeks. You moisten your lips, and prepare an elaborate sentence. But, no! he is not your man yet. Into a miserable little office he has slipped, and you have some more minutes of anxious waiting to go through.

Finally, he comes, talking to his boy, and looking neither left nor right. It is a little habit of managers never to see you by any chance, if you are seeking an engagement. Falteringly you stake your claims to be taken on, walking beside him as you talk, that is if you want him to listen to you. He usually regrets that no people are wanted for the first piece of the season. If there is anything later, they will communicate with you. Leave your address. Good morning!

And that is the last you will hear of it.

If you are chosen and admitted to the sacred ground of the green-room, most likely it will be because you are "fine and big", and will fit into some frocks already made for a lady of large proportions; or you are just the right size for a "march girl", or for some equally useful, but not very flattering, reason.

And so you become an "extra lady".

The shy young actress, hiding behind a pen-name, bursts into print. This article, published in the Melbourne Argus on 16 March 1907, was in one of the fat newspaper clipping books found buried among Mary Marlowe's personal papers along with the manuscript of this autobiography. The many clippings reveal what the critics thought of Mary Marlowe as an actress, author and broadcaster. Some of these reviews are reproduced throughout this book. Mary does not mention them in her text and even her best friends were never shown her clipping books.

came to Australia as lady's maid to the Speaker's wife. On the ship she met a rich man and married him. She was childless, a good gardener, a great cook, and a perfect needlewoman. She had the last of the mixed biscuits when she called on me. She took a look at our cooking arrangements and carried us both off to stay with her at Greenwich.

I would have loved her had she not wanted to kiss me all the time. It was her Swiss nature. Her aitchless 'usband adored her. He did something with bricks that made money. He had a marvellous 'eart.

The girl from Melbourne was recalled to her home in two weeks. They cut off supplies as she had failed to get work in Sydney. When she had gone, the Lady of Greenwich took me to her cottage in the Blue Mountains.

Between meals I explored the country. Every pass that was negotiable bore the imprint of my urgent feet. As I walked I began to weave words, frame sentences, speak them aloud to get the rhythm of them. I would lie for hours on a spur of rock overhanging the valleys with their millions and millions of eucalyptus trees. They gave me comfort, courage . . . country courage. The adventure of writing a book no longer seemed so remote.

The day we went back to Sydney there was a telegram awaiting me. It had come that morning. 'See Julius Knight tomorrow at eleven.' Julius had two weeks work for me in the same plays I had been in at Bendigo and Ballarat. Nothing further offered afterwards.

On the last night my tummy rumbled as I made up my mind to ask Julius Knight to take me on tour again. In the current play I made an entrance with him and we usually stood together for a couple of minutes waiting for the cue. As I moistened my lips to speak—heart on the jig from nervousness—he turned to me. 'Well, Mary, I'm taking you with us to New Zealand. You'll understudy. You know more about make-up than the other girls and I think you'll be more useful to us.'

Broken Hill and beyond

New Zealand again and then Broken Hill. Here I was afflicted with another misdirected attack of social service. I helped a woman to run away from her husband. Broken Hill is scarcely the place for it. The area is limited and there are few places to take cover. There was, for all that, my bedroom at the hotel, and here I hid the fugitive.

Social service was working in me like yeast. Ethics were sound enough but unconventional. The husband had beaten his wife. She showed me heavy black bruises on her breasts where he had thumped her when struggling to get her salary out of her womanly pocket between them. Elsie earned more than Rupert, playing more important parts. To deceive his fellow actors on salary day, he jingled a great many loose coins in his trouser pockets. But we knew.

Why should a woman be beaten by her husband and put up with it? When Elsie fell down a rickety old stairway in the theatre, trying to run away from him, and scuttled into my dressing room, asking for help, I took her home. We both finished early in the piece and he had to stay until the end.

In the morning she was feverish and semi-conscious. I thought she would die of pneumonia or something. In Broken Hill I knew a barmaid with a golden heart. I appealed to her and she hid Elsie in her hotel—in a conscious period we got her there—and then brought a doctor. The fever condition was nerves, he said. Ice on the head and light nourishment. After a few days of this she came back to my room. Another bed was put up.

On the last two evenings, when she had to appear in a play, I policed the wings for her so she should not crash into Rupert. We scurried home as soon as possible. Every night we discussed plans for her divorce and what she would do afterwards.

We booked sleepers on the train for Adelaide. We left the hotel so as to be at the station as late as possible before the train started, but the husband was on the platform when we reached it. He stepped forward to speak to Elsie. Elsie stepped forward to speak to him. In thirty seconds they had made it up and she spent the first part of the night in the carriage in his arms. I think they had both been rather glad of the week's rest.

Then there was Ethel, aged seventeen. On the stage she was seductive and progressive in nakedness. Off the stage she was a chocolate-box baby. She was loved by a fellow with a brawny figure and no brains. Round about ten any morning, anybody passing Ethel's bedroom might hear her calling in infantile tones: 'Stanie! Stan-EE! Isn't Stanie coming to carwee li'le Effie to her barfee? Stan-EE!'

Ethel married Stan-EE. He had a nice mind—or none—and did the honest thing by 'Li'le Effie'. They went to America and were swallowed up in Middle West stock.

Our star, Julius Knight, was the most glamorous figure on the stage and he knew all about the technique of heroes—every variety. Combined with this, his knack of blending colour in scene or costume, his knowledge of producing and getting the best out of an artist or actor, his infallible flair for selecting the right music as prelude or accompaniment to a scene, and his resonant voice made him one of the most outstanding players who ever graced the Australian theatre. In his spare time (there wasn't much) he knitted or made wood carvings. In both these minor crafts he also excelled. But the vision of Monsieur Beaucaire in his brocades and lace ruffles, or Napoleon in his cutaway turning a sock in the dressing room was a rude shock.

On ships, on trains, in hotels, in dressing rooms, the men always played bridge or poker. The scene shifters played craps or nap. Somebody's rug was borrowed for a table. It covered four pairs of knees or a couple of up-ended suitcases, and served admirably.

Of all people attached to theatres the scene shifters are the best. Sometimes I stayed in the same hotels and shared their meals. Always, then and now, they have been my friends.

There is nothing spectacular about the lives of the stagehands. They go on working until the job is done and, if it will make a better job, they will go on working a bit longer. They can make anything, from the Eiffel Tower to the Crystal Palace, from a bunch of dewy grapes to a circular staircase to hold a hundred people. They never grumble. They are never late. They are never lazy. They always have time to do that extra something for somebody that makes the tour more comfortable. They are up with the dawn, sleep with one eye open, never ask for an alarm clock, and they often travel with the luggage—on top of it, alongside it, anywhere but under it.

It was a lovely play, *The Scarlet Pimpernel*. Julius Knight had given me the soubrette part—Sally Jellibrand. We had rehearsed it on tour. We were to open an important season in Sydney with a new leading lady, Ola Humphries. She was American-cum-Swedish-cum-French. She flirted about the stage like a willie wagtail.

First rehearsal was called in Sydney for the morning after we arrived. Before we began my old friend, the stage manager, called me into a corner. 'I hate to tell you, kid, but you're not to play Sally. The office has sent round a girl. Her father's in the Firm and she has pull. Oh, don't look so tragic. I'll find a line for you in the ballroom scene and put your name on the programme.'

Several new girls were taken on for the ballroom scene. One of these was given the understudy of Sally. Another, Jean Martin, was handed the part of the ingenue to understudy. She was told to learn it quickly in case she would be called in an emergency to play it. Jean was a society girl from Adelaide whose family fortunes had recently crashed. Exquisite of figure, Jean had poise and grace, and society had put its mark on her. She was sure of herself. At home she had many suitors.

As an extra, Jean would have been earning two pounds a week. She retained the family habit of spending lavishly, and her weekly bill for the hansom from the theatre to her society friends in Edgecliff where she was staying as a guest was thirty shillings. In our communal chorus dressing room she flaunted her understudy part. She told me she had been promised a better one in the next play. That did not make me love her any better.

I hated Jean Martin, and all moneyed amateurs, but she took a fancy to me. She tried to be friends but I thought her immeasurably silly when she talked of her wealthy relations and associates. She found everything in the theatre funny, including us. What we thought of her did not enter her consciousness.

The Sydney season had not been going more than a week when somebody gave the company a picnic to the National Park. I did not go, being much too heartsick. The girl who was playing Sally and her understudy were both at the picnic. They were taken out in a launch on the river. The launch broke down. Word came through by telephone to the theatre that they had missed the train and could not be back in time for the start of the play.

A ring came through while I was at dinner. The stage manager told me he was coming for me in a car. I would have to play Sally that evening, and he couldn't find the spare part. Could I do it? Could I!

We ran through the lines in the car going to the theatre. The wardrobe mistress was waiting with the frock. I tore down my hair while running up the theatre lane. Somebody put a comb through it. A dry make-up was all I had time for: rouge and eyeblack. I was ready in two minutes, the orchestra having been told to keep playing the tunes over until I was.

The man whose wife I had helped to run away from him was in the wings to wish me luck. I flashed onto the stage just as the picnic party arrived at the stage door. They had rushed for their lives in a car to beat the curtain, but I had the part.

As soon as we left Sydney I had it for always. After that night the parts came galloping in on me. It would be Sally Jellibrand, rising eighteen; the Countess of Something or Other, falling eighty; a serving maid with a song at the spinning wheel in *The Corsican Brothers* (the song especially written for my voice); the Widow Melnotte in *The Lady of Lyons*, and so on.

The Widow Melnotte was an anticlimax. I had played Pauline Deschaples—the Lady herself—in our dining room. And here was I playing the mere governess in *A Royal Divorce* after being a howling success as the Empress Josephine in our dining room. Now I had to stand by and hear our leading lady chuck away her points every night. It was frustrating to be a court lady, entirely silent in *The Prisoner of Zenda* after my domestic triumph in the dual roles of Princess Flavia and Antoinette de Mauban. Producers can't see a yard before their noses!

London calling

Despised and shunned though she had been in the beginning, Jean Martin gradually insinuated herself into my life and my heart. Though I did my best to give her the cold shoulder she won me over. After long journeys without sleepers because they were beyond my means—though Jean always had one—she would come upon me stretched out on some uncomfortable sofa in a hotel sitting room and, even if there was only an old and jaded piano, she would play to me. Then she would sit beside me and play with my hair. She had a genius for banishing a headache.

Madame Carreno had been her piano teacher for some time and she and other teachers had advised a professional career. Her music broke down my reserve. She conquered me with a diet of Beethoven, Chopin and Schumann. She persuaded me to sing again and was ever ready to play my accompaniments.

We began to plan things. How about London? Let's save up for London! A new dress was an event, but London seemed nearer when my salary was raised one whole pound.

Jean was not strictly beautiful but always *bien soignée*. I admired her before I loved her. Finding me one day in the process of beautifying myself, she volunteered to make a job of me. My beauty aids had cost two shillings: sixpennyworth of sheep dip for my hair, sixpennyworth of peroxide and a sixpenny orange stick for the nails, and sixpennyworth of butcher's lard and bergamot for a face cream.

Jean threw the sheep dip down the sink and replaced the lard and bergamot with a pot of her own beauty cream and a bottle of angel-water. The orange stick remained, but now she manicured me and brushed my hair daily. She told me that sheep dip might be excellent but it was not comfortable to live in the same corridor with it.

Next Jean attacked my clothes. My underclothing had been made by hand (mine) for a long time, but Jean changed the patterns and sent to her home town for handmade Chinese lace imported by friends of hers from missions to save Chinese girl babies. It cost threepence per yard. Sarah Blessing had augmented my wardrobe with the gift of three flannelette nightdresses, costing two and elevenpence each. They were intended to keep me warm on the New Zealand tour and pure on the ships.

Jean changed all that. The new nightdresses were cut on a more audacious pattern. And our friendship endured. It bore all the tests of time and trial and trouble. We never had a real row. There was never an occasion when I needed comfort or encouragement that Jean did not give it readily.

When we returned to Adelaide Jean invited me to her home. I fell in love with her brother. He was a strong silent man, and I was at an age when such characteristics were desirable. We drifted into companionship and dropped behind the others because he was so silent and I was so shy. He was the social failure of his family, and I of mine.

London cooled my ardour. Today I look back upon him as the first man I ever regarded as a possible husband. He married a woman who was not so shy, and soon my heart was centred on a man who was not so silent.

Jean depended upon the generosity of her rich brother-in-law to help her get to London. I was steadily saving up that extra pound of my salary. We were joined in our enterprise by a young actress in the company called Eve. She was the typical First Woman.

My mother had left me nothing but her diamonds and the furniture. I sold the furniture and invested the money. The diamonds I put into the bank so that when the time came they would be there to bury me. They'll just about do that decently.

The Member of Parliament had died suddenly and there was nobody to stop me going to London. Our hearts light as quicksilver, we left on a penny-a-mile ship: Jean, Eve and I. Each of us had a letter to Dion Boucicault the younger, the English actor, manager and dramatist who was married to Irene Vanbrugh.

On the ship Jean and Eve fell in love. I was kept busy with tonsillitis.

Eve selected the ship's doctor and enslaved him. He came quietly. We called him Billgraeme, a contraction of his full name.

At Fremantle a young mining engineer came aboard. He had finished his contract with a Kalgoorlie mining company and he was going back to England, home and mother—particularly mother. An hour out from land he met Jean on deck. He knew and she knew that until the end of life—and after—they would be lovers.

He was tall and dark and sleek and had an air of being well-bred. We named him the Gibson Man but he had been christened Walter MacGrath. He used to make progress reports to me every day on deck and one morning he was observed giving me a butterfly kiss with his eyelashes. This was to show me how he was getting on with Jean. The worst was accepted in the smoking room. We were all bad.

If you don't like us that way don't go on with this story. It gets much worse.

London comes true

Inscrutable London! Indifferent London! Adorable London! So small and compact, so large and obtuse; so haughty, so friendly! A city of secrets with a beckoning finger and a whispering voice, murmuring: 'Come with me!' An aloof stranger that sneers a rebuff at the intruder—too busy to care whether or not you are trampled in the crush of her thoroughfares, too kindly to leave you in the gutter. London, the world's enigma!

I hated it. I loved it. I worship the memory of it. But London is not England. You must go to the country to feel the pulse of the English. You must know the trees of England to hear the voice of England. You must stand on the white frill of England to hear the song of England that beats below on her white cliffs. You must listen to the booming of guns across the English Channel to know the courage of her and her people.

We berthed at Tilbury.* The Gibson Man took charge and did not leave us until we were safe in the cheap suite of rooms a friend had taken for us in Upper Gloucester Place in London. The house was kept by an ex-actress. She reminded us of a busy bird. How she ever found time to manage her house amazed us. She was a rampant feminist by conviction and a landlady by bad luck. She had an invalid husband and a child to support. When she had time for it she was kind to us. She understood the artistic temperament.

We had a shabby sitting room on the third floor, where Eve's bedroom was. Jean and I had the attic above. Eve had a moveable bath which she shared with the drawing-room gentleman. Jean and I had a large frying pan under the bed and did the best we could with the can of water which a lisping little slattern brought up soon after dawn. Once a week we enjoyed an all-over bath downstairs for a shilling.

* It was 1910 and Mary Marlowe was twenty-six.

The landlady bought our food to our order, when she had time and remembered it, and another little slattern cooked it in the basement and carried it up three flights of stairs on a tin tray. On average this kind of living cost us twenty-two and sixpence each per week. Sometimes Eve drew out of the pool if she had been out much, dining at the expense of her many admirers. Both girls used my bank. By doing this the amount was just important enough to be taken seriously.

We rechristened Gloucester Place 'Grub Street' which was much more suitable. It was drab. London was cold. We resolved to hire a piano and buy a palm.

On our first Monday we went out to buy clothes. Eve's new gown expressed her personality: black velvet with gold lattice across the bust and a tiara to match. The gown was kept up by faith but swept the ground for a long way behind Eve. Jean ordered a marvel in misty chiffons like whipped cream mixed with soot. I was poured into a black satin sheath with gunmetal jet to lock me in. It looked like a Newcastle lode and saw yeoman service. After its leading lady periods it finished its frayed career in an auction room and brought six shillings during one of my 'perishes'.

When we had made our grubby little sitting room look homey we sent out our letters of introduction and asked everybody to tea. Most of our contacts replied that they were just starting for the country. But distinguished guests came now and then to Grub Street. My cousin, Major Percy FitzGerald (a son of the Member of Parliament), turned up. He took me to tea at Rumpelmeyer's and bought me a guinea hat in Hanover Square. Mine, he said, was frightful. We went to his tailor's in Saville Row. He paid a third of his bill and ordered clothes to twice that amount. That, he informed me, was how a gentleman managed finance. He asked me to go to Brighton with him and then said he didn't mean it. He left me to come home in the bus alone because he had an appointment with a duchess. Later he married her. She was Millicent, Duchess of Sutherland. Afterwards I inherited one of her hats.

The Major promised to write to Dion Boucicault about his 'little cousin', and tell the fellow he must do something for her. If he did, Dion Boucicault had forgotten by the time I called and presented a letter of introduction from Australia. I mentioned the Major and the Duchess.

'That marriage will never be a success,' said Dion. He was a seer. 'A woman, duchess or not, can't put a pin through a butterfly and make a domestic pet of it.'

Days after she landed in London Mary went shopping. She had herself 'poured' into a black satin sheath, sat for a studio publicity photograph and started calling on theatrical agents.

In turn Boucicault interviewed the three of us. We each wore Jean's pearl necklace and Eve's furs. Probably Boucicault did not notice. He was accustomed to pearls and furs, as he moved amongst that section of society that wears them in bed.

Boucicault was gracious to all three of us but he was most impressed by Eve. She was the prettiest. He told her to try vaudeville and advised Jean to become a mannequin. She had the figure for it. When my turn came and I announced that I was a character actress his eyebrows went up dramatically. A protesting cluck rose in his throat. 'My dear child . . . it would be madness. Wait until you are sixty before you take on character. While you are young go after leads. Say you can play them. If you can't, you'll soon learn.'

He did not offer me one.

Jean had the first of the luck. She had dug up the Earl of Kilmorey, who knew theatrical managers. He secured her a walk-on at His Majesty's in a Shakespeare play produced by Sir Herbert Beerbohm Tree. She was worried that she put her big chance in jeopardy because that day, as she was looking extra saucy and probably being extra saucy, the lead, Arthur Bourchier, had kissed her and she smacked his cheek. She came home and cried on my shoulder. That evening she was particularly kind to the Gibson Man. But we dared not tell him.

Jean was not needed for rehearsals for five weeks so she and I went on a walking tour of Brittany. We returned to Grub Street to discover that Eve had been married in Liverpool during one of the doctor's long leaves. Not content with that, she had engaged a partner and booked an act in the music halls. In the sketch she had a husband who did not behave, so she threw him over her shoulder and held his head under the kitchen tap. Eve had taken ju-jitsu lessons before she left Australia to prepare for the exigencies of travel overseas.

Jean was soon rehearsing *Henry VIII*. She had a small silent scene with Henry Ainley. She knelt and kissed his hand when, as Buckingham, he was on his way to the scaffold. She cried real tears. She had this knack. Ainley thought her clever, interesting, resourceful, imaginative. The tears told him that as they fell on his hand.

But Jean had an emotional attachment offstage. One day she asked me to stay out all the afternoon. She had invited the Gibson Man to tea. I obliged and when I reached home late he was leaving, smiling idiotically.

'It's happened,' said Jean when I went upstairs. 'We're engaged.'

'What are you going to use for money? Walter has none and no job.'

'He'll get a job in time.'

I was wondering whether *I* would as I travelled by train to Banbury to stay a weekend with another of the Member of Parliament's sons. He also had married into the aristocracy. The family lived in a glorified cottage at the Wroxton Abbey gates. The villagers bobbed to them. My cousin's aristocratic wife had a tragic face. She was my conception of Lady Dedlock in *Bleak House*.

We played cards after dinner, the eldest son humming a musical comedy tune with one finger on the piano. He knew another actress besides me, but she was also in the aristocracy now.

Next day we went to Stratford-on-Avon. In the Memorial Theatre how could I resist trying out my voice? It was a line of Rosalind's. The theatre was empty save for us, but my female cousin looked at me with an expression which conveyed 'These incorrigible Australians.' My male cousin borrowed sixpence from me to tip the waiter at the Shakespeare Hotel.

The aristocratic weekend cost me two guineas. The visit taught me my place was amongst the commoners.

The next time I saw 'Lady Dedlock' she was sitting in a basket chair in a lovely garden at a party given by the Countess of Something Or Other in Oxford. I was there as a member of the Visiting Pierrots, who had been brought down from London to entertain the guests. On an improvised stage in this terraced pleasance I danced and I sang 'I'm Such a Silly When the Moon Comes Out'. 'Lady Dedlock' was in the front row. I felt silly enough to swoon in the sunlight but she was too well bred to recognize me. That was my second appearance with the concert party at a guinea a time and it was my last.

Back in London I spent my days in theatrical agents' offices chasing the elusive job. It was a brutal business. Eventually I was sent to the Strand Theatre to be looked over by Stanley Cook. The little man was running a farce there and sending a couple of companies on tour in the autumn. He called me a 'colonial'. That enraged me. We had a heated argument and I was too busy being annoyed to realize he had started the argument to see if I would light up well. That terrible shyness was always a wall between me and managers, but Cook had broken through. He gave me a pass to go to his matinee that day and said he would let me know later.

I went to the matinee and arrived home late. Eve was furious.

She had wanted her furs. It was July but we were still wearing them. I could not eat tea. I went to bed to cry and count my money. Would it stretch to a fare back to Australia? What else? No jobs, the girls leaving me for their men . . .

The last post was delivered to Grub Street at ten o'clock. I heard the postman's knock and then the little slattern climbing the stairs. A letter for me in a long envelope. It contained a contract for six months to tour for Stanley Cook.

Part Two

David

My father's folks lived in Wales. They invited me to 'Glentrothy', their home outside Abergavenny, for a fortnight. There was comfortable time for that before rehearsals began for my tour.

My meeting with David was hastened by an omnipotent porter who thought it important that I should sit with my back to the engine. He was fussy about my carriage and walked me the length of the platform before being satisfied it would not be overcrowded. He put my suitcase in the rack, label hanging down. There was one other suitcase there already. 'A nice gentleman,' said the porter.

David noticed the label as soon as he entered the carriage. The train was then moving. David caught at the luggage rail to steady himself. The label was level with his eyes. He dropped into the corner seat opposite, and grinned at me.

'Well, I'll be damned! I almost missed the train on your account. Going to the Glen? So am I. Your aunt wrote me to look out for you—take care of you on the journey. Maybe you've heard of me?'

'Not a word. Who are you?'

'David Cameron. Friend of the Canada branch of the family. Going to the Glen to tell them about the boys over there. I travel the world. Business, shipping. You're the actress cousin.'

'Is that how they describe me?'

'They're inarticulate. You're not a bit what I have been looking for up and down the train. I've left a trail of outraged women on the platform. Gazed hard at each to see if she matched up with the description your aunt gave me of you.'

'What did she tell you to expect?'

'A slim kid with green eyes and a snub nose.'

'Fairly accurate description.'

His eyes—they were blue—had a mischievous look, like a dog's when he expects a game. 'Has nobody ever told you about yourself?

I had a mighty good look at all those ladies but I didn't go after the colour of their eyes. Are yours green? I'd figure them chipmunk. I've been looking for somebody like an actress as I'd so little to go by. That ring you're wearing? Does it mean you're engaged?'

'It was my mother's.'

'Ah, that's fine.'

He took my hand to examine the ring. Before we reached our change junction I had told him a good deal about myself and about the girls at Grub Street. He led me on.

At Newport we went into the town and had tea. The hour slipped by. In the end we had to run for our connecting train. At Abergavenny Cousin John was waiting for us with his dogcart. He drove us seven miles before the house came into view. The whole family were on the front steps.

Uncle Reggie Vaughan had married my father's sister. She gave him eleven children. Then she died. He had a suitable rest before taking a second wife, a niece of the Member of Parliament, that strong-minded uncle of mine by marriage on my mother's side.

Glentrothy was a comfortable home, an easygoing home. The hall door opened into the square hall. The hall fireplace could take a tree. The fireplaces were stacked with logs cut on the estate. Rooms were lived in. No grandeur, only comfort.

Beautiful old lawns, cut into terraces, sloped down to the River Wye. The drive to the outer gate was a mile long. The family said the Rosary aloud in the dogcart every time they went down the drive. The horse accommodated his pace so that the final Hail Mary could be finished before the dogcart reached the final gate. A sunken tennis court was kept to the consistency of velvet. Pigeons lived about. A big park cut off the road and the village. In the home acres there were a great many cottages, most of them with oak beams and some with oak staircases. It was a sweet-pea district and the cottage people vied to make their gardens showy. The flower shows were a feature of the county.

We were driven to the Shrewsbury Show the first day of our visit— Shrewsbury, so important, so urgent on show days, stepping out of the past to meet the present. Poor people came into their kingdom through their flowers, their jams, their pastries.

Life for me suddenly became all green and gold. The green of the astonishing little Monmouth hills, the gold of the summer. I was happy. At first I did not know why. All about me were dear folks full of kindness. In some ways they were as medieval as Shrewsbury.

An Irish judge, a bishop (one of the Vaughans), a shipping man and me: we were the house party. The judge had come to woo the youngest daughter, Gwladys; the bishop had come to prepare a series of sermons, so he said; David was here to bring news of the sons in Canada; and I was snatching a holiday from high finance and theatrical agents.

My cousins had known Mary Anderson and that made the stage acceptable. They took her as the standard. It made things easy for me. I did not mention the Pierrot parties.

With the bishop holding the book, sonorously reading Romeo and Shylock, I acted Shakespeare for them in the hall after dinner. Simple people, easily pleased, they enjoyed listening. Mainly the family concentrated on the judge from Ireland. They watched for the reactions of Gwladys to his elegant attentions.

I was falling in love with David Cameron. Nobody took any notice of that, except David Cameron.

I had felt a certain astonishment when he took my hand in the train to examine my mother's ring. His hand on mine had something of my mother in it. There was the same sense of comfort conveyed, the same feeling of ownership and protection.

David had a voice like an organ. The Canadians have. You can almost feel the floor vibrating beneath you when they talk.

Maybe you wouldn't call him good-looking, but I never was a judge of a man's looks. Gerald du Maurier and Arthur Mailey could have posed for the Apollo Belvedere as far as I was concerned. It took years and years to wake me up to the fact that both of them were plain men. A pair of whimsical eyes can play havoc with my judgement. David had those eyes. He reminded me of a Viking. Tall, broad, fair, with blue eyes that smiled on the slightest provocation. That is the best I can do to describe him.

We saw a good deal of one another because at Glentrothy we did things in mobs. We would go to see the cottagers, to admire the gardens, to inspect the horses, to praise the pigs, to speculate upon the turnip crops, to gather blackberries, to visit the shows, all together. Naturally we fell into pairs.

By the end of the first week we were in love. David was as silent— almost—as Jim Martin, Jean's brother, had been. I felt I was becoming reckless. He was probably the type of man who exerts his charm over every girl he meets. He might be a collector.

A county lady was organizing a bridge tournament for charity. The family had taken tickets for us all. My uncle thought it would be a treat for me to see the lady's treasures, her Mings and such.

After dinner that evening I asked to be forgiven, pleaded a headache, preferred a quiet night at home.

I wanted time to take stock of myself. I was rapidly arriving at that stage where I would have liked everybody to fall dead around me except David. The others were such a nuisance now. They seemed to have no meaning for me at all. Only David. There are more shattering things than war. Find yourself in a world of stars, the earth vibrating, your heart standing still at the sound of a footstep, and you will agree.

My cousins were complaisant and they never fussed. They drove off to the bridge tournament, leaving the bishop in the library to draft a sermon, David in his own room working on plans and specifications for some scheme of his company which was to take him abroad shortly, and me.

The bishop and I saw the family away. The bishop waved from the library window and I waved from the doorstep. He retired to his comfortable saddlebag, and I found my way to the flagged terrace overlooking the river.

The last of the pigeons had gone to roost in the pines. The twilight warmed the lawns to a richer green. The river was like green glass.

I curled up on a long cane lounge and watched the sky deepen from blue daylight to an indigo night. The stars seemed nearer and clearer than they had been since I left Australia. I fancied I could hear them crackle. Reality and I were complete strangers.

Before long Wye, the old one-eyed black sheepdog came around the corner of the house. He was respectful of my preoccupation and I of his. We were both chasing butterflies.

Through the French windows at my back David came out onto the terrace. My heart stood still. Wye's stubby tail thumped a welcome. David stooped to fondle his untidy ears and then sat down in the chair close to my lounge.

'Something told me I should find you here. Officially, I believe, you are in bed, drugged with aspirin. The stars muttered they had seen you on the terrace so I came along to cheer you up.'

'Shirking?' My heart was on the beat again. I had my breath now.

'I did try to work. Then the stars came between and told me I was a fool to waste time. Do you agree?'

When David took my hand everything had been said between us. I knew why I was born. Was it all spirit . . . that sensation of a bird in my body flying to the top of a tree? The bird in my body was now bursting its little throat with a song. I think it was a skylark. He sang his fool head off. I thought David must surely hear him.

It was some time before David got out of his creaky chair and came to sit on the edge of *my* creaky chair. Now he took both my hands and still he did not speak—except to say my name again and again. The way he said it made it sound wonderful. It was longer still before he put his head down to my heart and said, so softly that even Wye could not hear, 'I love you.'

The bishop was snoring when we went in.
'Go up, my sweet, and dream of me,' said David. I needed no telling.

We had a week of dreaming and building castles. The judge took the attention of the family. When he proposed they had no thoughts, no eyes, no interest except for him and Gwladys.

David and I were in agreement over essentials. I could go on with my tour because he had engagements on the Continent which would keep him away from me. We would travel to Town together and he would meet the girls at Grub Street. The future was a little nebulous. All I knew was there would be no settled home. I would travel round the world with him. If not, it meant long separations. My gypsy heart leapt at the prospect of a life of moving on. To be with David was home enough.

'Don't let us crash in here with our news,' I pleaded. 'Gwladys should have all the thunder, and I want to tell the girls in London first.'

We travelled up in an empty carriage. We held hands as though hands were jewels. At Newport the carriage filled up and we were not alone again until we reached Grub Street.

The landlady told me the girls were both away. Jean had gone to stay with her future mother-in-law. Eve had hastily travelled to Liverpool, her husband coming unexpectedly on a different ship from his routine.

We had a small meal served up by the slattern. David was amused at everything. Our makeshifts enthralled him.

In the morning he was to leave for the Continent. His journey would take three months. I did not know my tour dates so far ahead but when he returned he would come straight to where I might be playing. By that time he hoped I would have worked stage fever out of my system and be ready to marry him.

It must have been about ten o'clock when he commenced to pace our little sitting room in the way my Only Surviving Uncle did before he ceased to survive. David had something on his mind. If I had not been so much in love during the past fortnight I might

have noticed this before. When I came to think about it, there were
plenty of signs.

At last I spoke about Montreal. His life there. Immediately I felt
there was a fence up. Instinct warned me now there was something.

'You're worried about something. Tell me. Now. Don't write about
it. Now. I will understand.'

'Will you?' He came to the couch and sat beside me. Of course
I would understand!

He looked at me for a long time. He kissed me before he spoke.

'I didn't mean to tell you. I didn't want you to share this worry.
It's going to be straightened out as soon as I have time to fix things.
The fact is I'm still engaged to a woman in Montreal. I shall break
it off by letter tomorrow.'

My heart died in me.

'Men don't break engagements. Only women can do that.'

'You're incurably romantic, aren't you, dear? Men and women
make a save for themselves when they need it. Edith can take the
credit if she likes. I am not going to marry her. I won't marry one
girl while I love another. That's sheer fool stuff.'

In a kind of amazement I asked, 'Who is she? How long have
you been engaged? Does she love you?'

Piece by piece he told me the story. She was the same age as he,
thirty-one. They had been brought up together. Her father had looked
after him when his own father and mother died in an epidemic
while he was a child. Though his parents had left enough money
to educate him with something over for an income, Edith's father
gave him his first job in his own office, setting him on the road
to success and plenty. He had favoured marriage between him and
his daughter but he died before there was an engagement. Edith's
mother was an invalid and, though they had been engaged for several
years, the marriage had been postponed again and again so that
she might nurse her mother. She believed her mother was dying.
She had been dying for five years.

David pleaded in his defence that Edith had had her chance to
marry and again and again rejected it. He asked could she be really
fond of him since she put him second in her life.

Is it a curse or a blessing to be able to see the other person's
point of view? I saw Edith's just as clearly as if she were in the
room putting her case. She had grown up believing that David was
her man. Making sacrifices for her mother, she had always the feeling
of a safe background, an assured future when she felt she could
take her place beside David. She deserved a better fate than to be

thrown aside for a chit of a girl whom her affianced husband had met on a summer holiday. She should have a better fate if I had my way.

Unhappily I could also see David's aspect and my own. We argued until midnight. I did not cry until he had gone away.

His train left for the boat early in the morning. The continental tour was only the first stage of a journey that must take him out of my life. A telegram reached me with the breakfast tray.

'Do not make any more contracts until we meet in September. Am not prepared to accept decision. Have thought of three new arguments. Will go to Montreal myself to make things better.'

What use? Ethically he belonged to Edith. There was no argument. People said you got over things. Time did it for you. One thing, though. Never make a confidant. Tell nobody anything. Thank God the girls had no hint of what was happening to me. Stiffen the spine and pretend to be gay. Bluff myself first and then the others would be bluffed. Only that way lay sanity.

Edith would regard me as a vamp, a wicked witch. The world would agree with her. I knew myself to be neither vamp nor adventuress. My mind, my ethics, my whole outlook on life were set for the heroic. Whatever I might achieve on the stage as a heroine, I must be one for myself in private. David couldn't understand that. He didn't want to be a hero, just a happy man, a plain ordinary man, walking through life in an ordinary way with the woman he loved. He did not think of me as a heroine. He regarded me as a damned fool.

He was right.

Discovering England

After her brief appearance in *Henry VIII*, we married Jean to her Gibson Man one fine morning at Spanish Place. She changed her religion for his sake.

Before long Tess, her mother-in-law, set her wondering if there was a God at all. She exerted a terrible tyranny over Jean's life and from the beginning resented her and seemed to be set on separating her from her husband.

Jean had no conventional bridesmaids but I held things for her. Afterwards at the small wedding breakfast in the home of an Australian friend I took Tess into the next room, she said, 'to die'. A small dose of digitalis averted the catastrophe. Unfortunately.

Following a brief honeymoon, Jean and Walter went to Ealing to live with Tess. It was a small house. There was a small fat dog called Daddles. When Jean played the piano it was to the accompaniment of Daddles sniffing and Tess scratching her taffeta silk lap. Any musical person will know what that means.

I left Jean to her tragedy while I went on tour. Unthinkable, unmentionable things happened to her, but her brave heart and her love and loyalty to her husband sustained her. He went abroad to a job. She had to face her lonely life. Soon there was a child coming.

One day she sent for Eve. 'If I die in childbirth promise you will take my child and bring him up.' She hoped for a boy. A girl was born. She had Eve's faithful promise, and this made a bond between them that even I could not match with my love and desire to help. Eve was a married woman. She could look after a child.

Touring in England is a different pair of shoes from Australia. Out there we lived in hotels—good or bad according to our salary—or boarding houses. In England it was 'diggings', and they were mainly situated in the slums.

On tour nobody knew us. Nobody wanted to. We were merely the troupe that had come into town. The grocer recognized us before

Mary as the seductive Sally in The Man from Mexico.

the week was out. The local clergyman sometimes asked us to tea. In my particular company we gave each other tea parties two or three times a week.

The leading lady shared rooms with the ingenue. The character woman was married to the butler. The men went in groups or in pairs. There were only two people in our troupe who engaged rooms alone: the hermaphrodite and me. He had a combined room. When I could get them I had a bedroom and a sitting room.

The hermaphrodite was an unknown quantity and I remained ignorant during the tour. I put down his mincing walk, his waist, his falsetto voice to the fact that he was half French. He was a harmless creature.

We were a sober and well behaved company. We were as dull as mud.

My salary as soubrette was three pounds a week. Out of this each week I posted six shillings to the agent who had sent me for the job. It was his ten per cent.

Living at peak cost me thirty shillings, the rent varying from ten and sixpence to twenty-two shillings. Bacon and eggs for breakfast, a joint a week, tapioca pudding every day, a baby bottle of stout and a slice of cheese for late supper.

The tour, the diggings, the dull routine of a small theatrical travelling company fell into their right perspective by the end of the first week. Henceforth I set out to discover England.

Strange people came and went, types that no other kind of life would reveal to me. I went into the English slums that tour and lived with the people who are of the slums. As I moved from town to town, the lives of these people were woven into a pattern such as I could never find in any other way. Their homes, their aspirations, their desperate predicaments were open for me to investigate. I lived now among the people who struggled for a bare existence in factories and breweries and little shops; in coal pits and mills, in shipyards. These were my daily companions. I lived in their homes, passed through their kitchens. I was part of their daily life and I was— God be thanked—their rent.

So that the best portion of their small houses might be ready to let to theatricals, these families huddle in the back quarters. Often quite a number of one family ate and washed and slept in the kitchen. Mother and father had an upstairs room, only two or three of the children sharing it. The tails of my chops went into the stew pot, hard cheese from scraps was a common factor in their food. They came to my sitting room, talked of themselves and their hopes and fears. Some spoke in queer dialects. It was hard to follow their speech but never their hearts.

They did not cadge or pilfer or add percentages to the weekly bill. They made do with what they justly earned.

Lying in bed in northern towns, at dawn I would hear the knocker-up, his clackers rumbling out like thunder as he went from door to door, arousing the workers for the mills. Then would follow the clatter of clogs on the cobblestones. Two hours later my breakfast tray would be brought up. I'd think, 'Why don't these people hate and resent me?' Dumbly they accepted their portion and did not grumble. They were the stuff that, later, made the British Army.

Tradition caught hold of me. Coventry started it. I had rooms in the musty, dusty house of faded gentry: three old ladies who put coloured handkerchiefs round their heads to dust the piano. I managed to get all three a pass for the show. It shocked them. Miss Letty brought my tray in the morning. She let me see into her mind.

'You smoked last night. Is that necessary? So bad for your health. Couldn't you pretend? A sugar cigarette.'

When I asked for the truth of Peeping Tom and Lady Godiva, Miss Letty lowered her lids. Her mouth straightened.

'Not a nice story. She was a noble woman but was it necessary? Too impetuous, if you ask me. She might have used feminine powers of persuasion before she went to those lengths.'

Woman is woman's sternest critic.

There was nobody at Kenilworth the day I went; nobody except the gloomy guide and the spirit of Amy Robsart. I was the lone prowler at Warwick Castle; the caretaker raked in my shilling and showed me the ancestors with a certain proprietary pride.

Haddon Hall was sleeping off its past when I reached it. There was no one to open the great doors for an inquisitive wanderer, but no one to stop me from exploring the grounds. As I knew from pictures and books the door through which dashing Dorothy Vernon had slipped to her lover's arms, and the gate where the horses waited for that enchanting elopement, it was not difficult to call up the ghosts.

That night I was late at the theatre. The company was wondering if I had followed Dorothy's example. I had no more than time to scramble into my stage clothes and make a rush for it. In the last act the leading man missed his entrance. Though two of us talked furiously in high voices, which we hoped would carry to wherever in the wings he might be, he didn't turn up, and at last I walked off the stage, down the passage to his dressing room, dragged him from a game of cribbage, and marched him onto the scene. The spirit of Dorothy was abroad.

Eastbourne was well bred. Hastings, her slovenly sister, I found an endearing spot. At Eastbourne and Bournemouth we played on the piers; a strange sensation to hear water lapping against the piles beneath our dressing rooms.

So the tour went on. There was Burton-on-Trent, the home of Guinness, but I remember it best because it was there the landlady wrapped the tail of my chop in a parcel and gave it to me to carry to the next town. Wigan was the place where the lame clergyman had us all to tea. Huddersfield was, is, and always will be, the worst spot on earth. Somewhere along the tour we came to Southampton. Southampton meant the inevitable: it meant David.

In the forest

David arrived at my sitting-room door as the servant was clearing the breakfast things. His ship was to sail for Canada in the morning.

The servant discreetly left us but she looked back. I saw her over David's shoulder as I was crushed in his arms. She heard nothing because neither of us could find words for a long time.

It was many minutes before he said: 'Put on your bonnet and shawl, dear. I have a car below. We are going to spend the day in the New Forest.'

Almost before I knew what had happened to me we were away in the open car. David drove. The bird in my breast was outsinging every bird in the Forest. It was a sunny morning.

When we were deep in the Forest David parked the car in the courtyard of a Lindfield inn. 'First we'll take a look at the Forest but in case we can't find the wild honey and the strawberries and the other food for lovers we must be prepared to face a meal somewhere.' He ordered lunch. The innkeeper regarded us slyly. He seemed to be looking for confetti.

'Luggage will be all right in the car, sir. I'll see to it.'

David smiled wryly. 'You're wrong, mister. We have no cargo.'

The Forest showed her best. It was a day of ecstasy. My perfect hour.

David did not tell me the arguments he had thought out. He trusted to his personal appeal to win me from stubbornness, believing that this day together would prove to me how impossible life would be apart. He did not talk of the future. He scarcely spoke of the present. There was no detail of my past he did not want to know. The tiniest things. He told me much about his work and his travels but he did not touch on Edith. The day was nearly done before he said: 'When will you marry me so that we can come back here for our honeymoon?'

'In our next existence.'

'You won't be able to stick it.'

'I will. I must.'

'My ship sails in the morning. Edith expects me to marry her at Christmas. You must make up your mind before the ship reaches Montreal.'

'I have. You know that.'

That was all. Maybe it was impossible for a man to believe a woman could be so sure of herself in sorrow.

Later I said, 'You'll feel differently when you see her. Even if you don't, you have a debt to pay. I can't cut in.'

'I'll wait three months for a cable from you.'

'Three years wouldn't change me. I must be decent.'

'You don't realize yet how barren—and how long—life can be without the person you want . . . you love.'

I did not. That is how I mustered up courage to send David back to Montreal.

His ship sailed at noon. I watched it go to the open roads. There was a good view of the harbour from my window. Then I sat down in the old broken-down chair and I cried until there were no tears left in my heart.

Late that afternoon a packet was brought to me. Inside was a letter and a small box. The box contained a slim jewel case, the name of a Paris firm on the white satin of the inside cover. It held a slim necklet: two aquamarines on a thin platinum chain. The letter was brief. Hardly a letter at that. I read from the thin sheet of ship's notepaper words written in David's forceful handwriting.

There's in thee all that we believe of Heaven,
Amazing goodness, purity and truth,
Eternal joy, and everlasting love.

Everlasting love!

When you are very young it is tolerably easy to be good. My family had not had me until my fifteenth year for nothing. They had inculcated morality into me. I was not a normal human being even yet. Though the blood ran hot in me at last, I was still thinking along the lines of the best heroines, and had selected a pure white marble plinth, little realizing that the cold would strike from the feet up before long. In some remote region—surely?—Fate or Destiny or God, something omnipotent with a capital letter, would work on my behalf to bring everything right in the end. All true heroines, after much tribulation, live happily ever after.

Stevensonian philosophy taught: 'There is no cutting of the Gordian knots of life; each must be smilingly unravelled.' Sooner or later David's Gordian knot would be treated like this—smilingly unravelled. He would come back to me, free, and loving me more than ever. The notion possessed me that Edith would lead a very happy life with him but a very short one. She would die with a smile on her lips and gratitude for David in her eyes. There would be no children. We would have nothing to reproach ourselves for when he came back to me. David would marry me then and I would bear him six children, all sons.

While I was waiting for Edith to die I had the sons. They came rather quickly and close together. They were all well developed except the sixth, Robin. Robin was the baby, and he showed a Peter Panish obstinacy about growing up. He never grew beyond the age of three. We still play trains on the carpet.

David was on the high seas, heading for Newfoundland, when the first of my sons was born at Southampton. His name was David too; he was the image of his father. From the cradle he was determined to be a sailor. For him I dreamed life on a windjammer, sailing the wide oceans, blown round the world by the wind.

Roger, the second one, came to me at Bournemouth one sunny morning as I watched the ships go by from the pine woods of Boscombe. Did the pines point his future path to Canadian forests? He was my lumberjack dream son—big and dark and muscular, with a rumbly voice like David's.

Watching the children floating their small ships to France from Hastings Beach, I was suddenly aware of Peter. Only for a minute was he a blue-eyed baby. Promptly I settled him in Amen Corner, working amongst London's poor. Every time he smiled at a patient I could see David in his eyes.

John was my great engineer son. The crowning feat of his brilliant career was the tunnel under Sydney Harbour. Perhaps that was because I thought of him travelling from my rooms at Hoylake in the under-harbour train to the theatre, or perhaps it was because David had once told me that he had wanted to be an engineer. John had red hair with a kink in it.

Alan, the fifth of these imps, was a ready-made farmer. He had the flat voice of a countryman and he would have died for his dogs as willingly as he would have laid down his life for his country.

Robin, the baby, came because I seemed to need a baby most just then, as all the others had grown up so quickly. He was born—

the last of my dream-children—one Sunday evening after I had been for a long tramp in the country. There was a wire from David on the dining-room table, forwarded to me from London. It read: 'Edith's mother died tonight. Wire instantly if you have changed your mind. There is still time. David.'

My limbs were aching. My heart was heavy. Robin was born prematurely. He clamoured for his father as he lay against my breast. His brothers cried out to me to give them their father. I spent a terrible night arguing with my unborn children.

In the morning I answered the cablegram. The children had lost their father. I wired: 'Mind unchanged.'

On with the show

The younger set was on the way when I returned to London. A little Billgraeme was expected, though his prospective mother was still putting her vaudeville partner's head under the tap. She did not think Little Billgraeme would mind but he did. Emphatically.

Jean's child was nearly due. Walter came home from Russia and they had a flat in West Kensington.

My old theatre friend, Norah Delaney, had married a musician called Albert Cazabon, and while he waved a baton or a violin bow in one of the Wyndham theatres, Norah wheeled a little Norah in a pram round Hampstead Heath.

With natural modesty I refrained from mentioning my six.

Eve had taken rooms for me in Denby Street. Having fixed me with a London address, she went to Canada to be with her husband's people when her baby was born. She hated them. For the sake of the child, they put up with her, accusing her of incipient unfaithfulness every time she looked at a man. Eve could not help looking at men. She regarded them as the most essential ingredient of the universe.

The baby was a boy. He was born perfect and exquisite and he lived two days. Eve gave the baby clothes to the poor, packed her trunks and took ship for England. Two months after her child's birth she, also, was looking for a stage engagement. Africa supplied it. She went out to play Janet Cannot in *The Great Adventure* and resolved never to have another child.

I was with Jean the night before her baby was born. She played all evening and finished up with a fireworks display of a Chopin polonaise.

'Please go easy,' I implored. 'The baby'll be born on the pedal if you don't take care.'

Jean bade me goodnight, went to bed, and had her little Eileen. Walter sent me a telegram which reached Denby Street at ten the next morning. I replied: 'I don't believe it.'

A year later Jean had her second child. She called her Leueen. As I write, that young person, Leueen McGrath, is busily carving a place for herself on the London stage. I have her picture as a very young lady of the period in *French Without Tears*.

In the meantime I went out hunting London's actor managers. Blackmore's sent me to Derwent Hall Caine for Polly Love in the dramatization of his father's novel, *The Christian*. Derwent, reaching to my shoulder, said: 'Too tall.' He took my address without further comment.

Sir Frank Benson patiently listened to me while I read some of Rosalind to him in his office where typing was audible and young gentlemen standing about in groups were talking sport. The distractions held no horror for Benson but they paralysed me into mental pulp. He thought he might offer me work in three months time when he would be wanting two or three Rosalinds for his tours.

William Brady was over from New York, engaging people at Drury Lane. Hundreds waited for him three mornings in succession. So did I. On the third morning he saw me as he was going out to lunch. 'The type I wanted. You would have suited me exactly. Sorry, but I've just this moment engaged a girl for the part. Sorry, girlie.'

Jolly life, this play-acting!

My Welsh cousins asked me to go down to them again. It was an escape. It helped to conserve the little money I had left. During my first week there Cousin Roger wrote from Canada, describing a wedding—David's. 'It wasn't much of a beano,' he wrote. 'The bride was in mourning for her mother. They are off to Australia now. David is going on business so he's making a honeymoon of the trip.'

It was better to know. I hoped Edith was preparing for her early death. There was a hollow where I had believed my heart to be. It was difficult to get to sleep at night.

In the third week of the visit a telegram came. 'See me immediately. Derwent Hall Caine.'

The cousins packed me and drove me to the train, and I was at Whitehall Court at ten next morning. Blade thin, cheeks hollow from lack of sleep, and quaking, I faced Derwent when he came into the sitting room of his father's flat in that quick nervous way of his. He handed me a script. It was *The Christian*. 'Read Glory to me. I'll give you cues.'

I was still reading Glory when the housekeeper announced his

Mary as Glory Quayle, the Manx girl who becomes a music hall star in the dramatization of Sir Hall Caine's novel The Christian.

lunch was on the table. He gave me cold chicken and claret. Afterwards the housekeeper took me into Sir Hall Caine's bedroom and helped me into Glory's clothes, which were hanging up in his wardrobe. The gowns fitted except that they needed to be lengthened.

Back in the sitting room, I read some more of the part, Derwent explaining the 'business'. We talked salary. I didn't open my mouth too large, and he was pleased when I offered to sing off stage, so saving him another salary. I had the part.

Next day I read Glory all the morning. Derwent sent me to Gustave for a red wig. My expense. The wig transformed me. Except for my snub nose it would have made me a handsome woman.

On the third day, now word-perfect in Glory's ninety 'sides', I met the full company, minus Derwent, on a London stage and we had a rehearsal. The stage manager was an Australian, William F. Grant. He was a darling. He helped me through a great ordeal.

On the fourth day we travelled to Liverpool—still without Derwent. On the fifth he turned up, consented to run through his scenes with me on the stage and then we broke up until theatre time.

Billy Grant threw me the lifeline as I trembled in the wings. 'Go on and show 'em, little Australian. You are going to be grand.' Here at last was the chance to act my head off. I forgot everything else, even David Cameron.

In my hand was a dove or a cormorant or an eagle. They gave me all sorts of birds that tour and most of them terrified me. This, the first, cast upon me a bleak unfriendly look as I stroked its head and sentimentalized over it.

'Fly over the wide sea. Go to your freedom,' I cried, releasing it. The base creature double banked, flew out into the auditorium and settled on the rim of the gallery box.

I sang my song off stage in French. Liverpool had never heard such French! On that first night I let it rip. Derwent had to speak through my song, on stage. He crossed to the prompt wing and muttered to Billy Grant: 'For God's sake! Doesn't that girl know the people have come here to listen to me and not her?'

I had not thought of him.

As a leading man Derwent was a devil. If the callboy forgot his special and individual call he would take the time to lose his temper and keep the stage waiting. Sometimes he would walk offstage to stop a noise in the wings, leaving me high and dry to smile it through. Frequently I had to invent to cover the breach while Derwent poured his invective on some stagehand. I thought him a bad actor but this season I thanked God for him.

THE OPERA HOUSE

It is doubtful if there has ever been such a crowded audience to witness a farce at the Burton Opera House as that which assembled on Monday evening. Fully an hour before the performance was timed to commence there was a small knot of intending spectators outside the doors, and as time went on this increased, and by seven o'clock there was a queue which reached well into Guild Street. The house, in fact, was filled through the early doors, and so uncomfortably filled that a number of those who had paid the additional price availed themselves of the offer of the management and took a pass-out cheque available for another night.

The audience was kept in a roar of laughter from start to finish. The story all hangs on the doings of Benjamin Fitzburgh, who, after imbibing not wisely but too well, is sentenced to thirty days imprisonment. In order to keep this fact from his wife, his friend pretends that Fitzburgh has had to go away to Mexico. When he returns from his holiday(?) he finds that his people have been studying Spanish in his absence, and his attempts to converse with them are highly amusing. In this the title role, Mr Edward Coutts is splendid, for he has a style of his own, which at once marks him as a clever comedian. In his part he is ably supported by Mr Staine Mills as Roderick Majors and Mr Frank Powell as Timothy Cook, while among the ladies Miss Muriel Langley as Fitzburgh's wife and Miss Mary Marlowe as Sally Grace, her sister, are worthy of special note. The farce, which is in three acts, is preceded by a curtain raiser, "The Recompenses", an incident in the South African War.

THEATRE ROYAL

There can be no two opinions about Hall Caine's drama, "The Christian", at the Theatre Royal this week, for it leaves an impression on the audience that few plays can create. The two main characters are, of course, the Rev. John Storm and Glory Quayle, the Manx girl who becomes a music-hall star, and the story centres round Storm's endeavour to get her to give up a life he thinks unfit. In this way religion becomes a dominating feature, and on the one hand we hear John Storm preaching and living a Christian life among the London poor, while on the other hand there is Lord Robert Ure describing religion as a struggle against nature, and using other condemnatory arguments with a venom that robs them of their little plausibility. Sandwiched between the two is Horatio Drake, a worldly man with some honour left. There is one very moot point, however, when Storm visits Glory and tells her he has come to kill her—"better a life ended than a life degraded". One is inclined to use as a negative argument to this that while there is life there is hope, even of repentance.

Nevertheless, the whole drama was presented in such a manner that the feelings of the most susceptible person could not be hurt. John Storm is a strong character, and there was a force and sincerity about Mr Derwent Hall Caine's acting of this part that was bound to carry the convictions of last night's large audience: in fact, his was a masterly performance. For Miss Mary Marlowe, as Glory Quayle, we have nothing but praise, for she displayed great qualities, both in the prologue as a lively young girl and in the emotional acting necessary in the following acts.

Left: One of Mary's first mentions in the British press. Early in 1911 she played Sally in The Man from Mexico in the provinces. Later she would play the part again in London.

Right: For several months in 1911, Mary toured the towns and cities of England playing Glory Quayle in The Christian. The play was so popular that when it played at the Lyceum Theatre in London hundreds were turned away nightly.

We toured the big towns of England, playing *The Christian* and *The Manxman*. Then we came back to the Greater London theatres. At Hoxton—the Blood Tub Theatre—when as Kate Cregeen I laid my wedding ring on the kitchen table and prepared to take leave of my property child in the cradle, a woman in the gallery cried out, 'Oh, don't go, missus, don't go!'

On tour we had rehearsed *The Bondman* somewhat spasmodically. I was scheduled to play Greeba until Derwent became engaged to some unknown actress and gave her the role. Neither the play nor the betrothal had much of a run. Derwent married another woman and I was left high and dry because most of the theatrical companies were already formed for the new season.

Prospects were far from bright. I had been out of work for a fortnight when the landlady brought up the *Era* with the breakfast tray. A small advertisement leapt at me: 'Wanted leading lady for Australia. Dramatic. Must be prepared to sail Friday. Apply No. . . Henrietta Street.'

Here was a perfectly good leading lady, lolling back on the pillows and eating toast and marmalade. Ah, the significance of toast and marmalade! Not much butter under the marmalade. This leading lady was darned hard up. And she was homesick. It was nearly two years since she had left her native land and she was quite prepared to sail for anywhere on Friday.

Putting on my best tailor-made—a Bradley bought in better times for bad ones—I went to Henrietta Street. The man responsible for the advertisement rang up one or two London producers and asked for my qualifications. They had rehearsed me and they said enough to get me the contract. As it was tucked away in my

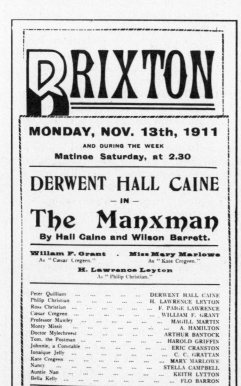

On the same tour as The Christian, *playing in the big towns of England and Scotland before opening in London, Mary also starred in* The Manxman *with Derwent Hall Caine, the author's son.*

'Mary Marlowe . . . gave a most pleasing portrayal of that fascinating creation of Hall Caine's, "Glory Quayle". She was delightfully natural amongst her native scenery in the Isle of Man and equally effective after her success behind the footlights in London. Possessed of considerable emotional qualities, her interviews with John Storm, and the spirited scene with Horatio Drake in the second act—the saloon of the "Philharmonic"—aroused the audience to enthusiasm.'

'Miss Mary Marlowe, who essays the character of Glory Quayle, is a young Australian, who, having met with much success in her native country, has come over here to achieve greater things. Her impersonation was of a highly satisfactory nature, and created a very good impression.'

'Miss Mary Marlowe, as "Glory Quayle" has . . . some difficult work, and the manner in which she portrays the part stamps her as the true artiste. She is certainly a clever actress as far as emotional work is concerned, and she has created a good impression in other parts of the provinces.'

'Miss Marlowe's Glory Quayle may be a little too boisterously buoyant in the first act, though as the play develops her undoubted powers as an actress emerge, and she creates an idealistic atmosphere round a somewhat difficult part.'

'Miss Mary Marlowe, as Glory Quayle, succeeded in her interpretation of the part in all but one thing. She did not realise for us quite the romp and madcap girl that the author . . . intended his heroine to be.'

'Miss Mary Marlowe is the Glory Quayle of the piece, and sustains the role very successfully, her naturalness throughout a trying part being highly commendable.'

'Miss Mary Marlowe as "Glory Quayle" was very successful all through. Her representation was a fine one from beginning to end, and won unanimous approval.'

'Miss Mary Marlowe, as the wayward but charmingly naive and good-hearted Glory Quayle, showed dramatic ability of no mean order, and, as the play proceeded, quite captivated the hearts of her audience.'

Applause from the critics up and down the British Isles for Mary's Glory Quayle.

bag I would not have changed it for the Koh-i-noor diamond.

The girl originally selected for the job had peritonitis or toothache or funk. Australia is remote to the English. Someone must sail on Friday. I would do. The fare was paid there and back and a six month contract carried a neat little salary.

The leading lady sailed on Friday. She had a kipper for breakfast. She spent her sinking fund on a new hat and some press photographs.

An Australian star

At Port Said the Arab said: 'Love and trouble are waiting at the end of the journey.' For two shillings, any Arab will shake momentous things out of his burnous for you. To balance the Terrible Twins, he predicted good fortune in work. He did not disturb my serenity. Ah, the soothing sea!

This leading lady job attracts lovers. They are inescapable; they go with the parts. No use getting uppish and taking it as personal. Leading ladies are supposed to have sex appeal or they wouldn't be chosen for leads. The men keep going until they find out.

In one theatrical troupe I had a torrid time. Five out of the six men thought it their duty to make love to me, certain that I would expect it. I believe the only reason the sixth didn't fall into the same error was because he was already attached to the heavy woman.

A woman on a ship alone, an actress at that, is fair game. On the outgoing ship I had three suitors. I have forgotten their names. One taught something at Oxford but I did not want to learn what he had to teach on shipboard. The second was a crook fleeing from justice, poetic or police. Every day before lunch he came to my chair and told me he had said too much but he couldn't help himself. The third was a Scottish engineer. A very hot-blooded fellow. I had to seek refuge by placing myself under the wing of a little Lancashire woman who was a match for him.

An exclusive boarding house had been selected for me in Sydney as suitable for a leading lady. They put me at a table with an elegant elderly gentleman. He was a widower and a bank manager. Even he was affected by the aura and the new experience. I thought he would 'declare' at every meal.

It was a reconditioned world I had come back to. Scene shifters with whom I had shared tables in small hotels on tour sent me telegrams on the opening night and there were flowers from strangers. The press interviewed me. Before, I had been acting myself stiff and

Miss Mary Marlowe's adorable hat—a dream in purple with an ostrich idyll in the same shade climbing over its roof—shook its dashing plumes in this office the other day. The girlish face under this imported millinery is sparkling with intelligence—a useful asset for any young person to carry about with her. Mary Marlowe came back to her native land under a six months' engagement to the new theatrical firm of Bailey and Grant. She leapt off the *Otranto* in time to take up a vigorous course of rehearsals for "The Squatter's Daughter". March 30 is the date of the girl's first appearance at the Palace Theatre.

"I didn't leave affluence to go on the stage," says Mary. "It left me—I mean the affluence did—for droughts followed the bank smash in Victoria many years ago, and my father's money gently subsided, or something of the kind. It's odd, of course, that my first part here should be as the squatter's daughter, my original role when I first toddled across the stage of life. I'm proud to say that any small success I snatched in London and the provinces was won by fisticuffs—*not* in the boxing sense—and not by influence of any kind. Managers in London, of course, have to be stalked with care by unknown Australian girls. When Eva Quinn, Jean Martin and I made the first great plunge for engagements on the English stage, we were not at all like the daughters of Croesus. However, we contrived to look so—an important matter. Eva had a very handsome set of furs, I had a silk underskirt that gave the right kind of rustle, also some good trinkets, and Jean Martin contributed her share. This gave us one prosperous-looking turn-out. We wore the combined wardrobe in turns when we interviewed managers. I often wondered whether it ever seemed familiar to the Great Power who saw it for the third time. They all doubted us when we said—in turn in our only affluent toilet—that we were Australians. 'But you don't speak the Australian language,' said they. 'You haven't—er—got the Colonial accent.' However, we provided an *alibi*, or whatever it is when you're bowled out in speaking the truth."

Australia 1912: Mary Marlowe charms the Sydney press when she returns to take up an engagement with Bailey and Grant.

"ON OUR SELECTION"

Encouraged no doubt by the exhilarating success of "The Squatter's Daughter", and, in a lesser degree, by the support extended to "The Man from Outback", Messrs Bert Bailey and Edmund Duggan produced another drama of local interest at the Palace Theatre on Saturday evening. It is a dramatised version of the well-written story "On Our Selection" by Arthur Davis ("Steele Rudd"), and is the collaborative work of Messrs Bailey, Duggan and Beaumont Smith . . . Viewed strictly as a drama, "On Our Selection" may be epitomised as a mixture of broad farce, comedy, and tragedy, while from the sentimental aspect an interesting love story meets all requirements. It is hardly necessary to mention that there was a large audience. Indeed, the greater portion of the reserved seats had been taken some days prior to the opening performance, and an hour before the curtain rose, the "house full" notice was exhibited. For a first night the drama went without a hitch, and uproarious merriment accurately describes the condition of the audience during nearly the whole of the four acts . . .

"ON OUR SELECTION"

GOOD AUSTRALIAN DRAMA

"And when the crops fail in the drought and all the stock is gone, what will you do then?"

"What will I do?" said Dad. "I'll do what many another man in Australia has had the heart to do before—I'll start again."

"On Our Selection", the play which was staged for the first time last night at the Palace Theatre, is Australian through and through. It brings to life again every laugh that Steele Rudd has raised in his most successful book.

The plot is a strong one; it has a number of dramatic incidents, but its sterling worth lies in the vivid truthfulness of the characters and the excellent way in which they are portrayed by Mr Bert Bailey's Company. There is not a false note in the wording of the piece—one may easily excuse a slightly exaggerated phrase here and there—and the acting brings out every humorous situation without spoiling it with over-emphasis.

The characters might have just stepped out of Steele Rudd's books. There is Dad and Mum, Dave and Joe, Sandy and Kate, Uncle and Malony, and Billy Bearup, just as they lived in the pages of the Australian humorist, and they bring with them the atmosphere of the bush.

The plot deals with the love of Sandy and Kate, the evil influence which Jim Carey, the son of the mortgagee over the selection, bears on their lives, and the murder of Carey by Cranky Jack. The story would serve easily by itself as the ground-work for an excellent melodrama, but the dialogue and the intensely human situation raise it above that, and place it in a class with the best American drama that has been seen in Sydney.

Sydney audiences enjoyed On Our Selection *which opened at the Palace Theatre on 4 May 1912.*

they had never noticed me. They gave me the star dressing room in the theatre where I had been an extra, dressing in with a mob of twelve.

After being associated for many years with an established Australian theatrical management, Bert Bailey and Julius Grant, the comedian and the business manager, had broken away and launched into management for themselves. This was their first venture and I was their first leading lady. They had taken a long lease of the King's Theatre in Melbourne and by arrangement with J. and N. Tait— a firm then starting to provide strong competition for the old house of J. C. Williamson—they were able to sublease the Tait playhouse in Sydney and allow the Taits to use the King's. This gave them two strong bases. In the other states and in New Zealand it was easy enough to book theatres and so they were sure of a long circuit. Julius Grant, please remember, was the manager who had told me politely when I was fifteen he had no possible use for me.

Our opening piece at the Palace Theatre in Sydney was a revival of *The Squatter's Daughter*, which Bert Bailey had written, and which had broken records on its first presentation. It was good melodrama and crowded with real Australian atmosphere. Except for a few horseback scenes that made me fidgety, I enjoyed the part. For the first time on the stage I found out that heroines must have a good deal of courage to face the situations of danger inseparable from real drama. The part of Violet Enderby called on me to walk narrow logs perilously poised above gushing waterfalls, shoot at people while I went in terror of the gun, hold a horse steady with his eyes to the footlights while a rope was attached to his neck and the other end thrown to a hero on a cliff who then proceeded to climb down it. I had to make my first entrance with a speech of six 'sides' describing a kangaroo hunt, and perhaps that was the worst ordeal of all.

Our second piece was Scottish. For no apparent reason it was called *Bonnie Mary* and the old tune was played softly by the orchestra every time I put foot on the stage. I wore my red wig to make up for my bad Scottish accent. It was becoming, and so was the white silk nightdress with the lavender bows for the bedroom scene. The bad man was hiding behind the bed curtains as I knelt and said my prayers and afterwards . . . well, it was very dashing. The villain was my old friend Jimmy of the Julius Knight company who later became a major in the Coldstream Guards.

On Our Selection (which opened at the Palace on 4 May 1912) was our third play. Bert Bailey made the play but the man who wrote the book, Steele Rudd (Arthur H. Davis), had been born and bred on one of my family's stations in Queensland. Here was I, come from the other end of the earth, to play his heroine.

The Davis family had looked after the railway siding and held a farm on my grandfather's land. The piece was written about the humble but doughty people whom he had noticed in his youth around the district. I had been born a squatter's daughter—like the heroine of our first piece—but it seemed an even greater coincidence to be playing Kate Rudd of the Rudds of 'Westbrook' railway siding.

On Our Selection proved a gold mine for the managers. It also gave Bert Bailey, as Dad Rudd, the finest and best remembered part of his long and varied career. No classic, this play, but it broke all records on the Australian stage, repeating that phenomenal success when it was made into a talking picture. Its success lay in its laughter.

During that year's engagement with the Bailey–Grant Company, my contract being renewed at the end of the initial six months, we played five pieces besides *On Our Selection*. Our company had a fine domestic atmosphere. There were several happily married couples in our casts and nobody quarrelled or grumbled. The two managers set the good-humoured mood.

The night before we left Sydney for Melbourne, the seat of my family, where I had been invited to be the honoured guest of the aunt who was now the Member of Parliament's widow, some friends and I were talking. One of these was a doctor who had pulled me through bouts of laryngitis in former days. He said to me, half in warning, half jocularly, 'You be careful now on tour and don't upset the balance of that happy company. You have a dash of flame in you. Look out!'

With the cheerful assurance of supreme ignorance, I laughed and replied: 'I have a simple creed. I try not to hurt people's feelings and I don't want any woman's husband. They are quite safe.'

The doctor laughed, too. 'All right so long as the husbands feel the same way. But, my dear, you eliminate the element of surprise. That's always risky.'

Forty-eight hours later we were in Melbourne playing at the King's Theatre. David was waiting for me when the show was over. He took me home.

Conflict and cobbers

A man seizes the passing moment for happiness. All men. Women
find happiness when it has foundations in the future. Like most
men in love David Cameron was an opportunist. Did he think about
the future at all? He was terribly urgent about the present.

Every night he was waiting outside the theatre to take me home.
Every night the old arguments were thrashed out. They were
threadbare but he went on using them, flogging them. It was the
age-old argument between a man and woman: 'You won't because
you don't care enough. When you really care for a man you won't
care a damn for the future.' Like a weed this argument cropped
up.

'When the time comes that you do love somebody you'll know
what I'm going through now.' Another weed.

I bore it for a fortnight and then I made a stand against my own
weakness, folly, love. This trinity controlled me. 'I won't see him
again.'

The resolution taken, for many weeks I passed David every night
in the street and refused to acknowledge he was there. I made a
point of leaving the theatre with one or two people who would
be walking my way towards the tram which took me to my suburb.
David was too proud to crash in and join me. Each night when
I saw him waiting for me my heart almost left my body. I told
myself I would get over it. Edith was in Melbourne and from stray
fragments of news I picked up about her it seemed that her untimely
death was highly unlikely.

I developed a distressing complaint which, for two guineas, a
Collins Street specialist diagnosed as nervous indigestion. Did he
guess what caused it? 'You feel things more than most people,' he
said. 'Ever since you were a little girl you have been feeling things
in a much more acute way than most people. Breathe deeply. You
can get this nerve mixture at the corner chemist, but the best I can

do for you is to advise you in time of trouble to breathe deeply.'

Having luncheon one day at the Vienna Cafe with my honoured aunts, I heard David's voice. My heart leapt so high I half expected to see it sitting with the beetroot on top of the lettuce on my plate. If his voice could do that I knew it was not safe to be within touch of his hand.

I was back among the people who did no wrong. Their standards were not mine any more, but I had my own. I must not hurt another if it could be helped. I must not take her husband. Stronger than the rage in me and the passion in me, was my inherited morality and that cheap little ambition I had to be a heroine.

Daily, hourly, nightly, I fought the fight. I lost my faith in eternal goodness—in God. I lost faith in everything. I had cried and prayed for help to a personal God and there was no help and very little courage in me. One thing only kept me to my resolution: horror of injustice. There was another woman in this. She didn't know. She mustn't know. Why should she suffer what I was suffering? One of us was enough.

The last week we were in Melbourne he rang me at my aunt's home and asked me to meet him at the end of the road when it was dark. I said I would. But the respectability of that household overcame me. When the hour struck I was glued to the hall. I could not bring myself to open the door. The family—unconscious of their influence—conquered. I stayed indoors and David wondered and waited in vain.

The last night of the season as I left the theatre—alone this time—David caught up with me. He had taken a risk and told me he was determined this night to separate me from any escort at whatever cost. We walked the full four miles to my aunt's home. The moon turned the silver birches on St Kilda Road to silver flame.

'You cannot escape me,' David said. 'I will follow you all over Australia . . . and then wherever you may be.'

It came out by slow degrees that Edith had made up her mind to go back to Canada. She did not care for Australia and she missed her friends. She had a baby boy. She did not like travelling with her husband.

'Can't you let her know it is foolish, dangerous?' I said.

'Why should I when I don't care?'

'A wife's place . . .'

'My God!' he cried, impatient, 'You know them all, Mary. Don't be trite. Be human.'

I couldn't be human. The family traditions were too strong.

When Miss Mary Marlowe entered the cosy parlour where I was waiting for her at the Hotel Cecil, I was struck with the remarkable resemblance she bore to Miss Margaret Thomas, another popular young English lady, who was such a success with J. C. Williamson's Comic Opera Company six or seven years ago. After greeting, I said:

"Pardon me, Miss Marlowe, are you any relation to Miss Margaret Thomas . . .?"

She smiled and answered in the negative. Then she continued: "I'm Australian born and bred, but I went to England some years ago."

Surprised, I said, "Then we cannot claim any credit for—"

With light, laughing brown eyes, the young actress interrupted me with—

"If there is anything creditable about my position on the stage, Australia is entitled to it, because I played with the Julius Knight Company before I went to England."

"Oh, I see; then you are quite an Australian?"

"Yes, indeed," she replied. "I am a native of Melbourne, and am proud of it, but, I love England and its people, for I made many friends there."

"Did you play leading parts in the Motherland?" I asked.

"Yes, I played Hall Caine's heroines Glory Quayle and Greela in the company which included the author's son, Hall Caine, junior, who is fast coming to the front in London. Then I filled a six months' engagement with 'The Man from Mexico' Co. at the Strand Theatre, in a leading part."

"Were you specially engaged by the Bert Bailey Co. to come to Australia?" I queried.

Miss Marlowe smiled and said: "Yes, 'The Squatter's Daughter' was the first piece I appeared in. Then we played 'The Man from Out Back', and after very good business we played 'On Our Selection', which has been quite a triumph. As the play has almost a personal interest to me I am quite happy at being one of the company that has helped to make it famous."

. . . Miss Mary Marlowe should reach the highest pinnacle on the dramatic stage, as she has all the attributes which go to make a famous actress. Tall and graceful in figure, with large brilliant eyes, aquiline features, an impressive mouth which when smiling, reveals two gleaming rows of even teeth, she is indeed endowed. Miss Marlowe expressed her keen desire to visit India and the East before returning to England, and at the conclusion of her present engagement it is her intention to do so. Miss Mary Marlowe, we wish you well wherever you go, and as fellow countrymen, are proud of you.

—Kildare.

Australia 1912: The local press interviews Mary.

THE
SQUATTER'S DAUGHTER

It is four and a half years since "The Squatter's Daughter" was first produced at the Theatre Royal, but time has not staled its popularity. When the piece was revised for the fourth time on Saturday night by the Bert Bailey Dramatic Company the enthusiastic reception of February, 1908, was repeated and again many were turned away. Mr Julius Grant was posting up "House full" at 8 o'clock, a notice by-the-way, that has been frequently used during the present season. "On Our Selection" had a fine run, and when the management reluctantly withdrew the comedy the attendances were large to overflowing . . . "The Squatter's Daughter" bids fair to rival the general patronage of the first of the company's repertoire, although there will be only five more nights to do it, for "Bonnie Mary" labelled in advance, "a new play and a good play" is announced for next Saturday evening. "The Squatter's Daughter" was excellently presented and the best testimony to its capacity to keep the crowd at the right pitch of enthusiasm was supplied by the detonations of applause that alternated with the booms of laughter. Add the pistol shots to these and also the emotional exclamations of patrons who were completely carried away by the thrill of the episodes, and it may well be imagined what a lively time there was. Certainly the members of the company got out of the melodrama quite as much as the authors had put into it and the scenery imparted a stirring spectacular interest to a story which need not be retold . . . The principal roles were most satisfactorily presented. Mr Guy Hastings made the part of Tom Bathurst an attractive one for its courage and dignity as the overseer, and manly tenderness as the lover of the squatter's daughter, Miss Mary Marlowe. Her impersonation of the heroine was bright and wholesome, without being especially vigorous or winsome. Mr Bert Bailey was Arebie MacPherson, "of the clan MacPherson" from head to feet, and all over, and if he did accept some apparently tragical situations with surprising flippancy, the intention was creditable. He was funny, anyway, and that was what he was intended to be . . .

'Miss Mary Marlowe, as Kate Rudd, had a difficult part, but she did it ample justice.'

'Miss Mary Marlowe invests her work with quiet dignity and appeal. The emotional parts are perhaps rather too subdued, but altogether Miss Marlowe has an easy, pleasant style.'

'The acting was equal to the requirements of the piece. Miss Mary Marlowe, as Mary Melrose, well sustained her mournful role. Her path was a veritable "Via Dolorosa".'

With Bailey and Grant, Mary toured Australia. As Kate Rudd in On Our Selection, she pleased most of the critics in the cities visited. The review above appeared in the Adelaide paper the Register on 19 August 1912.

Never since the world began, never until it ends have there been or could there be more considerate or more kindly theatrical managers than Bert Bailey and Julius Grant. They were two honest-to-God troupers who hadn't been spoilt by financial success. They did unto their actors as they would be done by. Over and above that Bert Bailey is the best character actor that Australia has produced this century. He has made 'Dad' of the outback live for as long as those who saw him play it have memories. After that he will pass into stage tradition.

Julius Grant is the type of man who couldn't be other than kind. There is a story told of how he acquired enough money to go into management with his friend, Bert. 'Jules' Grant was house manager of a Melbourne theatre. Night after night an elderly man, who seemed to be in poor circumstances and was palpably a lonely fellow, haunted the street in front of the theatre. He would get into conversation with Jules. They would talk of many things, the house manager always affable, ready for a quick laugh, full of pleasant anecdotes, a sympathetic listener. And from this a friendship grew. Sometimes Jules put the stranger 'in front' in some odd seat that nobody wanted. After the show ended, the yarns would begin again, always in the street. He never asked the stranger's name. To Jules he was merely a lonely man who was badly off, a man at a loose end, a man without friends.

Then came the day when the stranger died. Jules heard more of him, for he had left him his modest fortune, a matter of a couple of thousand pounds. Jules had the capital to go into management.

He made big profits and saved them. As I write now, he lives in bachelor ease on his apple orchard at Olinda in the Dandenong Ranges, troubled only by the raids of itinerant birds and the codlin moth. Once a week or so he comes to town for a yarn with his old friends or to attend a meeting of some society formed to erect statues to that gloomy English poet in exile, Adam Lindsay Gordon.

Years after that theatrical season, Jules met me on the doorstep of a literary society which had made me a member, not for my qualities as a writer but because I had been able to help them a little in the press. That evening Jules stood up and spoke for me. He did me proud. He told all those who had come to see the author before they read the author—a peculiarity of literary societies—that his firm had been proud to import me from England to be their leading lady and together we had gone from one success to another.

Bert Bailey also lives in luxurious retirement with his daughter. The profits of *On Our Selection*, play and film, have made life

The cast of On Our Selection. Top row (from left to right)—Lilias Adeson (Lily), Queenie Sefton (Mrs White), E. Duggan (Maloney), Guy Hastings (Sandy), Alfred Harford (Billy Bearup); middle row—Arthur Bertram (Joe), Alfreda Bevan (Mum), Bert Bailey (Dad), Mary Marlowe (Kate Rudd); front—Fred MacDonald (Dave), Laura Roberts (Sarah) and Willie Driscoll (Uncle).

MISS MARY MARLOWE

"THE BEST THING ON EARTH"

Miss Mary Marlowe—with an E—who plays Kate in "On Our Selection" is much in the public eye at present. Kate is one of the few parts in the piece which is not a character study—but what drama is complete without a heroine?

And Miss Marlowe makes a most charming and sympathetic one, such as the minds of the dramatists, Messrs Bert Bailey and Edmund Duggan, conjured up, when they traced her in with such delicate artistry. In fact as "Steele Rudd" himself says, "I wouldn't change a line of the play." . . .

The English-Australian actress (for Australia is her birth place) confesses to doing a little scribbling. She wrote a melodrama when she was in her early teens, which she laughingly "threatens" to produce. She has just written a sketch adapted from Anstey's "The Tinted Venus", which tells of a statue in a barber's shop coming to life and falling in love with the barber. There are two outstanding characters in it and it was the actress' intention to present it at one of the music halls, when she received an engagement by the Bert Bailey management for this Australasian tour. "The Squatter's Daughter", "Bonnie Mary" and "The Man from Out Back" were included in the repertoire together with "On Our Selection".

"That has been our trump-card," said Miss Marlowe enthusiastically. "Seven weeks in Melbourne to phenomenal business, and in Sydney they simply 'ate' it! They came from far and near to see Dad and his family! It was very funny, too, to hear the remarks made by the spectators from way-back, as they analysed and recognised the various characters portrayed on the stage. Australian colouring to the life! It caught on marvellously. And I see no reason why it should not do likewise in New Zealand. Life in the back blocks is essentially the same everywhere—the same privations and hardships—the same indomitable spirit which makes for pioneers—a little laughter to leaven the load. Laughter is universal. 'On Our Selection' is bound to provoke it, whether it's presented to Australians or New Zealanders.

"My only regret is that I haven't got a laugh in it! I'm always cast for the emotional, and I should just love comedy. To be able to make people laugh, either on or off the stage, is I consider, the best thing on earth."

After their Australian tour, the Bailey and Grant company toured New Zealand. One critic there wrote: 'Miss Mary Marlowe is an ideal Kate, interpreting the role of the heroine with a quiet dignity and lovableness that win her the sympathy of all.' Here she is interviewed by the New Zealand Sporting and Dramatic Review, *21 November 1912.*

pleasant. Today he looks the benign patriarch because he refuses to part with the beard he grew for the screen version of Dad Rudd, but his eyes are young.

They are matchless fellows in comradeship, these two. I shall love them always.

We travelled from Brisbane to Perth, from Sydney to Tasmania and on through New Zealand; from Broken Hill to Melbourne. We played to capacity houses almost everywhere. We toured the country after the cities. We played on the largest stages in the Commonwealth and some of the smallest. We had six pieces in our repertory but unless the season was lengthy we did not need another after *On Our Selection*. It coined money wherever we played it. It went on coining money long after I had left the company.

Every now and then David and I would be in the same town. We always met and we always went over the same old arguments. They were poignant hours that led to no conclusion.

Now I had come to the end of my journey. My passage to England was booked. Presently twelve thousand miles would keep me out of mischief. It was London for me and Australia for David. Edith was still in Canada. She must have been conscious of something lacking in her relationship with David or she would not have left him at the mercy of his passing emotions.

It may have been an ordinary germ, but I think it was the abyss stretching ahead of me that caused my vitality to ebb during the last weeks of our tour. In Broken Hill three doctors did their best for me on the assumption that I was suffering from influenza. I had no understudy so I had to crawl onto the stage. I would leave it to vomit in the lane.

I felt close to death when we jolted out of Broken Hill by the back streets. There was a railway strike and we were afraid the strikers would stop us. We were all crowded onto a large lorry. Some of the men sat on top of the luggage and the property master clung as best he could to the ropes which bound it. Every little while the lorry was pulled up to retrieve some piece that had slipped its cable.

It was fiercely hot as we bumped over the desert, over dead and half submerged trees, past the bleached bones of animals. There was no track. It was sunset when we reached the railway, the sky a purple and crimson smear. We had a rough meal in a wooden shed called the 'Railway Refreshment Rooms'. We sat up all night in the train bound for Wallaroo on Spencer Gulf.

From Wallaroo the trade ships go to the outer world. It is a runt of a town but there was a bathroom at the hotel. Actors on tour ask no more.

We played three nights and moved on to Adelaide, taking in Gawler for a one-night stand. We left the hotel there in a horse vehicle like a prairie schooner with thick straw on the floor. The golden bangle that I had worn since a child dropped into it, but as we only just had time to catch the train, it was never found. To my highly-coloured imagination it seemed an omen: the past was past.

When the train ran into Melbourne at last, I said goodbye to the company in the carriage. In the afternoon they were going on to Sydney by the express. A local actress had been engaged to take over my part. My aunt, the ex-Speaker's wife, had invited me to stay with her until I sailed.

David was waiting for me outside the Melbourne railway station. I sent my luggage by the carrier, and David and I walked down the long stretch of Collins Street together. He told me he was sailing for New Zealand that afternoon at four on his company's affairs. He had come to the train to make a final plea. Would I go with him or wait for him to return from New Zealand?

'You really didn't expect it,' I said. 'This is goodbye.'

It is a long way down Collins Street from the railway station to the Town Hall. Too long if you are saying goodbye.

A street seller held out some violets on our way down. David bought a bunch for me. We walked on in silence to the Town Hall. My tram left from there. We waited silently, side by side, for a few minutes until it came.

David helped me onto the open car, the dummy we used to call it. Hand over mine, he said: 'I will never forget you. I will never be far away from you.'

I remember lifting the bunch of violets to my lips as the tram started. I could not see David any more.

As the tram went on relentlessly for the four miles between the Town Hall and the street where my aunt lived, I recalled all the comfortable, smug married women I knew. They were so sure of themselves, always so quick to judge those less fortunate than themselves. I wondered if they knew—many of them—how close they lived to the invisible danger. I wondered if they had any idea—all of them—of what was going on in the minds of the husbands lying by their sides. Then I thought of the hundreds of women who were in a similar predicament to mine. Maybe they were saying to themselves, just as I was saying, 'Why should this happen to me?'

I thought of my friends and my relations, of all who had tried to bring me up in the right way and form my character and stiffen my morality. Of each I could say, 'You are happy. You have the husband you want. You have children and their love. If you have not now you have had in the past. Your man comes home to you after his day's work. He is working for you and your children. These things you have accepted as your right. Or you? You have a lover who will one day be your husband. Who are any of you to judge me in my struggle? Who are you to judge me if I stop struggling and send for David?'

Yet the tram took me further away from him and I knew I had come to the end of the struggle.

When I reached my aunt's house I collapsed. For two days I lay like a dead log on a bed on the balcony. Influenza was as good an excuse as any other. My Unmarried and Emotional Aunt sat by my bedside hour after hour, her eyes on my face. At last she lost patience. 'For goodness sake, wake up!' she said. 'You can't lie there and sleep all the time. You're being ridiculous.'

When the month was up I was on my way back to England and there was nobody to tell me, or nobody to mind, whether or not I was ridiculous.

At a terrible price I had conquered myself. I had not been guilty of the sin of taking a woman's husband from her but I wondered often on those quiet nights at sea if the same thing were to happen again would I be able to go through the struggle a second time and win.

Being a good wife is a full-time job and not, as so many regard it, merely part-time work. When I hear them talking about their husbands as though they were household jugs I think: 'Have you any idea how near you may be to the danger line?'

Dying is hard work

We three—Jean, Eve and I—arrived back in London within the same month [December 1912]. Jean came from Russia because she was going to have another child. She had amazing tales to tell. One that lingers in my mind is about a housemaid. Having shown her how to clean the washstand, the following morning Jean came upon the little Russian scrubbing the toothbrushes.

Eve, who had been a stage success in South Africa in the part of Janet Cannot in *The Great Adventure*—a character not unlike her own in its practical approach to life—had developed a social complex. To catch her at home in her Bayswater rooms you had to call before breakfast. When she wasn't being social she was buying clothes for parties.

I had two rooms next door to her but I kept my troubles to myself. That is the way I can always best bear them.

First Derwent Hall Caine sent for me and offered me Glory again. But I asked for too much and they found someone else. Then Rufe Naylor engaged me to go to South Africa at a week's notice to play ingenues in his new stock company. The engagement was to last six months with the option of six more. I signed the contract on a Friday in green ink.

At the first rehearsal—in a bar parlour in a remote suburb—the stage director handed me a sheaf of printed plays and told me to learn the leads. I would be playing them. Then I panicked. I went to a doctor and asked for a certificate to release me from fulfilling the contract. Africa was so distant. Supposing we crashed? What would I do for money? The doctor, who conscientiously examined me before issuing a certificate, told me that I was so thin my kidneys had come loose and I was on the verge of a nervous breakdown. He gave me an address in Wales and urged me to stay there for two months.

The girls were surprised. They did not regard me as the sort of person who cracks up with hard work. Yet what else could it be? Exactly! What else? The stars were for me. In South Africa the company went on the rocks.

I finished up at Horton Burrows in South Wales. I went there to die. I hoped to die, prayed to die and was expected by the villagers to die. But the climate was too salubrious.

The first room they gave me was in a lime-washed cottage up the hill from the sea. Kneeling on the lumpy feather bed, I could touch the ceiling. To look through the dormer window one had to stoop a little. There were sunflowers in the garden and the sea was ahead—the Bristol Channel, it is true, but there were sea-going ships upon it. The sun baked the lime-washed cottages to radiance. It seemed a waste of time to die.

The village dog made friends with me. He knew the best of the walks and the quiet places where a dog might find a rabbit and a woman solitude. He knew the nicest people in the cottages and through him I was made welcome.

When, a week later, the village was free of visitors, I moved down to a big house facing the sand dunes and sea-grass. I was the solitary boarder. The cook was rising seventy, with a white beard, a crumpled forehead and a laugh full of fireworks. She talked to me as I went to the kitchen for my morning glass of milk.

'We thought you had come to die,' said the cook. 'It seemed a shame—a nice, plain lady like you. Once I wanted to die, like you, but there was too much work to do.'

Here was an idea! As I loafed on the hot sand, skylarks overhead singing of hope, the shush-shush of the sea at my feet, the words of the old cook belaboured my mind: there was too much work to do.

Philosophy for the timid and the discouraged! From the working people can always be learned the best lessons. The cook was right. Soaked in sunshine, I jumped up at the last, walked to Porteynon and bought a fat writing pad from the postmistress. I was out of things until my strength came back but I could start my book. It had been working in my mind for some months.

Every evening when dusk fell, a lamp was brought into the sitting room. To the sound of the sea through the open French windows I began the tale of our adventures: Jean's and Eve's and mine. It was not half as hard as I had imagined.

I spent a month in this forgotten corner, then the money question began to worry me. Since I couldn't die and cease to bother, I must get back to work.

The Three Arts Club in London was my next home. It sounded friendly but, unless you belonged to one of the inner cliques, it wasn't. Everybody was important and each girl took herself seriously. They all dressed like posters. We each had a cubicle and no man was permitted to put a foot on the stairs.

It cost nineteen and six for the cubicle and there was a set rate for breakfast. For a small sum you could have a kipper, a sausage or an egg. The crockery was ultra-floral, which made it seem better value.

In the cubicle next to mine Gwen Richardson spent several hours each day saying 'Ah!' in strange ways. She called the noises tonal exercises. She was the protegée of Ellen Terry, and spent weekends with Ellen and her daughter at their country cottage at Hythe.

Through Gwen I met Ellen Terry. Ellen was Personality Girl Number One. She couldn't help making you feel you were the only other girl in the world she really wanted to talk to—and there was so much to say. Australia, for instance. Lovely Melbourne! Melbourne for homes. Sydney for a holiday. Couldn't remember my words, my dear, but they were always wonderful to me in Australia. Incorrigible Ellen!

Gwen Richardson flamed into sudden success at the Old Vic as Lady Macbeth and then deserted the stage to hunt diamonds in Brazil. She wrote a book about her adventure and the stage lost an interesting personality.

Louis Meyer was engaging companies for Canada and Australia to play *The Glad Eye*. Somebody told me. I thought I could do with Canada, and put on my long feather—the leading-lady one bought in Shaftesbury Avenue on the eve of sailing for home. It worked. I went to the Strand, interviewed Meyer, and came away with a contract for Canada.

Canada and a bite of the Big Apple

Meyer had said: 'There will be a second piece, *The Real Thing*. Phyllis Neilson Terry is playing it for me here. Watch it. I've engaged a girl for the lead in that, but I have a hunch you'll be playing it when it comes to the point.'

Before we left London I almost knew the play by heart.

That year [1913] we were the last ship up the St Lawrence. We could almost see the river freeze behind us. Canada was deep in snow. The sepia-tinted trees on the banks were bare. This new world, bright with winter sunshine, was like a fine etching.

We arrived at Quebec just as the lights went up in the Chateau Frontenac and on the ramparts of the old town. We came into Montreal in the early morning: sun up, and the sidewalks brushed; snow piled many feet high on each side of the wooden broadwalks. The roads were hard under white carpets.

In the afternoon we rehearsed at the Princess Theatre and that night we opened our season. We were keyed up for a thrilling premiere. We got it but not the sort we expected.

For the past four years the students of McGill University had not been allowed to attend a theatre in a body. That ban was lifted at last, and lifted for our first performance. This was their grand renewal of their ancient rite, 'Theatre Night'.

Mr S. Morgan-Powell, critic of the *Montreal Daily Star*, has better described our first night in Canada than I could hope to.

McGILL STUDENTS BEHAVE SO BADLY
THAT THEATRE IS CLOSED

When Mr Wright, manager of the Princess Theatre, accepted the word of honour of McGill University that they would behave like gentlemen on the occasion of the 'Theatre Night', he took a big risk. He will never take another. Neither will any theatre manager in Montreal if he has any sense. The McGill student body laid itself out to convince Mr

LOUIS MEYER introduces

The full All--Star British Company

direct from the Strand Theatre London
in

THE GLAD EYE

(A farcical Comedy in three acts, adapted
by JOS. G LEVY from the French
Le. Zebre by MM. Armott and Nancey.)

THE CHARACTERS

Gaston Bocard	Douglas Greet
Mauaice Polignac	Fredk Meads
Galipaux	Augustus Wheatman
Chausette	Walter Hicks
Ferdinand Flowuet	Reginald Fry
Tracassin	Walter Linsday
Comte de la Beuve	Colsten Mansell
Francois	Grenville Darling
Police Sergent	Martin Henry
Lucienne Bocard	Mary Marlowe
Suzanne Polignac	Eve Walsh-Hall
Kiki	Katie Yates
Juliette	Irene L'Estrange

THE SCENES

ACT I. Morningroom at the Chateau de Vercottes.
Mons. Galipaux, House in the country, near Paris.

Schmitz London

ACT II. The Library at the Chateau de Vercottes.
To days later-

Bull London

ACT III. Same as act I. The next morning

The play produced by E Dagnall.

Dresses by Cuthbert 50 Margaret St. London

Stage Manager	Martin Henry
Business Manager	Graham Pockett
Canadian Manager, Ahead	H Armitage

One Canadian newspaper reported that The Glad Eye was 'presented by a splendid British cast' and had 'admirable settings and stunning gowns'.

Wright—and everybody else who was present at the disgraceful scene last night—that its 'word of honour' is not worth ten cents.

It was simply pandemonium from 8.25 p.m. when the curtain went up till 9.40 when it was finally rung down on Mr. Wright's orders. The student body laid itself out 'to guy the show', to make things unendurable for every decent person present, and to distinguish itself in rowdyism.

Bags of flour were flung at the actors and actresses on the stage. Small bags containing sand and lead pellets were dropped upon the audience from the galleries; pepper-laden snuff was scattered about; hens, pigeons, frogs, and other missiles were thrown about; occasionally offensive shouts further polluted the air, and not a single sentence was audible from the raising of the curtain until one of the actresses closed a speech with the apposite words . . . 'Call the police!'

I was the actress. With a laugh in my voice and a breaking heart, I let them have it over the footlights, as though it were a line from my role. They gave me a rousing cheer for it. That was our opening night in Canada.

When the acrid experience of the McGill student body had lost its pungency I began to love the Canadians. More or less they all reminded me of David and St Bernard dogs.

We went west to Winnipeg, where we were forever diving into shops and hotel lobbies to thaw out. Icicles formed on our eyebrows and crisped the thin hairs inside our noses. We performed for the One Hundredth Regiment Winnipeg Grenadiers. What a difference! The theatre was profusely decorated with their colours—red and royal blue and white. The men were in their 'scarlets'. This time we faced an audience in gala mood.

At the end of the second act a very small boy appeared from the orchestra pit, saluted smartly and placed a sheaf of American-beauty

Scenes from The Glad Eye.
Above: Act I—'Galipaux' exhibits Chausette to the ladies
Below: Act II—An amusing end to the second act

Above: Dressed for the part of Lucienne Bocard in The Glad Eye.

Below: Baggage day. The company went through the Rockies and back again playing at places like Moosejaw, Medicine Hat and Nelson at the far end of the Arrow Lakes.

roses in my arms. He was no taller than the stems of the flowers. Another perfect salute from him brought down the curtains, and the house.

Next day I wrote a thank-you note and said I would keep the colours I had souvenired until they fell apart. The colonel of the regiment replied that this gesture was appreciated and it would be a future pleasure to send me the Grenadiers' Christmas card. I received one only. By the second Christmas the entire regiment had been wiped out in the European War.

At Regina the Canadian Mounted Police had a 'Theatre Night'. They did not clap, they stamped. The noise was like herds of moose rushing down a hillside.

In Calgary we commenced to rehearse *The Real Thing*. The woman who had been engaged for the lead was slumberously beautiful with latent fire smouldering beneath her classic surface. She had studied Greek drama and she had known Rupert Brooke. She was a highbrow with a goddess complex. She had just married a gawky schoolboy who was also with the company. They quarrelled all the time and towards midnight she grew intensely Greek. Every night we could hear her private interpretation of Medea, as she tried to break in her husband. Naturally, this young woman was a little contemptuous of French farce and she had difficulty memorizing her lines. The rehearsals suffered in consequence.

One night Medea overdid it. Both she and her husband missed the early morning train, the only one that day. At a conference in the corridor it was decided that I was to play the lead in *The Real Thing*, opening at our next stop in four days. I retired to the remotest corner of the long, swaying train to study the part. Medea and her husband arrived the next day. She watched the rehearsal for a few minutes and somewhat abruptly left the stage. She was back a few hours later to tell me she had the part back. Our business manager, Graham Pocket, had said so.

'He's still in bed or he'd have come round himself,' she said.

I went straight to Graham's bedside. He had no idea that I, too, could give a fairly decent imitation of Medea. I said my piece, swept to the door and delivered my ultimatum. 'Take your choice. I play that part or I go back to England tonight on the outgoing train.' God only knew where the money would come from but my air of sincerity and outrage made little Pocket sit up and shiver.

I played the part. It had been written for Yvonne Printemps by her husband, Sacha Guitry (the actor/playwright who had taught all his five wives to act), and it had everything in it that an actress could

KEPT HOUSE LAUGHING

"THE GLAD EYE" SCORES AT THE RUSSELL THEATRE—IS FULL OF FUN

"The Glad Eye" is a very English version of a French vaudeville. The old time tricks of two gay young husbands who give their wives in the country the slip to trot off to Paris are its theme. Of course, an excuse has to be found for these delightful excursions, and the balloon of Monsieur le Comte de la Beuve, whom neither gentlemen have seen, serves this purpose. So Messieurs Gaston and Maurice are making balloon ascents with their dear friend the Comte de la Beuve.

Now Maurice has a credulous wife in Suzanne, and the tale does for her, since Maurice is glib of tongue and lies; but when Gaston starts in to balloon, too, he arouses his shrewd wife's suspicions. And Gaston is the usual vaudeville jackass, who is always putting his foot in it to make the audience laugh.

Such are the elements of which "The Glad Eye" is compounded. The play itself last night was a little slow in getting off, but once started it did what the advance notices said it would—that is, it kept the house laughing. It is all good, clean fun, and you never know what will happen next.

As Madame Lucienne Bocard, Miss Mary Marlowe was the pick. Her dresses alone are worth a visit to the Russell. Further, she can act, and further still, she looks very fascinating in her wonderful dresses, which entitle her to the claim of being "the best dressed woman in Paris". She should go far in this country . . .

'The work of Miss Mary Marlowe as Lucienne Bocard, one of the wives in the dual situation, also approaches very close to the line of true comedy. Miss Marlowe is both apt and dexterous. She is at times more than this, and then there is a haunting sincerity about her callousness and her sophistication that draws near to fine art.'

'Miss Mary Marlowe, as the wife who unravels the machinations of the deceiving husbands, was very charming, and she had good support in the person of Miss Eva Walsh-Hall.'

'Miss Mary Marlowe and Miss Eva Walsh-Hall, as the two wives, one wise but the other trusting, are both admirable in their parts. They have attractive personalities, are bright and vivacious, and interpret their roles with splendid effect.'

Canadian audiences enjoyed The Glad Eye. The reviews were accompanied by headlines such as 'The Glad Eye Makes Big Hit', 'Kept House Laughing', 'Most Hilarious Comedy' and 'Glad Eye Winks Way Through a Rollicking Farce'. The review above appeared in the Ottawa Evening Journal, 5 December 1913.

STAR OF "THE GLAD EYE" VOTED ONLY ONCE, AND THEN "FOR A REASON"

The ardent suffragist claims entry of the polling booth as a right. Miss Mary Marlowe, who comes from Australia, where the women have the vote, says that the polling booth is at least a convenience.

"Have you ever voted?" asked The Herald reporter of the pretty little lady who is playing the leading part in "The Glad Eye" at the Princess this week.

"Only once" replied Miss Marlowe, "and that was for a very feminine reason. Shall I tell you? Well, one election time in Melbourne I was walking along the street when my petticoat became unfastened and seeing a polling booth I went in, well—and recorded my vote. That was the only time I ever used my right in Australia."

From the happy, carefree life of a bush girl in the backwoods of Australia to the role of leading woman of a touring company, and all within the short space of six years, has been the experience of Miss Mary Marlowe . . .

"It has been the dream of my life to visit Canada. I have not seen very much yet, but what I have seen I like. When we go out west we are going through the Rockies. I am sure I shall want to get out and let them leave me behind."

In speaking of Monday night when the McGill students caused the curtain to be rung down at the conclusion of the second act, Miss Marlowe said that while she expected something of the sort, as she was used to such things in Australia, she did not think matters would have become so unruly. "It was the funniest expression of animal spirits I have ever witnessed," she stated.

The Canadian press interviews Mary Marlowe.

desire. The real meaning of many of the lines only dawned on me when I heard the fat chuckles of the elderly men in the front stalls.

We went through the Rockies and back again. We played Moosejaw, Medicine Hat and Nelson at the far end of the Arrow Lakes. Then back across the continent to Montreal. The carriages were hermetically sealed. A stove at the end of each carriage gave out great heat. There was no change of air. We travelled in a fug.

As the train slowed down coming into Montreal, there were kisses all round. The company was going back to England that day. With two young men, Freddie Meads and his pseudo-brother, Tim, I was going to New York.

New York, I was sure, was just the thing for my aching heart despite the many warnings of the wickedness in the streets there. 'Beware the tomato juice ploy,' I was told. The advice was to keep walking if tomato juice was splashed on you from an upstairs window and, by every means, to resist an invitation into the house next door to be cleaned up. This was the way 'they' got you in their clutches.

Just short of the United States border all three of us were ordered off the train into a world of snow. We were without visas. When we had booked at Regina on the other side of Canada we had been told not to worry about them because we were British. It was midnight. The warm train vanished into the night and we trudged through the trackless snow for a mile to a godforsaken village where the stationmaster lived. Sleep did not come easy with the lumpy mattress and thoughts of David. Here was I in his country while he was in Australia. My life was a mess.

Before dawn we were back at the whistle stop to catch the first train to Montreal. I walked in on Eve who was living there then with her husband, Billgraeme.

'Of course,' she said after hearing my story, 'you were put off the train because that inspector thought the boys were white-slaving you.'

However, New York still beckoned. The boys and I took the first train out, complete with visas.

New York smiled the first day. I was offered two jobs. The first was to play the mother in *The Blindness of Virtue* on tour. I thought I could do better. The second was to play leads in stock in the Middle West. There was to be a change of play every week and five costumes on average wanted for each. I had no stock wardrobe. I could not afford to buy one.

After that New York turned mean. Freddie, Tim and I found

inexpensive rooms at a residential called 'The Florence' in Thirty-Second Street. It was dilapidated but spacious. In the basement was a popular cafe where, for twenty-five cents, you could get a meal of lettuce and vinegar, garlic sausage, deep apple pie with cheese and excellent coffee. For forty cents you could have Chicken Maryland.

Under the moulting wallpaper on my bedroom wall, in the middle of the chipped marble mantelpiece, I placed my little silver clock. It stood for home in the desert of that room until Tim, all too soon on the financial rocks, pointed out that it had pawning value. Would I be a pal and lend it to him? The clock went to 'Uncle'. Tim had a feast of Chicken Maryland washed down with rye whisky and lost the pawn ticket. As the weeks went by one had to be a pal with other small treasures but at least some of them were retrieved later.

A gentle negress made up my bed every morning and swept the surrounds once or twice a week. When she had finished her morning's work at the Florence she went to her Harlem flat where she cared for a husband, several children and nine boarders.

'We are saving up our money to make a religious mission and it will cost a great deal,' she told me.

'Where are you going?'

'To Australia . . . to convert the Australians.'

I did not own up for fear she might start on me.

Soon we had collected a small circle of other Britishers—all young men out of work and living on a bone. Sometimes they brought a contribution to the communal meal—a piece of cooked sausage, a spill of popcorn, a couple of grapefruit, a piece of pie. We cooked or warmed up the meal on the gas ring and used the boys' big double bed as the dining table.

Among the boys who came to the bed-table dinners was Kenneth Gordon Spables. He scratched a living posing for commercial artists and writing short stories and, now and again, he got a day's work as an extra in moving pictures. Put him in a dress suit and immediately he looked like the Crown Prince of any mid-European royal family. In rags he was still handsome enough to be the hero of a melodrama. He had the best kind of English manners and beneath that aristocratic armour he possessed an inflexible character and a heart in a million. He was as real as the other boys were rolled gold.

When they dug him up and brought him to the Florence Kenneth was finding it difficult to stay alive. He spent two days in every seven in bed and depended on the kindness of his landlady to bring him food. In my American years he was the best friend I had. When he was in funds he would take me to a gallery seat—half a dollar for the two of us—a music hall or a picture house because these were the cheapest. Afterwards it was to the nearest automat for a cup of coffee and a pie.

I used to fear he would die before I saw him again but he always managed to cheat death and come back with a new dollar and a laugh. If he had nothing else to give you he brought laughter. I was often lifted from my private slough of despond by our fine friendship. What did I mean to him? A bit of his England, broken off and floating in a cruel sea; a lone puppy that wanted to be bucked up a bit; a girl who made a good cup of tea.

Desperate for a job I was now calling on picture managers as well as theatrical agents. The film people kept demanding 'stills' so there was nothing for it but to spend a morning at White's on Broadway with my picture hat and a few yards of Mr White's stock tulle. He took twenty pictures, all excellent reproductions of the feathered hat but not particularly like me. I became horribly self-conscious as I handed them out. I was afraid one of the picture managers would ask whose photograph I was using.

I broke into moving pictures as a hard-faced, grim, middle-aged landlady demanding her rent from a working girl. The Jewish director instructed me how to apply my make-up, handed me a severe gown and an apron, told me to scrape back my hair and to look hard. I spent the afternoon in that Bowery studio while they shot me in various attitudes of menace. They gave me four dollars for the job. It was Chicken Maryland for me and the boys that night.

I died in the snow in my next film part. Pathé Frères hired me for a couple of days work in the Catskill Mountains. 'I need a girl of your type,' said the director, Frank Powell, 'but don't fatten up before next week. You are to be mistaken for the heroine and you will die of starvation in the snow.'

We all went up the Hudson to Albany in a little steamer. At dawn next day we were called, made up by candlelight, served a scrappy breakfast and packed into an open motor car. We were already dressed in the clothes we were to wear in the picture. Mine were practically rags. My make-up was chrome yellow and crimson lake with blue shadows under the eyes and around the nostrils. It was icy cold, the organ pipes of the Catskills completely crystallized with snow.

Starvation and cold were the two emotions I was told to register while my part was being filmed. Frank Powell stood beside the

Above: From Mary's North American photo album. Apparently there was not much fun in her life at this time. She wrote of thoughts of David: 'Here was I in his country while he was in Australia. My life was a mess.'

Below: The company goes swimming.

cameraman and, in a gentle undertone, he gave me directions.

'Cold . . . cold . . . you're so cold. You wish you were dead, you're so cold . . . you're shivering . . . your teeth are chattering with cold. You're hungry . . . Oh God, is life worthwhile? . . . cold . . . so cold. What's that? . . . a purse? . . . a purse in the snow . . . whose purse? Never mind whose . . . Money. . . is there money in the purse? You want money . . . money means food . . . if you had food you wouldn't be so cold.' Frank Powell spoke the words and I recorded the emotions. It amounted to a form of hypnotism.

There were other scenes where I was not expected to need his direction. The death scene was one. So long as I died on a certain twig, to keep in focus, he did not interfere. I came to a gruesome end registering waves of emotions on my face and enjoying myself thoroughly. I stumbled to my knees in the snow and swayed and swerved. Then, turning my body in a semicircle, I went limp and died with my face towards the camera. Some such dramatic end had been mine in one of my childhood dining-room dramas.

On the journey back to New York the cameraman said: 'Frank was raving about you to us last night after you'd gone to bed. He thinks you have a future in films.'

'Did he?' Eager for more of that stuff, I naively asked why.

'Because you died in exactly the same spot every time. He was able to get back to New York twenty-four hours ahead of schedule.'

Frank Powell had left word at his studio at Hoboken that I was to be given regular work while he was on location. Just enough to break me into studio lights and methods.

I was booked to play in a small ballroom scene for which we supplied our own evening gowns. I wore my black ninon and jet. The assistant director, Mac, gave me a few individual 'bits' in the scene. I acted my head off—silently.

At the end of the second day Mac came to me after the rushes were screened. 'I like your landscape,' he said. 'May I call?'

Surprised at the sudden sortie, I blundered: 'My place is not suitable for callers.'

'All right. You know best. We'll be finished your scenes after tomorrow.'

'You're not serious? Mr Powell said . . .'

'Frank won't be back for a long time. I can't see how we can use you. If I could come and discuss it with you . . .'

My black ninon and jet had done me a bad turn. For stooping over that balcony in the film ballroom, it was just a little low in the bust.

Fighting dragons

Every day I went off to fight dragons. Every day the dragons won. They clawed a little more out of my soul each time and sent me home with my face a shade whiter. Fear had set up house with me.

I could not sleep at night unless the fur collar of my outdoor coat was drawn over my head. It was a form of dope. Every morning when I awoke I would ask, 'Couldn't I afford not to fight dragons today? Just one day off from the dragons!'

They had to be fought. Out of my furry fastness I must come, day after day, and take up the battle.

The rent was seven dollars a week; reduced to six later for a back room. Breakfast at the German bakery round the corner on Eighth Avenue cost fifteen cents—coffee and toast or some form of American bannock with butter. A midday meal of two courses at a small Italian restaurant—also round the corner on Eighth—cost twenty-five cents for two courses with coffee. The coffee was all right, the food filling. Dinner, as an alternative, at the same restaurant cost thirty cents— three courses and coffee.

In the apartment there was a gas-ring. Sometimes that served for all the cooking I could afford. I looked at it often and speculated. Would that be an easy way out?

Above the gas-ring I had hung my favourite picture, 'The Avenue at Middleharnis' by Hobbema. It has long perspective and avenues that lead into the future. It saved me from the gas-ring. I recommend it to all who live in one room.

I resolved to be a bootblack. Surely the novelty of a woman bootblack would draw custom? In Canada and the United States I had frequently heard the jibe thrown at the English for allowing their women to clean their boots. Come then, let me startle the nation. Since they would not be at my feet why shouldn't I be at theirs?

I wrote to one of the principal hotels on Broadway and put it to them. Installed in a corner of their vestibule with a shoeshine chair, I was prepared to work on salary or percentages.

The reply came promptly: 'My Dear Madam, Why choose us? We have had our quota of publicity this month. There have been two suicides on the premises.'

My next scheme was to sell newspapers from a street kiosk. Somebody warned me in time that I would be stoned to death by the newsboys. Licences, ground rent and the permission of an association formed to protect newsboys would be necessary before the first paper could be sold. Kenneth didn't think I'd have time to sell a second.

Freddie went on tour and sent me back some of the hundred dollars he had borrowed. I paid in advance for a course on beauty culture and hairdressing at the Wanamaker School on Thirty-Second Street. The full course was fifty-five dollars and a certificate was guaranteed.

Australian actor O. P. Heggie secured a part for me in a spectacular play called *The Garden of Paradise*. By mischance his letter notifying me of this reached me a day late. I missed the first rehearsal and lost the part. The company rehearsed without salary for three months. The play closed on the tenth night.

I saw Heggie act in Galsworthy's *Justice*, playing the lawyer's clerk, with John Barrymore as the convicted man and Cathleen Nesbitt as his wife. It was too perfect. The realism was horrible. The man who was with me put his head on my shoulder and sobbed. I did not sleep for nights afterwards.

One day I found the dingy offices of two middle-aged men who supplied acts for the Marcus Loew circuit. They offered me thirty-five dollars a week to play in a potted sketch of *The Heart of Maryland*, a play in which Mrs Minnie Maddern Fiske had made her name many years before. *The Heart of Maryland* is founded on the legend of the young woman who muffled the curfew by swinging on the tongue of the bell far out over the city. I was to be the heroine who swung on the bell. The vaudeville agents had experienced great difficulty in securing an actress with the nerve for the act. It had sensational appeal and I was engaged to be the sensation. I was frightened almost out of my wits at the prospect but nobody needed to know that. After all, it might be fatal on the first night and that would be one way out of my difficulties.

The day before the first rehearsal the agents had news for me when I went to their office. They had found it impossible to get the rights of the play and they could not present the sketch. I was not to carry off the bell, nor the bell carry me off, that season.

The two men, grateful to me for being ready to risk my neck

Time off from the tour.

in their service, decided that they must do something about me. They found a dramatic sketch for three people, two men and a woman, and they engaged me for a month to play the Marcus Loew Circuit round Greater New York.

The name of the sketch was *Retribution*. I was a young married woman who had had an illicit love affair with a planter in the South Seas before her marriage. Planter turns up. Dumbbell husband, who can't see what is happening an inch before his nose, usefully turns his back when planter and bad wife make signs to each other about their past. Husband is successfully humbugged and everybody lives happily ever after as planter announces his intention of returning to the South Seas.

We tried out the act in Albany, scene of my picture experience, and nobody stopped us playing it twice that week and four times a day at the Greater New York theatres later on.

The Ben Greet Players were looking for somebody who could speak English to play Adriana in *The Comedy of Errors*. They found me. This meant three months permanent work, with a change of town every night and Sundays to do the washing. We combed the Middle West playing in a large tent and dressing in another at the back, the grass our carpet. Ben Greet, the actor–manager who had founded the company, had gone back to London to help found the Old Vic. We were a happy troupe of twelve. A woman playing a minor part acted as wardrobe mistress and packed our stage clothes at the end of each piece while the rest of us went off to supper. We changed our hotel every morning except Sunday.

Helen Hancock, a red-haired wench who played the courtesan, became my friend. Had I been a man I would not have been able to resist her red-gold hair, her pearly skin and her flaming heart. At this time she was waiting to be divorced from her English husband, a journalist. She had the grounds but no money. He had the money and no grounds. In time she saved enough to bring the case. By then she had fallen in love with a married man. She waited ten years before he could persuade his wife to divorce him. Then he married Helen. The marriage was successful for a year. Helen divorced him to permit him to marry the woman who had come between them. I never told Helen about David. She might not have understood.

When we returned to New York at the end of the season, we had played *The Comedy of Errors* in seventy-eight towns, all of them with a public square in the centre. Those which had given birth

When the film people in New York kept demanding 'stills', Mary took herself and her feathered hat to a Broadway studio. 'I became horribly self-conscious as I handed them out. I was afraid one of the picture managers would ask whose photograph I was using.'

to some great man had erected his statue in the middle. Those who had no local hero grew cactus plants.

I had saved thirty dollars every week out of my sixty-dollar salary.

When we disbanded in New York Helen Hancock introduced me to the Rehearsal Club. The club had bedrooms for eleven women and provided breakfast and dinner. The luncheon cafeteria served on an average four hundred a day, and the residents, if they had pennies to spare, usually took a midday snack from the counter. Most of us had an electric plate of our own. With ten cents we could do wonders on it. The club was full of eager girls who lived on currant pie and hope.

Jane Hall, founder and manager of the Rehearsal, was a deaconess of the English church, working in the world. She had first founded a club for boys who went out to work young, and then one for girls which became affiliated with the London Three Arts Club. Finally she had put her heart into the Rehearsal. She listened to the ambitions of thousands of us through the years. We cried on her shoulder and she saved us from despair.

One morning I noticed a new theatrical office in a large building where there were others; on the door was a placard with the words 'Enter without knocking'.

Inside a tubby, bald little man was interviewing scores of people. Presently I caught his eye and he smiled and beckoned me. He was Gus Tannehill. His daughter, Myrtle, had once been a star in Australia.

Gus had a thick neck and a ruddy temper. This day he was in an affable mood and he engaged me to play the heavy woman in a comedy-drama with music called *It's A Long Way to Tipperary*.

There were dozens of people at the rehearsal next morning. The cast was small, so from the outset we knew we were on trial. Mr Tannehill sat at the prompt table with his legs crossed and his hat on the back of his bald head. There are theatrical managers like him on the screen. He must have been the model for the films for I have seen no counterpart.

We read the play. Those who pleased Gus were told to come back in the afternoon. Those who did not were told they had better be car-conductors and saleswomen and give up the idea of acting. Gus told me he had changed his mind about me. I was to be the heroine, Kathleen, the sweetest girl in Tipperary. 'Go and sign your contract with our agent,' he said. 'You will pay him ten per cent of your salary.'

'He didn't send me to you. I don't know that agent.'

My protest was squashed. 'That makes no difference. We book through him and he gets the ten per cent anyway.'

The agent collected it weekly for four months. There was no way out of it.

Gus was the roaring bull type. He swore at everybody and yelled his instructions. I escaped, but, being no better than the rest, I wondered why. One day he told me.

'I can't swear at you. I'd get nothing out of you if I did. You're too sensitive.'

Unfortunately he forgot at the dress rehearsal at Newark. We rehearsed all night, broke at seven in the morning, and opened at the matinee. During the night Gus swore at me. With typical Tannehill expletives he yelped: 'Don't cross your body with your hand.'

I stopped the rehearsal while I told Gus I might be a fool but not that sort of one. He was in the stalls and I was making a dramatic exit up a ramp. The company held its breath.

Gus cried: 'All right! All right! Get on with it. All this worry on my mind and you object to a simple direction.'

'Given that way, I do.'

After a few hours sleep and a bath, I wrote to the managers in New York before going to the matinee, asking to be relieved one week from the opening day. I would just have my fare back to New York.

We played Newark and went on to Buffalo. Before our curtain went up in Buffalo, Gus came to my dressing room. He had an open letter in his hand.

'I've had word from my principals in New York that I must apologize to you. You've given notice?'

'I have.'

Gus was not used to leading ladies who did that sort of thing. Grumbling at me, apologizing to me, he asked forgiveness.

'Well, don't go off the handle again,' I said, as though I had never heard a swear word in my life before.

Gus was recalled at the end of the week and a new producer sent into Canada to pull us together. He did not know any bad words. It was a dull tour. But I saved my fare to England.

Shakespeare, the South and Bowery nights

Jane Hall said: 'You're not going back to England now you have friends here. Even if you go broke again you won't be the first girl the Rehearsal Club has franked. Buy a new hat and go round to see the managers.'

The very next day I signed up for the part of Katherine in *The Taming of the Shrew*. It was for a summer tour starting in six weeks and they were keen for me to go to London to be rehearsed for the part personally by Ben Greet. The World War was hotting up but nobody in New York seemed to be taking it seriously. So off I went.

When my ship berthed at Liverpool I was arrested. No passport. Spy? Actress!

Two grave, tired-eyed men interrogated me in the ship's saloon. I was the only suspect. Two charming English lads who had squired me through the voyage now cast oblique glances my way. A policeman took me ashore and systematically went through my trunk. He pounced on my photographs. Then I was put on the mat before a suave young Englishman with a twinkle in his eye.

'Now, what have you been up to?'

I told him, roughly, that I had been brought up in the belief that I was part of the British Empire and it hadn't occurred to me that a passport would be necessary. The shipping company had not warned me. They were just trying their darnedest to get me a berth quickly because I had to be back in New York in six weeks.

'What for?'

'To take up a theatrical engagement.'

That stunned him for a moment. He then turned to the photographs which had been taken from my trunk.

'My word. You did have a good time in America. I am obliged to keep a few of these for my files.'

Mercifully he did not choose any of Mr White's masterpieces. He preferred a carefree study of me in the corn fields of the Middle West with windswept hair and one of the company posed like an ancient frieze against a camel on a wild animal farm.

'Sorry you've been troubled,' said the officer. 'We need to be careful in wartime. The ship due in this morning after yours has just been torpedoed in the fog off Ireland. And now, when we are all on our toes, an Australian sounds rather like an Austrian to us. However, if you don't get a passport you will always miss the boat train to London.'

Ben Greet rehearsed me for two mornings on the empty stage of the Old Vic. He was a most debonair Petruchio in spite of his stubby figure, white hair and kind round face. We had a table and two chairs for furniture but in no time he had Katherine and her truculent wooer alive for me.

The stage curtain was up. I had never seen such a shabby, decaying theatre in my life but I felt the ghosts of its great past lurking behind the crimson velvet furnishings. Ben and I had lunch together twice and then I was on my way back to New York to tour the northern states for three months.

When we returned to New York Oliver Morosco was reviving his big success, *Peg o' My Heart*, there and I heard he was sending out several road companies immediately. I was at the office of Oliver's manager, Dan Frawley, bright and early but was still surprised at the speed at which I was ushered into his presence.

'Sit down,' said Frawley. 'I want you for the southern tour. We start in two weeks. The salary will be seventy-five dollars. We'll provide the clothes. Here's the contract.'

The sad South was a revelation. The railway stations were littered with dirt, banana skins and foraging pigs. The trains crawled. Often we got off and picked cotton in the fields for amusement. The country was a sleeping beauty awaiting the hand of a prince or a dictator.

Magnolias in the dusty gardens. Blue starry nights, pregnant with perfume and romance. Broken chandeliers. Holes in the carpets. Shattered, worm-eaten banisters leading to spacious vestibules and musty bedrooms where the taps did not work. Decaying palm trees flanking the crumbling porches of colonial mansions that now took paying guests. A sense of hopeless desolation over everything. We had four months of this decayed grandeur, and then we disbanded in New York.

The theatrical temperature was low that season. My third American 'perish' set in. Tracking the elusive job, any path that led to money lured me. Some days I typed envelopes, the contents appealing to the women of America to wake up and take notice of the war in Europe. This paid my rent for a fortnight, but the women of America were not overly impressed.

With my trunk dragged across the door, for there was no lock to any room in the Club, I wrote a book. Because it dealt with the adventures of Australians in England, *Kangaroos in King's Land* seemed an appropriate title. There in the Rehearsal Club bedroom, the world shut out by the trunk, it was hard to keep on with the story when I came to write the parts about Australia. I would write until I couldn't see the page through my tears, and then I would throw myself on the narrow, lumpy bed, and sob them out of my system. Though grief was almost killing me—grief and despair— I told the truth in that simple story about four Australian girls seeking work on the stage in England.

Kangaroos did the rounds of the publishers. 'Too British for American readers,' they said. I was advised to put it aside for a year and write another with more story to it. So I started a wartime romance called 'The Toll Gate of Mars'.

In the club an aura formed around my unworthy head. I was pointed out to strangers as the girl who could write. The rejection slips helped to keep my balance.

One day Jane Hall sent for me. Two men were talking with her. One was lame. He had eager blue eyes and an ascetic expression. The other was fat, obviously a promoter.

Jane Hall said: 'Here's the girl for you.'

The two represented the Madison Square Settlement Home for Boys, a Little Brother movement in the Bowery. The lame man was secretary–manager and lived at the home. Each year a theatrical show was presented by the ex-members to raise funds. They wanted a producer for *The Christian*.

The lame man said: 'Your actors will be young fellows from eighteen to twenty-five. They are elevator-drivers, car-drivers, engine-men, mercery-sellers and such. You'll find them raw but willing. The girls' parts are always taken by a society of young women who do slum work. The leading one comes back every year.'

The salary was ten dollars a week. This covered my room and two meals at the club. The rehearsals were to be held at night. Six weeks hence was the date fixed for the performance in a large downtown theatre.

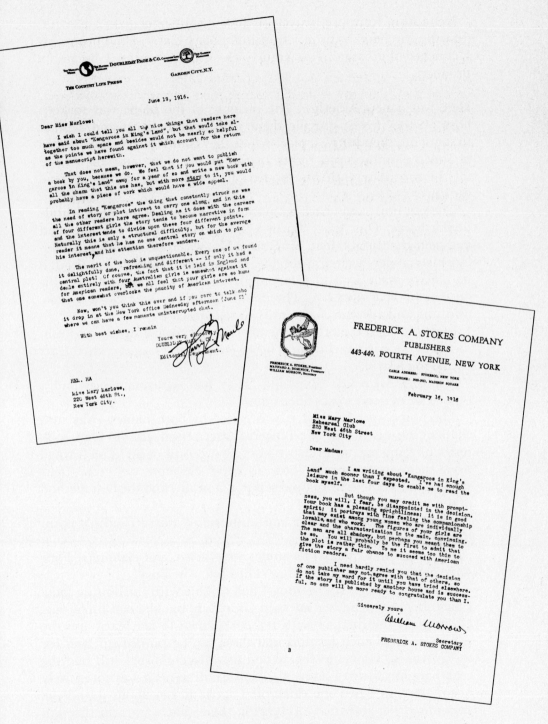

Gentle rejections from two New York publishers for Mary's first novel Kangaroos in King's Land.

Refraining from impulsively embracing the lame man and with-drawing my hand with tact from the podgy clasp of the promoter, I clinched the bargain. At eight o'clock that evening I became a producer.

Here was a new America. The purpose of the home was to keep boys off the streets, provide them with healthy sport and a place to shout out their lungs, a place where they could learn to box instead of holding impromptu fights in the gutter. The lame man lived on the top floor with his mother. In their sitting room we read the play.

The old boys came back to help the younger fry out of gratitude to the home. Our John Storm was a good-looking elevator man and he had natural talent. Sir Robert Ure was rocky on his aspirates but his manners were impeccable. Drake was a likeable lad though he always made love to Glory with his hand splayed out on his knee as he bent over her. These and the others were eager to take direction and all were charmingly unselfconscious.

I met the boys, the present members of the club, downstairs. From them the Mob were chosen. They were young emperors in the art of making a row.

The girls were less adaptable. They had settled incomes and a certain air of good works about them.

The home—or club, for it was called by both names—was in a challenging district in the Bowery. After rehearsals the boys took turns at seeing me home. As we went by street-car or on foot I learned from them many things: how to drive elevators, sell sox (their spelling), make ice cream (and sell it at a profit) and the best method of the shoeshine.

I had six weeks of them and enthusiasm was at boiling point the night of the performance.

The stage was huge. The scenes were heavy and elaborate. Four stage hands were engaged. They called me 'The Boss'.

Halfway through the evening I had trouble with the leading lady. I had offered to lend her my own Glory wig but she had hired one. Glory plays the first act with red curls down to her waist and the wig is made in such fashion that these can be pinned up later for the grown-up Glory. In the second act Miss Suburbia still had the curls hanging down. This being a music hall scene, it was not entirely unsuitable but when she came off I spoke to her about it and she announced her intention of wearing them that way right through the play.

When the third act started I went up to Miss Suburbia's dressing room. The curls were still waist-length. She looked pretty and girlish and she had not had a chance to look girlish for quite a long time, being, I judged, in the late thirties.

'I prefer them this way. I will wear them this way,' she said with an obstinate eye.

'You put them up or you don't go on,' I replied grimly.

'There would be no play,' she retorted with dangerous placidity.

'There would. My wig is in the theatre and I know the part.'

The curls went up. There was no more trouble.

I become an author

I went back to dragging stories out of my typewriter. My literary instincts were definitely sprouting new shoots. By painful degrees I was learning. Eventually, there was a note on my breakfast tray from Bob Davis of Munsey Publications. He wondered whether I could find time to drop in and talk to him about 'The Toll Gate of Mars' and three other stories I had bundled off to him with low hopes.

Without preamble he said, 'I like your work.' Before the flush had died from my cheeks he picked up the manuscripts one by one and, figuratively, tore them to pieces. When he reached 'Toll Gate' he flung the manuscript on his desk and swivelled his chair around to face me.

'Forty thousand words there,' he said. 'Take it home, girl, get it down to twenty thousand and I'll publish it. I'll give you one hundred dollars for it—when the junk is out.'

A hundred dollars! Twenty pounds!

He went on: 'You have a heap to learn but you can write. I don't want war things. I don't want to publish anything about that war but this has feeling. Let me have it back in a week.'

In a week 'The Toll Gate of Mars' was twenty thousand words. It was a better story. I posted it off to Bob Davis. His cheque for one hundred dollars came by return mail. It was published in the *All Story Magazine*. I was an author!

The idea for the story had come to me in a New York church. I had drifted in there heartsick, down and out, convinced that I would never be able to earn a dollar with my typewriter. I was on my knees, praying for courage, using that primitive formula of my own that comes from an overcharged heart when the world is too big for me. I prayed: 'Oh, God, make life a little easier.'

In a flash the theme came, practically complete, as though God had replied: 'There you are. Work for it. Make life a little easier for yourself. You can do it.' From the church I had rushed back to the club and started on the story. And now I had my fare back to England.

Ben Greet's American manager asked me to play Rosalind in *As You Like It* on a summer tour. I was tempted. I even rehearsed for a day but I withdrew by letter the next. London called.

The war was still ripping up Europe when I reached England but there had been no dropping of standards in South Kensington. My Aunt Marianne, the late Speaker's wife, visiting from Australia, was staying there at the Royal Court Hotel. Foolishly, I joined her. Three days of it made a monstrous inroad into my meagre capital.

To make matters worse, my aunt, declaring my American clothes outrageous, guided me to a little French shop around the corner and goaded me into buying a complete outfit which would not disgrace her and her friends. I looked as though I had stepped out of a canvas by Greuze in a Leghorn straw hat that sang out 'Follow me, lads'.

My aunt's second youngest, Percy, now a brigadier, came to call and, of course, brought along his wife, Millicent, Duchess of Sutherland. The Duchess was a beautiful lady deeply sunk in mascara and face paint. She told me of some brown Windsor soap made specially for her by a man in Burlington Arcade. I was to mention her name when buying it. The price was three and sixpence a cake. It would do my skin the world of good. I considered it very matey of her.

At this time Millicent was in charge of her own hospital in France. She had run across to see her Brigadier. She invited me to join her staff when my aunt mentioned my writing. 'There you'd find plenty of material for your novels,' she said 'I would write some myself if I had the time.' I restrained myself from accepting the invitation. To work under the Duchess, I knew, you must be rich and pay your own expenses.

She must have loved the Brigadier very much at that time because she was so nice to her mother-in-law. After a while she divorced him and had some scalding things to say about him in her memoirs.

The Brigadier was a realist. He knew what had made him the white-headed boy in our family in those days. I suspect we were born peasants but success turned the second generation into inflexible snobs.

'You have always known the Right People,' I teased as he kissed me goodbye.

The Brigadier's moustache went up whimsically. 'You always can if you don't care a damn about them.' So maybe it was that—plus his eyes and his soft impertinent voice—that landed him in English society.

My aunt took me to Sunningdale for two weeks. Soldiers were in camp nearby, Canadians were hewing down the timber and, now and again there was a rumble of guns. Still, I heard the thrushes in the dawn. England is never so sure of herself as in Windsor Forest.

The holiday renewed my spirits. My aunt was returning to Australia. She told me she was not worried about me because I had fended for myself for so long. If I wouldn't find a man and get married then . . . She washed her hands of me with a ten-pound note.

I found a cubicle in the Three Arts Club in London and started job-hunting. Recasting *Kangaroos in King's Land* with a happy ending, I sent it to one publisher after another. When it came back the fourth time I offered my services to the War Office, St John's Ambulance and a bank. Nobody wanted an ex-actress.

Aunt Marianne called to say goodbye before sailing. She had news. The Australian Comforts Fund office in London would give me a job and pay me thirty shillings a week. She had been using her influence. I was going to be a comfort.

London was bitterly cold. It was drab and dreary in the Comforts Office. The routine got on my nerves like a file on a thin nail. The staff talked in initials. I had never been in an office before.

The following week I got the sack . . . and deserved it.

Part Three

War from the wings

Next I found myself being sworn to secrecy by the Canadian Pay Office. I worked at a table with three other women and forty men in a large room in Millbank, all smoking at the same time. Twice a day the windows were opened for five minutes to clear the air.

The job was precis writing and it paid thirty shillings a week. We were dealing with compassionate pleas from Canadian soldiers and their womenfolk. Our job was to boil down to their pith 130 letters a day each to make it easier for the hierarchy to pass judgement. If there was a baby coming we were allowed to pin a red 'Urgent' tab to the letter. The 'Urgents' were picked up every hour and received immediate attention.

At the end of a month I had neuralgia all over. The only doctor I knew was a baby specialist. He came but said he could not be sure. I looked myself up in the Red Cross manual. I had the mumps.

The manageress of the Three Arts Club got wind of it. 'We can't risk keeping you,' she said. 'There are three hundred girls in the club. You must be out of here by tonight. Haven't you a friend who can take you to a hotel after dark? They wouldn't notice your swollen face then.'

My temperature went up and my pulse raced. 'When I'm up I'll report you to your committee,' I cried. 'You shouldn't be in charge of pigs, let alone girls.'

Next day I went by train to Sunningdale after one false start when I fainted on the club hall floor. The lodging house where I had stayed with my aunt was empty. They nursed me there for a month. By the time I could crawl—rather like a fly that had been retrieved from the inkpot and given a fresh start—I resolved to go back to the Canadians.

Three days later I fainted into my letters. Bronchitis and a barking cough. It was back to Sunningdale. I was sure I was heading for pneumonia.

'You can't stand the rest of the London winter, my dear,' said the local doctor. 'Go to the Forest when you can walk and try to draw strength from the earth.' Then he plopped on another mustard plaster.

I was beginning to think life was too much bother. Perhaps I might help a bit and get the damned thing over. There was not much left to pawn.

While I was thinking over these plans the post came in. *Kangaroos in King's Land* had been accepted. There would be a cheque for twenty-five pounds in the mail, an advance on royalties, as soon as I signed the contract.

Taking the edge off the ecstasy was a paragraph that said 200 copies were to be allowed the publisher by the author before royalties commenced. This was grossly unfair. I put on my warmest clothes and went up to London. To hell with pneumonia!

Ignoring the agent, I went straight to the publisher. I was prepared to meet a lion and met a lamb. He conceded my point. Royalties would start from the first copy sold. Then he set before my astonished eyes the coloured jacket for the novel. Leaving out love, that was the greatest thrill of my life. It was a bad jacket, crude in colour, wretchedly drawn, but it looked like a million dollars to me.

In the morning I started another book. I spent the best part of each day exploring Windsor Forest and then wrote far into the night. One afternoon I was sitting resting when a horseman rode up on a fat, speckled Shetland. He dismounted and sat beside me. A cheery little Cockney, he was one of the grooms from the Royal Stables. His mount was Bella the Second, at that time a favourite of King George V.

The groom had heard about Australia. We grew chummy. He told me a lot about the Royals and how they rode and never baulked at a ditch. Bella the Second was pot-bellied because His Majesty fed her on sweets.

'Get up on 'er,' said the Cockney. ' 'ave a ride. That'll be something to tell your friends in Orstralia.' I would have enjoyed the experience more had I not been aware that my bloomers must be showing as I sat astride the plump pony. My feet were almost on the ground but Bella was amiable.

Eventually, I was well enough to accept an invitation to lunch from my Uncle Reggie, who was visiting London from Wales. Over an excellent meal at the Gobelins he told me about the family. He had news from Canada . . . a letter from the family over there. He read it to me.

Suddenly my heart thumped. The letter was saying: 'David Cameron has gone to the Front. He has joined up with the Australians.' To me, 'You remember him at the Glen?'

Yes, I remembered him.

The letter went on: 'He was in Egypt with his regiment for a while and now he is in France. His wife is back here in Canada with her old friends. She means to stay until he is demobbed. She doesn't care about Australia.'

There was more of it but I could not take it in. I tried to sound casual when I asked Uncle Reggie the name of David's regiment. The war was going to be more horrible than ever now that David Cameron was in it.

Jean had taken a cottage at Birchington-on-Sea while Walter was at the war. She wrote asking me to come and stay while I built up my strength. Her two small daughters, Eileen and Leueen, their nannie and the cook made up the household. Walter and Jean had been in Russia during the early part of the war. Jean had worked in a Russian hospital. They left when Walter was sent to England as a King's messenger.

I had been at Birchington about a week when a telegram came to say that Walter had been admitted to a London hospital. Jean went up to London to see him.

The proofs of *Kangaroo* came that day. While I was correcting them in Jean's little white guest room which had a wide view of fields busy with the first urge of spring, a strange noise came out of the sky. Nannie rushed upstairs to the balcony followed by the cook, panting heavily. From the balcony we could see a crowd round the village pump. Against the intense blue sky there were black specks—enemy aeroplanes.

In the next few minutes three of the planes were shot down. One fell like a stone and landed in the sea beyond Margate. One exploded and burning fragments came to earth close to Manston Aerodrome, about a mile from the village. The wings of the third were shot away, the body hurtling into a field. On the balcony we were not concerned about the airmen or the British victory. Leueen was safe in her cradle in the garden but Eileen was in the village kindergarten. Was she safe? While the English guns were still muttering Nannie ran to the village to fetch her.

Some days later I joined Kent Auxiliary 178 and became afternoon nurse in C Ward at Quex Park Territorial Hospital, nervous in my blue print uniform down to the ankles. Quex had accommodation for forty-six patients. I had only a fragmentary knowledge of Red Cross lectures to help me.

The hospital occupied a stately mansion, Georgian in style, and it had all the traditions. There was a White Lady who walked in the moonlight, two other ghosts and a cricket pitch bounded by fields yellow with buttercups in the spring.

Major Powell Cotton, the owner (I can't be sure if he was the rightful heir or a wealthy interloper), had spent his early life shooting big game and his middle age writing books about it. The victims were stuffed and displayed in a private museum attached to the mansion. There were two large rooms with glass ceilings and walls and trick lights. They were set up to represent an African jungle with a watering pool in the foreground. Around this the stuffed creatures were grouped. On wet days the Major removed the scrim screens which shut off the jungle and gave lectures on his adventures. The beds were turned round to face the jungle.

'Straighten the beds in here first and then the other twelve on the long verandah,' said the nurse I was relieving. 'Then empty the cigarette trays and scald the sputum cups. Fetch two large cans of water from the kitchen at the other end of the house. Don't spill it. The men might slip.'

'What do I do with the water?'

'Wash the bandages. They are in soak now in the surgery sink. They will be boiled afterwards but you must get the pus off first in cold water. You'll find clean bandages drying in the conservatory. Roll them . . . Oh, by the way, there's an appendicitis in the far bed. I didn't have time to change his dressing. You do it. Just a dry dressing. He's wearing a many-tailed bandage so you won't need to move him. Goodbye, good luck.'

I washed the dirty bandages and felt sick. The appendicitis was an Australian boy from Forbes, New South Wales. He had kind eyes and the helpful spirit of a man from the outback. I am never likely to forget him. His name was Paddison.

He opened his pyjama jacket and took the pins out of the many-tailed. The dressing underneath had slipped. I had not seen a man's naked body before. My hands were still shaking from carrying the heavy water cans. I picked up the dressing with the forceps and gently dropped it on the patient's navel. That looked like the scar I was seeking. Paddison moved the dressing to the right spot and held it in position while I did up the many-tailed.

My cheeks were flaming. I was ready to run out of the hospital. But when the last safety pin was in Paddison said: 'Very comfortable, sister. My word, isn't it grand to have an Aussie nursing you!'

We voluntary nurses received no pay and we provided our own uniforms. The afternoon nurses were given tea and bread and jam at four o'clock but we took our night meal in our own homes. We bought our own thermometers, our own surgical scissors and we were invited to contribute small prizes for the bridge tournaments. We worked Sundays the same as weekdays.

Towards the end of my first day a Canadian walking patient called me behind a screen. There was a young man on the bed. His dressings were off. The whole of his hip had been blown away by a German shell. Where the hip should have been there was a mass of raw, bleeding flesh like uncooked steak. He was lying on his right buttock so the wound would not be touched by the bedclothes.

'There's a dandy hole for you,' said the Canadian. 'Fritz did that job well, didn't he?'

My bread and jam turned over inside and started to rise. Could I stand it? The men were not aware that this was my first day in hospital and that I had never seen raw flesh before. To them this was just a wound that a man could have and still be alive. They found the young man's tenacity a fine thing, and wanted me to share their admiration.

Matron appeared around the screen to finish the dressing and looked surprised to find me there. 'Help me, now you're here,' she said. 'Soak that pad in the saline. Use the forceps, please.'

When we had finished, when all the men had settled down for the night, the Matron called after me as I was leaving. 'Tomorrow, nurse, when you come on duty and have done the bandages and made the wards neat, take the methylated spirits out to Corporal Dow on the verandah. He is in the third bed from the far end. I want you to give his head a thorough doing. He's got nits in it.'

'Yes, Matron.'

I lost the bread and jam as soon as I reached the park gates on the way home. This, indeed, was war.

The other nurses had homes in the village and bicycles to ride there and back. I had neither and made my lonely way a mile across the fields at the end of the day to my rooms at Copeland House— high-sounding but humble—where Mrs Sharpey 'did for' me above the village china shop. My sitting-room windows looked over the cornfields which still—courageously—breasted up to Birchington's main street. Beyond the fields you saw the hills of Canterbury.

There was a good-sized bedroom at the back but the bathroom was filled with Mr Sharpey's tools. Every morning Mrs Sharpey brought a large jug of hot water to the bedroom. There was an oilcloth mat. There was a wash basin. There was a pail. Wash the upper part of the torso first, empty the water into the pail, wash the lower part of the body, and there you were . . . clean.

In eighteen months I had four baths. Two were stolen at Quex on days when I was on a twelve-hour shift. Matron sent me to lie down on her bed for an hour and the bathroom was next door. It was worth taking a chance. The other two were taken at the house on the cliffs where our quartermaster lived after we had been swimming from the thirty-nine steps which feature in John Buchan's novel.

At five o'clock in the morning at Copeland House, Mr Sharpey, a house painter, would climb the stairs with a cup of tea for Mrs S. He would then get his own breakfast, mount his bicycle, and ride five miles to Margate to commence work at seven. When he reached home at night he would be so tired and irritable that his children would not be allowed to talk above a whisper. Eventually he went mad.

At eight Mrs Sharpey would bring me an egg on a tray to my bedside, and a good pot of tea. When I was not on morning duty I breakfasted in bed. Mrs S. would relate the village news while I ate the egg, giving me a vivid description of the air-raid of the previous midnight. We spent our first few air-raids together but I soon got tired of that. It went like this: when the 'Take cover' alarm boomed out, Mrs Sharpey would rush into my room and wake me up. She would sit, trembling, on the side of the bed, with me holding her hands, telling her that you could only die once and that now was as good a time as any. She would sit on until the silvery siren of the 'All clear' rang out and then return to her own bed. By then we would both be thoroughly exhausted. At length I had to be ruthless and tell her that I could not do my work at the hospital properly the next day if I had to spend the night waiting to be killed.

Breakfast over, the penny section bath, a think-walk on the chalk cliffs with the skylarks overhead and by ten o'clock each morning I and my little Corona were at work in the window that overlooked the cornfields. We never stopped until Mrs Sharpey came in to set the table for the midday meal.

At 1.30 p.m. I set out for the hospital, walking a mile across the fields. After a few weeks they trusted me to do the real things at Quex. Nurse Hilda handed over the trench feet case in B Ward. She had had the stench of them in her nostrils for weeks and she was glad of the relief. Black stumps, suppurating freely; bandages to be soaked off for every dressing. You need enthusiasm for trench feet.

The chronic lung case in C Ward was in my care from the beginning. He was a seventeen-year-old lad from Liverpool, a thread of a boy who had lied about his age to get to the war. It was touch and go with him for six months. He was not a spectacular hero, poor little, cross-eyed, demi-man. He grumbled a lot, but I grew fond of him, for all that. We made him well enough to go back to his humble home in Liverpool. With so little left to fight for life, we knew he must leave it early. But we got him home.

The night nurse who patrolled the wards with a storm lantern every hour was a Cockney widow. She was a capable nurse, jocular with the patients. She sat on their beds and predicted their futures. She was engaged to a jockey who had been at Quex. He had a piece of shrapnel in his heart. When her annual holiday came she went north to meet him and he came south to meet her. When he ran for his train, the shrapnel moved a fraction and he died on the spot.

Of course, we mended many soldiers who went back to be killed by the guns in France. Mostly they would write when they went back. Then there would be no letters. Eventually we would hear what had happened to them.

I had applied for duty in France. Twice my call came and both times the commandant asked that it might be postponed. It was Mozart to my ears to hear her say I could not be spared from Quex.

Fomentations were my strength. One day I heard a patient say— when I was out of sight but not of hearing—'She drops a bloody red coal on yer bloody wound and looks up, so flamin' innercent, and sez she, "Is that comfortable, laddie?" I 'aven't the 'eart to tell her it 'urts like 'ell.'

There was Bradley who had a wound in his side the size of a saucer. So deep was it and he so weak that sometimes the functions of his body operated through it. He was not my case but he liked to talk to me. Bradley was a Lancashire lad of medium mentality who resented the war which had sent him back to England a bit of human flotsam. Latterly he was transferred to Herne Bay. I sat beside him in those last few minutes at Quex—he knew no other home now and seemed to have no people—and in those final moments he said to me:

'When I'm better, sister, I'm going to have a full bottle of wine all to myself. I'm going to drink the whole bottle.'

The ambulance came to the hall door. We waved until it was out of sight, lost down the long winding drive. Two days later Bradley died. Sheer inability to face the future? Homesickness for the only home he had known for nearly two years—Quex?

In the two minutes silence every November it is Bradley who comes to me and stays until the noise of the world breaks through. I hear him say: 'When I get better, sister, I'm going to have a full bottle of wine all to myself. I'm going to drink the whole bottle.'

Of all of them, why should it be Bradley? A lonely man without a family. Is it that? He was a ghost in life. He is my ghost in November.

Kangaroos in King's Land came out. The publishers flooded the Australian camps with postcards—me on one side and reviews of the novel on the other. After that it was impossible at Quex to disguise my past. Some of the patients had been in the camps and seen the postcards and they told the others. It was not only the name that seemed familiar. There was the face on the postcard bending over them. In a fortnight the publishers brought out a second edition.

Jean and Walter were disappointed. They thought I had completely missed their characters in the story but they told me I had captured Eve to the life and another little actress, called Patricia for the purposes of the novel.

Eve was disappointed. She thought I had her all wrong but congratulated me on perfect delineations of Jean and Walter and Patricia. Patrica's opinion never reached me. Supporting her sisters and their small families, she had overworked and died before her time.

Every morning in the window at Copeland House, overlooking the cornfields, I worked on my second novel, *The Women Who Wait*.

When it came out the publisher had a surprise for me. I had suggested a large question mark for the design for the jacket. But bursting out of the encircling question mark was a portrait of me, as Mr White of Broadway had seen me. The publisher was a Scotsman but he could turn a pretty compliment. Said he: 'I was searching for a good-looking girl to break through the note of inquiry and suddenly I had it. "What's the matter with the author?" I asked myself. Do you favour it, lass?'

He did, anyway, and so went further with the propaganda. He had a large poster in three colours struck of the cover and these were posted up in every London Tube station for a month.

A big push in France meant a large convoy of Australians to Quex. As the stretchers were carried through the hall the Major said jokingly:

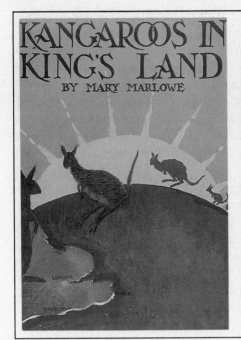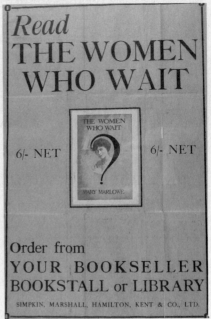

Left: Eventually Kangaroos in King's Land *was published in wartime London. The publishers promoted* Kangaroos *by flooding Australian army camps with postcards which had Mary's face on one side and reviews of the novel on the other.*

Right: The Women Who Wait *was also published in London during the war. It was intended to impress British women with the need to produce children. Posters advertising it were plastered in every London tube station for a month.*

'Seems we have the whole Australian army this time. Nurse Marlowe will be glad.'

Yes, I liked to see plenty of Australians come in. For them Quex was a haven after hell; for me their coming was a small chance to hear something of David Cameron. I knew his battalion. As each wounded Australian came in I searched his identification card, hoping to find that battalion number written on it. Then there was a second chance. Sometimes two battalions met. My ears strained as I bandaged the broken men, strained for a word of him. One never knew. One always feared.

Soon after that push, Australian soldiers in a Margate hospital were driven across to Quex for a little relaxation. Amongst them was a reckless fellow with the spirit of a skylark and his leg in a splint. As I was a fellow Australian, he asked, 'On your off day won't you come over and take me for a walk?'

Soon I fulfilled that promise. He was waiting in a wheelchair on the pavement outside the hospital when my bus got into Margate. I turned the chair for the heights of Clifton and the esplanade.

We were having afternoon tea in an open-air cafe on the front when the Hun aeroplanes came over Margate. 'Better get along,' said my soldier, paying the bill. 'They'll be windy at the hospital about those who are out. The nurses will be scurrying round after us. Let's go as fast as we can.'

As fast as you can is not making much pace when everybody is rushing for cover in an air-raid. A wheelchair is unwieldy at the best of times. All the way down the esplanade my soldier was shouting out reassuring things to the bewildered and scared women who were hurrying hither and thither like ants, not knowing where to take cover. 'Make for the beach,' he told them. 'The bombs won't be dangerous if they hit the sand first.'

When we turned into Queen's Square the first bomb was dropped. Fritz seemed to be immediately overhead and I—in swift vision— read my death notice in the newspapers. The soldier held other views.

'While Fritz is directly on top of us we needn't worry. Oh, yes, he'll drop a bomb but bombs don't fall straight. Here it comes. You'll see.'

The bomb came. It struck the sand twenty yards in our rear and burst with a muffled sound. I rushed the chair across the square. Then the second bomb was dropped. It fell on an empty house directly behind the picture house for which I was making. Not very reassuring! But I kept on, my soldier arguing with me all the time to leave him and take shelter. Immediately we came to rest in the theatre

'My soldier' Mary calls him; the name 'Jack' is written on the back of the photograph. Nurse Marlowe was taking him for an outing in his wheelchair in Margate when German bombs started to fall. With his leg patched up Jack returned to the Front. He wrote to her and then silence. Was he killed? Mary never found out.

lobby he hopped out of the chair. We clung together under the impression that I was giving him physical support. A third bomb was dropped up the street.

My soldier wrote from London when he went on leave, his leg patched up for him to return to the Front. Then he wrote no longer. The last I heard of him was from another Australian who had been in the Criterion Restaurant in London when my dauntless fellow gave cheek to three English officers. He was marched off to the clink. He went laughing.

Was he killed? Did he go home to Australia? I never found out.

In the great drive in France that sent us the biggest batch of Australians there was a boy called Stares. He had joined up in Melbourne when he was fifteen. He had had two years in Egypt and on Gallipoli and then a third in France. He was eighteen when he reached C Ward—febrile, wasted, ghost-pale.

Stares had developed malaria in Egypt. Recurrent attacks in France made the army doctors believe he was malingering. They gave him light duty and number nines. He finally got his blighty through a shattered finger. He was walking wounded when he came to us.

On his third night in C Ward I took his temperature; it was 103. I showed the thermometer to Matron and she said: 'Probably he put it in his soup. That finger wouldn't cause that temp.'

There had been nothing hot within his reach; he had refused the soup.

'Then he's been chewing cordite,' said Matron. She knew all the tricks.

I persuaded her to come to Stares. When she asked questions he answered wearily: 'Nobody'll believe me. The doctors in France don't understand it. I have malaria.'

The erratic temperature chart soon proved it. Month after month this had happened but only his finger sent him out of the lines. The iron had entered into his soul. He knew that he would be sent back to be killed. He confided to me that he did not mean to let that happen. Neater to finish it for himself in England.

Each day when I tried to clear the bogey from his mind he would say: 'I know what I'm in for. I'll be up before Charlie Ryan. He'll send me back. We all know him. He's harder than Big Bertha. None of us have a chance if we come up before him.' Such was Sir Charles Ryan's reputation among the Australians until he lost his own son in the war; then he softened.

Once at Horseferry Road HQ—when in a moment of temporary madness and at the instigation of Charles Nevin Tait—I recited at a soldiers' concert—I had met the officer in charge of soldiers on leave. He left with me the impression of a good fellow with a great heart. I wrote to him about Stares. I mentioned the threat of suicide.

It was not in vain. The officer arranged for Stares to be examined by another medical board. In a month he was sent back to Australia. That, I think, was the best thing I have done in my life.

A new life

When the war was over I went to London. On the first day I ran into Cousin John from Glentrothy, and had tea at a Lyons cafe. He had seen David Cameron the previous day and had the news that he was going back to Australia to live. He passed on David's business address in London.

In my cubicle at the Three Arts Club that night, I fought a war of my own. The battle was over at dawn after I had raked myself fore and aft with a probing searchlight. I had lost because I had a rent in my spiritual armour that left me vulnerable.

In my narrow bed I sat up and wrote to David. An ordinary little note went into the envelope. I asked if we might meet in friendship before he returned to Australia. The floor was littered with less restrained messages that had been abandoned. The letter thudded into the pillarbox outside the club before anybody was astir.

A week went by. No letter from David. He was right. Stronger than me now. Time had healed his hurt. Being a man he would know that in love you do not travel the same road twice. No heat in old ashes. Disturb them and what happens? Why, you raise a troublesome dust.

The night David's ship sailed for Australia I wore the necklace, his necklace. I wore it over my nightgown with my hand upon it as long as I was awake. Towards morning, I slept. When I woke the necklace was broken. The past was past.

I sat on the edge of the bed and gathered up the fragments. You go on living whether you want to or not. Take the courage of the men I had been nursing. Take the Australian fireman with his leg off at the hip and his arm at the shoulder. I remembered the day when I overheard him cheering a little lad who was grouching about the future. 'You mustn't lose heart, son. You must never lose heart.'

I wrote and wrote to pay the rent and the midday meal of sausage and mash or eggs and bacon. A Mrs Jones advertised in *The*

Gentlewoman for a pair of suede shoes. I sold her mine for thirty-five shillings. A cheque for seventeen guineas from the *London Magazine* kept me going until I was shipped back to Australia, courtesy of the British Red Cross.

It was dark when we steamed into Port Phillip Bay. I could smell burning gum leaves on the shore. There is no sweeter perfume. They carried me off the ship and put me in hospital. I had rheumatic fever—1919 did not look like being a very good year.

While I was getting back my vitality—the hospital doctor said I was also suffering from malnutrition—I rewrote my third novel, *The Ghost Girl*, and sent it off to England. Six months later it was published and I had a new contract for two more but royalties do not come by return air mail.

I was existing on the proceeds of a few short stories when producer Gregan McMahon called me out of the blue. 'I have a part for you. Come in and talk salary with the Taits. We're going to the West.'

The play was *The Luck of the Navy*. The part was a German spy with a French accent, Marie Ney was the ingenue, and Frank Harvey was the male star. This play reached Australia too late and failure was inevitable, but still we got three months out of it—Adelaide, Perth and Sydney, where our notice went up on the opening night. We were sacked on the advance bookings.

Disappointed? No. I was through with the stage. The war had changed my sense of values. I was going to be a journalist or die trying.

I took an attic in one of Sydney's old homes turned into a boarding house. From my window I could see Venus and she tried to tell me that the world was still beautiful. Through the opposite window a coral tree poked its leaves. It was a good place to set up my Corona.

In my first month of trying I applied for forty jobs and started on another novel. I fled to the Blue Mountains for a month of solid writing and returned to make a fresh onslaught on Sydney editors. Finally, I aimed at the *Sun*. I sent my scrapbook to Campbell Jones, the managing editor, who showed he was a man who recognized energy and enthusiasm. 'Go out and find the human things in this city,' he told me. 'That's what the public wants. There's a pantomime coming on at the Tivoli. Write me an article on that. Go and watch the kids rehearse.'

The kids were a joy. My article was published in the next *Sun*.

For my next assignment I had to play the part of a spy. A women's football team was being formed. The first secret training run was

If Miss Marlowe had never read a novel (as well as never having written one before), she would have made a better book of *The Ghost Girl*. She is intelligent enough to have invented better methods than those conventional ones she has adopted. It is, no doubt, her reading that is to be blamed for the strength and silence of her hero, for the unnatural villainy of her villains, and for the fact that coincidence is obliged to rush to the help of her plot. The scene is Australia, but though Miss Marlowe might have had the great advantage of a background that would interest and enlighten her readers, she has not been able to make good use of it. The book contains hardly any real observation, and not a single item of information about Australian station life beyond what one might get by making inquiries at an emigration office. But if Miss Marlowe would put down all her odd thoughts instead of all her even ones, with her facility and feeling she would write a good novel.

The Daily Herald, March 1922

The Ghost Girl. By Mary Marlowe. London: Collins, Sons, and Co. Pp. 290. 7s. 6d. net.

This is a first novel, and it is written with such facility and gusto that the experiment is obviously one that will be tried again. The next should be better, for the more obvious faults in this are of an exhausting kind that would hardly bear repetition. A good deal of it reads like a paint-box. It is a story of Australian life, and all the colours of skies, eucalyptus trees, and plains are splashed on with no ungenerous hand. The very first chapter, indeed, opens with a sunset and a dizzying burst of splendours and emotions. The heroine at that moment is asleep and happily oblivious of it and of all the blue veins and brown hair and deep rose tingeing the brunette skin which she is contributing to the canvas. On this scene the hero enters—faded blue shirt and sunbitten arms—bites hard on the cold stem of his pipe, and loves with every fibre of his being. So the tale goes on through the old familiar ways of misunderstandings and intercepted letters, till finally his arms go round her in a starlit darkness, and the author, presumably, rinses her brushes. Of its kind the book is not without a certain merit, and at least it is vivid. On cold grey winter evenings these hectic exhibitions of nature and mankind may prove to have a comfortable glow to read about.

The Sun, 30 April 1922

Australia 1922: Mary Marlowe, novelist, takes it on the chin when The Ghost Girl *is published.*

to take place that evening. The press was excluded.

'Join 'em,' said the news editor, who was as tough as they come. 'Get me the inside story and have the copy in by nine in the morning.'

I smiled, but my knees trembled. God help me! I knew nothing about football. I had never watched a game nor had I even read an account of one, but I found a schoolboy at the boarding house who explained it to me.

Off I went to the football ground. It cost sixpence to join the new club and soon I was talking with one of the stars, Maggie Mitchell, a brawny lass. 'I was weaned on Rugby,' she said, 'so I'm looking forward to ternoight. Aren't you playing?' I was in a white sweater and a tam.

'Couldn't afford the boots.'

But when the girls trooped onto the field, moon-green under the fierce electric lights, I was one of them. We had a male coach who showed us how to dribble and scrum up. He and the secretary of the New South Wales Rugby Football Association were the only men allowed inside the gate.

After training, the secretary stood on a rub-down table in the dressing room and told us to stick to our dribbling until we had full control of our legs. 'You'll be training in secret right up to your first public match,' he shouted. 'The idea is not to give anybody a chance to laugh at you. And if any girl here tonight gives any information to the press she will be instantly disqualified. Remember that.'

All night I sat up writing my story but I had to wait until the boarding house was awake to type it. Since the girls were so scared of being overlooked at their game by some outside male I gave myself the by-line 'The Man on the Moon'. That effort got me a permanent job on the newspaper.

In the old *Sun* building on the corner of Martin Place, seven floors high with a sunny roof, I was the seventh woman on the staff, including secretaries and telephonists. In its handsome new home, we have fourteen floors, two roofs, two towers, parquet floors for the higher-ups and a marble hall for the public. There are more young women than windows. That is progress.

In the beginning I was handed over to the social editor of the *Sunday Sun* to fill the gaps in her staff during holidays. Writing for the social pages was anathema to me. I had a tiresome tendency to tell the world what women were doing instead of what they were wearing.

So I was relieved to leave the beaded paths of crepe-de-Chine for the dusty realities of life. I became secretary and assistant to the editor of the *Sunday Sun*. This position I retained under the caliphate of seven editors, not including the holiday stopgaps. On the side, I had a regular theatrical column each week under the by-line 'Puck' and soon I was doing book reviews, reports of scientific lectures (because the rest of the staff hated covering them), news interviews for the daily paper, charity sob-stuff and taking dictation from the editor until it was discovered that I did not write shorthand and was typing the letters mainly from memory.

J. C. Williamson's, the theatrical firm, offered me the job of their publicity manager in Sydney at twice the salary. As this had been one of the forty jobs I had applied for, it gave me some secret joy to refuse. J.C.W.'s general manager, Charlie Westmacott, was so impressed with what he called my 'uncommon loyalty' that he made a special visit to the *Sun* to tell the editor what I had turned down.

The life of a barmaid had always intrigued me. I wanted to find out what it was like pulling beer taps. Action always followed impulse when I had an idea for an article.

As the paper would not arrange it for me—the managing editor strictly disapproved and I waited until he went to England—I had to make the arrangements myself. I made a bar-to-bar canvass but every hotelkeeper turned me down. One spoke for them all: 'This is specialized work. We couldn't afford to subject our customers to the errors of an amateur.'

At last a man who knew a barmaid whose brother-in-law owned the hotel where she and her sister worked fixed it for a day. He told them he knew a girl who wanted to see if she liked the life.

Dressed inconspicuously—as I believed—in a plain black crepe-de-Chine frock, at 9.30 a.m. I arrived at the bar. Before very long I realized that the simple frock made me as flamboyant as the Mona Lisa in a school art exhibition.

When I turned up the second barmaid said: 'Oh, now you're here I may as well take the day off. I want to get my moles cut out.' She left. Her sister Gladys and I were in charge of Sydney's thirst.

The hotel was close to the Town Hall; we got that trade. The wharves were nearby; we got that trade. The markets were round the corner; and we got that trade. Others came, mere passers-by, because the beer was good.

At the end of the day Gladys muttered in my ear: 'Look nippy. We'll never get 'em out by six if you don't get a move on. Look at 'em! Jest rolling in now when we should be closing. You go into the hall and call Frank. He'll have to come and pitch out the ones that can't drink any more. They're taking up too much room.'

They were. Some of them were on the floor. Some of them were sparring, made grouchy with drink. The windows were in danger. There wasn't an inch between elbows at the counter. I called Frank. He came, coat off, red-necked with purpose. He had strong muscles and he soon cleared the bar of the drinkers who were too full to drink any more.

After tea Gladys and I went off to spend the evening at a sixpenny dance hall. At the dance hall the law of the caveman held good. We dispensed with gloomy chaperones and no girl needed to be a wallflower if she knew the rules: the caveman shall choose and the woman on whom his choice falls shall look for no other partner; neither shall she talk between dances to the male of the species; nor shall she expect him to pay for her ticket nor buy her refreshments. If she does not suit his step she must be prepared to be dropped forthwith.

At my sixpenny dance hall men and women took their pleasure seriously. They were there to dance, not to flirt or to get acquainted. They went for exercise and relaxation from their daily grind and the floor, which we called 'swift', was the natural exercise ground of hundreds of factory girls, shop assistants, office servants and others who led sedentary lives. A flashy barmaid turned up now and then but the dude and the demi-mondaine were not encouraged and should any of either sex appear in evening dress we would not be answerable for the consequences.

The music of the sixpenny dance hall was always weird to the verge of prehistoric. Brass clappers, a jingle of bells, a thundersheet and explosive outbursts on the piano suggested that the pianist had substituted his boots for his digits, while a clarinet and a pair of castanets supplied strange syncopations. Bedlam set to rhythm.

On that evening the musicians occupied the gallery at the end of the tin-roofed Gothic hall. Lemonade was sold in a sort of catacomb beneath them. Any gent would get a lady's liquor on receipt of her sixpence. To drink out of the bottle was quite in order, as after the first fifty were served the glasses gave out.

In the dance hall three punkahs played; incessantly rustling out a contrasting tune to the band. These canvas shutters, covered with deep-sea blue wallpaper, ran the full length of the room. The lights were high in the roof and the body of the hall was dim, cool and 'swift'.

I was warned by Gladys not to exchange names with my partner, if I had one, and to remember we met for a common purpose, to dance. Curiosity would be considered bad taste. At the end of the evening you might say, 'So long!' or 'See you next Tuesday?' No more.

With these instructions, Gladys led the way into the hall. She was one of the regular Tuesday habitués. Tuesday was old-time dancing night and anybody who tried to introduce jazz would be ordered off the floor.

The floor *was* swift. It was waxed to the consistency of glass. As I gaily tripped across it to the low bench against the wall where the women sat between dances, I measured my length and cut the soft flesh beneath my chin.

The cut was so deep that I had to retire to the dressing room and stay there for the next half hour, staunching it with cold water. Gladys showed me the way and then went back for a partner. She told me if you were late on the floor you mightn't get one.

Anxious to get a story out of the evening, I returned at length to the hall and cat-footed to the bench. Everybody was dancing, as far as I could see. Gladys was 'up'.

Feeling faint and deadly sick, my head throbbing, a handkerchief pressed to the recent wound which had now more or less congealed, the room and its occupants swam before me.

In what seemed like the next minute an Elderly Gent stood in front of me and held out his arms. 'Shall we try this one?'

The Elderly Gent was wearing white flannel trousers, a chocolate brown Norfolk coat, and a variegated bow tie with an Irish diamond pin poised like a dewdrop on a spring flower. He was bald, and he was just as high as my heart.

He led me through the intricate mazes of the Larinka. On a certain rhythm of the music I was passed under the arch of his arm; this was chassé and reverse. I felt like the camel having his memorable experience with the needle.

The Elderly Gent had a sympathetic thumb. He kept time by pressing it against my shoulder, automatically releasing it on the third beat of each bar. For a long time we said nothing but breathed heavily. One of us had had onions for tea.

At the end of the Larinka the Elderly Gent put me down on the womens' bench—sexes did not mix between music—but when the band struck up there he was again, waiting for me, and in silence we plunged off.

My headache was awful and my head swayed unconsciously to the music. Several times the Elderly Gent said, 'Keep yer eyes on me shoulder' (several strata below). I couldn't concentrate on it, and at last his wrath broke under me. Lifting a horny hand, he delivered a sharp blow on my right cheek and growled, 'Will yer keep yer 'ead straight! Look at me! I keep my 'ead straight whether I'm drunk or sober.'

One learns to be grateful for small mercies. After all, one of us might have had onions and beer for tea.

He came for me a third time. We broke into the Alberts. I endeavoured to be social and chatty. I felt we knew each other much better now. Little response came from him, and suddenly he said, breathing hard, 'Been gassed in the war. Can't talk and dance.'

We continued to hold the floor and the Alberts changed into the Jolly Roger. I did not know the way of it, and when the music ceased abruptly and there was no Elderly Gent beside me I thought it was my cue to drop out and sit down. The Jolly Roger changed to a waltz and immediately another man was in front of me.

'Shall we try this one?'

I gave the right reply this time: 'Don't mind if I do.'

He was a young fellow. Spent his life mainly behind a counter, I judged. Had the air of pleasing women together with a simple faith in us. I was almost swooning by now but he piloted me round, he with his expert feet, I a dull dummy, limp in his grasp. The Young Fellow reversed. Evidently he fancied himself as a reverser. Soon we were doing nothing else but waltzing round and round the room the wrong way. Now and then he would turn me for a rest and the spin in my head would take a leap to the right . . . to the left . . . to the . . .

'To the seat, please.'

He guided me to the deserted bench. Sat there with me, holding my hands, his eyes inquiring. 'What's the matter? Is this my fault? Tell me, please. What can I do to make you better?'

Gladys chose that moment to turn up: 'Are you all right? I saw you digging your tootsies into the floor. Swift, wasn't it? Well, we'd better be getting along.'

The Young Fellow dropped my hands and stood up. The look in his eyes was the sort that would come if somebody gave him a blow between them.

'Thanks so much. Goodnight,' I said.

The Young Fellow knew how far you could go in the sixpenny dance hall: 'See you here next Tuesday?'

'I shouldn't wonder,' I replied in the language of the place.

Fictions

When I had decided that my fourth novel should be about an actress, the title came to me first: *Gypsy Royal, Adventuress*. The world looks upon actresses as adventuresses even in these enlightened days, though frequently they are much less sophisticated than the cocktail babies of Society. Charming, but weak in the morals, is the general opinion. Well, my Gypsy should walk a straight line but the world—her world and the bigger one—would not give her the credit for it.

The plot came one dawn when Venus was shining through the ragged limbs of the araucaria tree at the bottom of the boarding-house garden right into my attic. Venus twinkled at me and seemed to say: 'What about your own story as a plot?'

There it was! Suppose I were to make the two halves of me into two women and let them, thus separated, fight it out? Each would have plenty of opportunities to put forward her own views.

So the story began and so it marched. The two women were the reflected images of my own mind and the outcome of my own struggle. The novel wrote itself and, as usual, the characters soon took charge and did what they liked with my plot.

When it was published a man wrote to me. 'Write a sequel for goodness sake and set our minds at peace. Kill Margaret [the woman who thought the world well lost for love] and make John marry Gypsy [the woman who was my better self].' Starting with the men, the world is very conventional.

A curious experience followed the publication of this book. For the scene of the argument between the two women and for sub-sequent emotional climaxes I had chosen a house in Yarranabbe Road in Darling Point in Sydney, which was at the time owned by a friend of my aunt. One visit had been sufficient to prove its suitability and afterwards, by making exhaustive tours of the vicinity, I gathered all the details required. Thinking she would be interested to know this, I called the owner one Sunday morning to tell her about the novel.

The lady was away from home but her son and a friend were living there and they invited me in. There was a tremendous downpour of rain just as I reached the doorstep and they could do no less.

When they became interested in the story they asked me to stay and share their sausages, just about to be cooked, and suggested that I might like to powder my nose upstairs. I accepted. What an opportunity!

Having paid a brief Sunday afternoon visit before, I had not been upstairs. Now, while the two young men cooked the sausages, I sat on the bed where my Margaret had sobbed herself to sleep so many times, looked from the window through which she had faced hopeless dawns, powdered my nose in the mirror she had used to make herself beautiful for John. I had gone through agonies of emotion with her in this room and now I was actually in it. It was the most eerie sensation I have ever experienced. Everything in the room was precisely as I had written about it in the book. The room was the spare bedroom of what I called the Stable House. I called it this as the place had been converted from the stable of the original Hordern family mansion which still exists above the high wall that flanks the little house.

Over the sausages the son of the house, who used the title of major, inquired about my characters. When he learned that John Oliver, my hero, was, to say the least of it, a complete man of the world he said: 'Good Lord! I expect you have done in my reputation. Everybody will say I am John Oliver as I live here.'

Blandly I replied: 'They can't. John is an architect.'

'I am an architect,' said the bewildered host, 'and what's worse, I am responsible for converting the original stable into this house. Now all my friends will think I have a wife on the other side of the world who refuses to live with me. You have done me in the eye.'

He explained that his military title was an honorary one, given for voluntary work at the Victoria Barracks, but he forgave me.

Lunch over, I led the two young men to the window where Gypsy made her escape from surrender in a fit of moral funk.

'Can you escape from our dining room without breaking your leg?' asked the astonished host.

'Easily. First put your foot there . . . and there . . . and there. See? You can escape quite comfortably as long as the Chinaman is not watching from the outside attic. You wait until he is sunk in his

'An Unofficial Rose,' by Mary Marlowe. London, Collins; Sydney, Dymock's. 6/.

It does not matter a hang whether you are Australian or not, as long as you are Australian. Which superficial paradox is merely another way of introducing Miss Mary Marlowe for the sixth time to Australian readers of good novels. There are minor faults by the dozen in her newest story, 'An Unofficial Rose,' but they are as specks of dust upon the larger virtues of her work.

Miss Marlowe is a proper cosmopolitan. Fate has settled her in Australia. Yet she has not lost her cosmopolitan perspective. In this novel she transcends all the pettiness of either English or Australian insularity, and shows, by means of something approaching genius, that men are men and women women, whether they are reared in back-blocks or Belgravia. (By the way, is there a Belgravia nowadays?)

The central phrase of her novel is on page 118—'Tragic, Inconsequent Fanny Brown.' In those four words is expressed all the attraction of her novel. Fanny Brown is a funny little wanton, who before marriage bears two children; one, a girl, is adopted by English parents, who, childless, have settled in Australia, the other, Max Brown, half-brother to the girl, becomes a vaudeville athlete. Thus, Miss Marlowe provides herself again with the opportunity of exploiting her knowledge of behind the scenes, and magnificently does she make use of that knowledge.

The intertwining of the destinies of stage folks, aristocrats, and comfortable middle-class people will be bewildering to those acquainted with the colonel's lady, but not with Judy O'Grady. The story is worked out to a correct conclusion, and its philosophy (for every good novel has an underlying philosophy) is entangled in the words of the heroine's husband, who says, after he has safely captured his woman:

'So the main thing is not to let things get you down—to keep a stiff upper lip—come what will. All in the day's work. When we come to examine the time book at the dead end of everything we'll see the system was pretty fine, I imagine. In working out our destinies we humans are on as definite a routine as the stars.'

Daily Telegraph Sunday Pictorial,
27 November 1927

An Unofficial Rose. By Mary Marlowe. 7¾ x 5¼, 307 pp. Collins. 7s. 6d. n.

The Australian author of this story shows a cunning pen and understanding mind in depicting the crude but vigorous types whose fortunes she tells. Fanny Brown, an immigrant into Australia, has two, if not more, bastard children. Of the two the girl, Charmian, is adopted by an Englishman of high degree and goes to live in glory in Kent; the boy, Max, grows up a genial rapscallion and earns his living on the trapeze. The advent of the troupe of acrobats in which Max figures is the end of Charmian's grandeur, and back she goes to Australia, full of pride and adaptability, to meet her outrageous and hitherto unsuspected mother. The return to Australia ends in her marriage to a good fellow who is much better suited to her than the English aristocrats with whom she has been hobnobbing. A story full of sense and humour and containing vigorously written scenes from the life of a trapeze artist.

The Times Literary Supplement,
8 December 1927

An Unofficial Rose, *published in 1927, impresses critics in Sydney and London.*

opium dreams before you start.'

'You appear to have done everything but burgle this house. But we haven't got a Chinaman.'

'Yes, you have. He smokes opium and goes to bed directly he has washed up. He shuts his attic door always before nine.'

'There's no attic,' protested the host.

'It's outside in the walled garden at the top of the stone stairway. There's just room. I've built it.'

'It's an idea! Yet I'm an architect and didn't think of that. Next time you come we'll have the Chinaman for you.'

An Unofficial Rose, the novel that followed *Gypsy Royal, Adventuress*, was written to tell the story of that unwelcome baby born to the pitiful chorus girl in the next room to mine in Auckland. That old promise to myself was fulfilled at last. When she grew up she took charge of her own affairs in the determined way of novelists' brain children.

There was more to the story because, not long before, when on a holiday in Adelaide, a strange case came to my notice. A child, like the chorus girl's baby born illegitimate, her mother a servant, her father a passer-by, had been adopted by some rich people I met.

The child played on the carpet while we drank our afternoon tea. She was the spoiled darling of a childless elderly couple. Their servant, meeting another passer-by, produced a second child, a son. He was faced with a stern life and the necessity of picking up a living as best he might. Supposing these two met in later life, children of the same mother, but reared in quite different ways? Suppose the boy knew about his sister and, finding himself in tragic circumstances, made an appeal to her on the grounds of their relationship? I knew so much about these people and my chorus girl that the story simply had to be written.

An Unofficial Rose *was Mary's fifth novel. Years before she had promised herself she would tell the story of the unwelcome baby born to a pitiful chorus girl who toured with Mary in New Zealand.*

Soon after this book came out, a little story written in London for a competition, 'A Child By Proxy', was taken for serial publication by the *Woman's Mirror*, an Australian weekly magazine, published by the *Bulletin* and then in its first year. Mine was the second serial used, and followed Ethel Turner, who wrote their first.

Pavlova, Melba and Sweet Nell

My third *Sunday Sun* editor, Harry Cox, made a ghost of me. He believed, not the old joke that everybody has a story to write—their own—but that everybody has a story they cannot write for lack of literary skill. He sent me after these stories.

Ghosting for important people is another form of acting. You must be able to project yourself into another mind, produce in words the reflections of that mind and the personality enveloping it. Your own vernacular is of no use when somebody else's name appears over the article.

You must listen for the tricks of speech and choose the literary style which will best suit the personality. Quite often the person being ghosted has not a thought in his head. Then you invent his thoughts for him, cram them ready-made into his cranium, and presently you persuade him to hand them back to you. By that time he thinks they are his own.

Ghosting Anna Pavlova was like being in an express train, leaning out of the window, pulling flowers from the trees against the wind and throwing them on the seat behind you, hoping they would be there when you came to sort them out—not bruised or broken, but just as you had plucked the lovely things.

She had so much to say and she said it all so quickly. She moved into such pictures as she spoke—melted into plastic grace—that it resolved itself into a memory test for the interviewer. The trained mind must and does remember and you trust it on occasions like this.

I had come to her in a peak of excitement. Just before I left the office the news had come in that Kingsford Smith and Charlie Ulm and their two American companions had been found at Coffee Royal in Western Australia after being lost for a month. The town was in a ferment and in our office we were hysterical. In this state of mind I went to Pavlova.

Pavlova was just about to leave her city hotel for a cottage she had taken overlooking the harbour. Everything had been cleared from the suite except two large cages full of lovebirds on the window-sills. She would not trust them to be moved except in the car with her and, when she came from her bedroom, she spoke to them before she addressed me. She spoke in a voice like theirs.

Monsieur Dandré, her manager, ever anxious to spare her, offered to answer all my queries, giving me permission to ask Pavlova just one question, as was their custom with the press. Luck was with me. I asked one question but it was a fortunate choice. Did she approve of a very young child learning to dance on her toes?

She talked for an hour, transporting herself and me to Russia and the Imperial Ballet School. She explained the methods and the discipline. She followed the child who would dance through all the stages of the ballet as she had known it in the service of the Czar.

I did not speak again. The right chord had been struck and Pavlova talked because she wanted to. After first emphatically stating that no child should dance on the toes before the age of twelve or thirteen, she went on: 'There is nothing so jealous as art. It requires from us who follow it a lifetime of devotional self-discipline. The life of the classical dancer is not normal. The mind, the character, the physical life must be studied and developed until they are as near perfection as it is possible to make them. Little meannesses of the character, personal ambitions and vanity and the desire to show off must all be rooted out from those who would follow the straight line of the dancer's art.'

Her hands fluttered, touching her own body and then mine. Her eyes were alight in her skull-like face; a beautiful skull with the white skin stretched like thin parchment. Her voice was chromatic.

'Great art must be built up on fine ideals, Madame. You must work along the straight line. Let nothing turn you to right or left. Be good if you can and if you

An Australian Women's Mirror advertising poster featuring Said the Spider.

Becker & Maass, Berlin W 9, phot.

This photograph of Anna Pavlova always hung in Mary's bedroom at Newport. The ballerina was the only person to whom Mary ever told her love story.

want to. Be bad if you must. But never pretend. Do not wear a cloak to cover your real self.'

When we went down in the lift together she took up a coloured macramé bag I was carrying. 'That is a pretty bag.' She turned it in her hands. 'Why do not the stripes match exactly?'

'I do not think that is possible in that kind of pattern.'

'There must be a way,' said Pavlova in a reproving tone. Anything less than perfection was not acceptable to her.

On her previous visit to Australia I had gone to the theatre for an interview. Monsier Dandré had deflected me to the stalls and told me everything an ardent journalist should want to know: why she ran her orphanage in Paris—having no children of her own this was an outlet for suppressed maternity; how she worked; the kind of stages she preferred; her method with her company. He had answered all my questions without hesitation.

'I spare her interviews. You shall have one minute with Madame for a personal impression and to present your roses.'

He had led the way to Pavlova's dressing room when the rehearsal was over. Already she was in street dress, prepared to leave the theatre. She complained of a headache and asked him to go to the chemist's next door for some remedy. He disappeared.

Pavlova took the red roses from my hands as a mother takes her baby from a stranger's arms. She found a vase, filled it with water, and arranged them on her dressing-table. Then she pulled forward a chair for me and sat opposite.

'Now tell me, are you married?' she asked impulsively, her bird-like eyes surveying me. 'Not married? For goodness sake, why not?'

I told her the story I had kept in my heart for a long time. She was the first and the only one I ever told until I began these reminiscences. Perhaps I sensed she would have something better than sympathy and her fine discernment immediately supplied it.

'Then that is over and there is nothing to stand between you and your work. You can make your work your ideal. Madame, we are the vase to hold the beautiful thought. Our work must be ideal, consecrated to the best in form and expression. Now your life is your own. When we would work it is better so.'

Melba had been my golden dream since childhood. She had gone to school at the Presbyterian Ladies College and her friend and school-mate of those days was the mother of my former playmate, Gladys, from the end of our street.

They had kept in touch all through the years. Whenever Melba

came back to Melbourne she called or had the family up for the
day to Coombe Cottage and always sent tickets for several of her
concerts. She took an interest in the growing children and was just
woman to woman in this old friendship. Once in my extreme youth
I caught a glimpse of the tail of the great diva's skirt as she whisked
through the front gate of Gladys's house. Her perfume still permeated
the hall.

There was a legend in Gladys's family that her mother sang better
than Melba when they were girls. Of course that was not true, but
she sang louder.

When the Melba–Williamson Grand Opera Company came to
Australia in 1928, I was lunching at the home of the principal tenor,
Angelo Minghetti. The telephone rang during the ravioli and Louise
Minghetti answered. She returned to tell us that Melba was coming.

In ten minutes she appeared. Medium-sized, alert, eyes bright as
jet, vivid in her crimson coat and skirt and jaunty hat to match.
She had come from a rehearsal of *Thais*, with John Brownlee singing
the monk, Athanaël. She told us that the secret of his success was
the same as her own. 'We have the same formation of the throat.
The high arch. It enables us to hold the note with perfect poise.
If you have that arch you are a great singer. Nature has made you
that. Paris knows it already in John's case. He must be one of the
greatest singers of the world.'

She talked to me of Gladys's mother and her affection and respect
for her. She also told me of the precautions she was obliged to take
over her voice. 'I have never dared to sing when I am out of voice.
Sometimes this has been misunderstood but a singer with a world
reputation must not risk the public saying, "Melba has gone off".'

That day she had a new toy—a picture of early Australia, a large
canvas by Ray Lindsay, son of Norman, then on show at the Society
of Artists. Angelo must ring for two taxis and we would all go with
her to see the picture. 'What I will do with it, God knows!' she
said. 'Coombe Cottage is full. I shall have to lend it to picture galleries
for years.'

When Melba died they gave me her obituary to write—two columns
of it—and bade me commence with the story of her first concert
when a little girl. Flushed with her triumph on that small and insecure
concert platform in the local hall of her native country town of
Lilydale, next day at school she selfconsciously awaited the praise
and approbation of her schoolmates. The glory went out of the
morning when a little comrade said, 'Nellie Mitchell, I saw your
drawers!'

In the Sydney Botanical Gardens there is a garden of roses dedicated to the memory of Nellie Stewart. In death, as she was in life, she is Australia's most romantic stage figure.

Wistful and sweet, that was the essence of Nellie Stewart. After she had created the title role in *Sweet Nell of Old Drury* in Australia she was known universally as 'Sweet Nell'.

Nellie was true theatre. She commenced as a child with her father's 'Rainbow Revels' troupe. She played in pantomime, burlesque, musical comedy, and made one excursion into grand opera as Marguerite in *Faust*. In middle age she turned to drama, comedy and Shakespeare. She adorned them all. She had no interests and probably no thoughts for anything outside the theatre, though later in her life she raised a vast sum of money to buy radium for the public hospitals.

Nellie married early—the man's name was Dick Row— and it was common tradition that she left him at the church door. Hardly that, but not long after. She went to George Musgrove, one of her managers, and lived with him as faithfully as the best of wives until he died. She made fortunes for him which he lost in theatrical speculations. Nellie merely looked a little more wistful and went on to make more fortunes for him.

There was one child. Musgrove's wife would not divorce him but the Stewart–Musgrove scandal became sanctified in public opinion by its durability. Nellie asked for no social status and she never put herself in a position to be snubbed by the moralists. She was a creature of tantrums, childish vanity, plaintive charm, astute audacity, and capable of self-abnegation where those she loved were concerned. When she lost her temper, frequently, she called it 'having the mads'.

My meetings with Nellie Stewart were like flashes from Paradise in my childhood. I adored her. She was Romance.

The first was in her private suite at the Grand Hotel in Melbourne. My Actress Aunt took me to call at about three in the afternoon. Nellie was eating her midday meal. With her fabulous golden curls, her childish blue eyes—a stare in one—her Cupid mouth, and dimples dappling the wedge of face she allowed to appear from the frame of curls, she was the typical fairy princess. Her gown that day was a soft white flowing thing embroidered in Bulgarian stitchery. On the couch beside me was her coolie hat with masses of cherries.

The morose George sat at the other end of the dining table. The little daughter danced around. Nellie was saying: 'You know, Blanche, it's dreadfully vulgar of me but I adore tripe and onions. Would you like some?' We had lunched. We just sat round and adored.

BEGINNING NEXT WEEK!
A NEW SERIAL,
'SAID THE SPIDER'
BY MARY MARLOWE

No more popular serial has appeared in the MIRROR than Mary Marlowe's 'A Child by Proxy', so the news that her latest novel is about to appear will be welcomed.

'Said the Spider' is of a very different type, but is no less interesting than Miss Marlowe's previous serial. The heroine is found as a girl among the natives of Papua, and the development of the story of her life and love there, in Australia and in the U.S.A. makes a most fascinating and appealing study. First Instalment Next Week.

SAID THE SPIDER

One of the thoughts that will occur to most readers as they come to the end of *Said the Spider*, by Mary Marlowe (Collins) is: 'Here, at last, is the perfect film story.' It begins on the banks of the Fly River. Nao, a lovely half-caste child, the orphan daughter of a white woman who was captured by Papuan savages, is to be married to Ho—

> A sullen boy with deep-set eyes and fleshy eyelids under curling brows that were the brand of an evil temper. A monstrous growth of bulbous flesh served him for a nose, and his thick, bunching lips, coloured like the pinkish-purple top of a swede turnip in decay, were puckered into grotesque folds as he slobbered upon his flute. A mass of matted lime-bleached hair rose abruptly from his forehead and temples like the corrugated sides of a ravine.

David Wrixon, a 15-year-old Sydneyite, and his friends rescue Nao from this horror and we see her in a Sydney convent; in the New York 'dwelling-room' of a cocaine-taking aunt; as a dancer in Hughy Hughes's cabaret. And then David, whom she has always loved, comes back from the war.

The book is much more than a picturesque romance. It has atmosphere—the hot, tired atmosphere of the jungle; the slick, noisy atmosphere of New York—and the characters live. This reviewer has only one grievance against Mary Marlowe, who is steadily advancing in power and beauty as a writer. She could have kept her delightful heroine in Sydney, and she took her to New York. About the most vital of the minor characters is Bob Nawn, an Australian journalist—but he practises his profession in America. *Said the Spider* appeared with some of the realism cut out in the WOMAN'S MIRROR.

Above: Mary Marlowe's serials were very popular. This advertisement for the serialization of 'Said the Spider' is from the July 1928 issue of the Australian Women's Mirror.

Below: In 1929 Said the Spider *was published as a novel. This review appeared in the* Bulletin *on 5 June 1929. Sydney's* Sunday Sun *reported in its book column that the London paper* John O'London's Weekly *described* Said the Spider *as a 'brilliant literary achievement' and that other English reviewers were equally cordial: 'You can almost imagine Miss Marlowe's brain children chanting "we are seven" for this latest book is the seventh novel from the same source—a notable achievement for an Australian woman.'*

'The doctor has ordered me raw beef juice every day on bread,' said Nellie. 'It makes me wince but it's good for me.'

'Beer would be better,' said the square dark man at the end of the table.

'Oh, George, don't!' cried Nellie. 'You'll shock Blanche.' In my family we thought beer was Awful.

The second time I saw Nellie Stewart was from the manager's box at a matinee of *Zaza*. There was a retiring room behind it and here, in the interval, Nellie sent a tray of cakes and wine. George came, too, sent by Nellie to look after us.

George was soaked in his beer, unsteady with it. His speech was slightly thick, his language maudlin as he poured the wine for us. 'Nell is a good girl, Blanche,' he said. 'Good girl. Hot tempered. Gets mad sometimes. Flares up. Unreasonable. But she's a good girl. Give her her due, she's a good girl.'

Some of the glitter went out of the day when I thought of Beauty having to put up with the Beast.

When next I met Nellie I was a humble extra lady in her company. For one glorious month I saw her every evening and twice on Saturdays. One day I watched the dress rehearsal of a new piece from the stalls. Nellie was on stage in a Margueritish gown, a golden plait round her head.

Came George's mutterings from the darkened stalls and then Nellie burst into tears. 'I can't help it, George, I can't help it!' There was some play with a handkerchief.

And George said gruffly, 'All right, all right, Miss Stewart. Do it your way. It's wrong but we'll call it stage licence.'

Nellie did it her way. I think she had no intention of doing it any other.

Years passed. When her daughter had a child it was my duty to ring Nellie and ask would she care to tell us who was the father. The phone went dead.

Next morning's post brought a letter from Nellie, written on rose pink paper in a rose pink temper:

Neither Nancye or myself seek for publicity and cannot see why our private lives should be intruded upon—or commented upon. I am sincerely regretful to think what little etiquette and courtesy is observed in making use of as copy one's private affairs. It is most distressing. Faithfully, Nellie Stewart.

Nell becoming a grandmother was news to all Australia but she did not see it that way. Grandmother, be bothered! Resilient to the last, when an old woman she played Romeo in purple tights with a jaunty swaggering air. The voice that had captured several generations was still beautiful. For special charity matinees she played the balcony scene at the Theatre Royal to her daughter's Juliet. Her face took refuge behind a curtain of golden curls but her legs were impeccable.

I featured her legs in a newspaper article. Having written to ask if she had been the first to wear tights in Australia, I received another pink reply:

> No, I certainly was not the first to wear tights in Australia, but I was the
> first to wear fleshings and *tights from foot to neck* without a break both
> in London in *The Forty Thieves* at Drury Lane, Xmas 1899, and as the
> Prince in *Cinderella* here in 1901. In London I just wore fleshings and a
> green and white carbon diamond serpent. It caused quite a sensation
> and looked magnificent and certainly not one bit immodest—I don't
> think my public would ever accuse me of being that! A shapely woman
> is beautiful to behold—and she need not be naked to exhibit her
> shapeliness!!! Sincerely yours, Nellie Stewart.

She wrote her reminiscences and came to my office to be interviewed, realizing that anything personal written about her would be a better advertisement for her book than the stereotyped reviews. She chose the seat in shadow behind my door. She was a ghost with golden hair, her sub-deb's gown of floral muslin sashed in baby blue. She wore a girlish hat, wreathed with daisies.

'Don't let them tell you that anybody else wrote my book,' she said. (There was a current feeling that the late Frank Morton, a fine journalist, had done so.)

'Such as it is, the book is my own and no journalist has manufactured it. Frank Morton wrote some chapters and brought them to me. I found a brilliantly written story, but all trace of Nellie Stewart had gone. I put the chapters aside and began again. I am a Christian Scientist and I must be truthful in all things. Morton flattered me. He called me witty. Yet whenever I feel in keen sympathy with a person—or with an audience through my parts—although I may be really quite happy and gay a little lump comes into my throat. I think in me tears and laughter are akin.'

Here was the secret of her elusive charm.

The final scene was set for me in her home, 'Den 'o Gwynn' on the North Shore, Sydney. This day, I was taking tea with her and old Johnny Wallace, a veteran actor on the verge of being a nonagenarian.

Johnny was to be given a benefit by an amateur musical society. It was arranged that I should be present at the meeting between the actress and her former teacher and stage manager, and I made a story out of it to advertise Johnny's benefit.

Nellie took Johnny's arm. 'This way, Mr Wallace, love. I'll put you in the comfy chair. Mind the slippery mats. Nonsense! There's nothing wrong with your sight.'

Nor his memory. They plunged into the past with complete enthusiasm. Nellie sat with her back to the light but that was her only concession to the passage of the years. Throughout they were 'Mr Wallace' and 'Miss Stewart' to one another.

Re-enacting old scenes, reviving old triumphs, Nellie declared that Mr Wallace's training was responsible for her ultimate success.

'Forgive me, Miss Stewart, for saying what a sparkling little drummer boy you were in *Tambour Major*. The girl before you was so lumpy.'

'Forgive you, Mr Wallace, dear! The idea! Do you remember the night someone threw a bouquet on the stage for the leading lady and it fell at my feet? I picked it up to go down on my knees and present it to her, and the leading man snatched it from me and said, "How dare you! That's not for you, miss!" '

Johnny remembered. 'And do I remember when some gay spark threw a bouquet at you and for your next entrance you came flaunting along with it stuck in your cap? "Go back, miss, and take that out," I said. You refused. "While your father is away you are my daughter," I said. "He told me to look after you. Go back at once!" You cried but you went.'

'Oh, but I was so frightened of you, dear,' returned the husky-sweet Nellie. 'You were so strict with me. Ten hours in the theatre every day, and if a lady pretended to faint to get off, you'd say, "I know all about that, young woman. There's a man outside waiting to take you to dinner but you're not going." '

Johnny chuckled. He had enjoyed being a czar.

On they moved with the happy ghosts of a glamorous past. The stage of today is carrying on with a broken back because there are no more players who live their private lives in an aura of romance.

In the car on the way home, Johnny Wallace confided that he was going to the city in the morning by ferry and on foot.

'Must you?' I asked. 'The traffic is pretty dangerous in the city these days.'

'I must,' said Johnny obstinately. 'I must borrow a wig for my benefit. I put it to you, could I appear before all the people who'll be there with this old bald head of mine?'

As I was writing of this meeting, calculation brought up Nellie Stewart's age to sixty-six. (She had admitted that it was over fifty years since she and Johnny first met.) Remembering that on other occasions she had been sensitive on the matter of age, I rang up and asked if she knew what she had said and did it matter.

'Sixty-six,' replied Nellie over the phone. 'Did I say sixty-six? I'm seventy, dear, and of course I don't mind anybody knowing if it will help Mr Wallace.'

Having heroically owned up to being an old woman, Nellie had her own wig re-dressed and sat in the stalls at Johnny Wallace's benefit.

A year later she died. Johnny outlived her by several years.

Psalmist of the Dawn

When the Great Depression came to Australia many in our newspaper office were reduced in status and took a drop in salary. We lived on a mental seesaw, expecting to be sacked every Friday. Writing about the theatre had been my real work and now the theatre was beginning to slide downhill. That gaudy, bawdy Jezebel, the Film, was replacing it in large expensive advertisements and public taste.

It seemed a suitable time to write another novel. I wrote two for good measure: *Psalmist of the Dawn* and a sequel, *Island Calm.* They were both set on Lord Howe Island.

I was introduced formally to the lovable little Yellow Bob, *Eopsaltria australis,* colloquially known as Psalmist of the Dawn, by Donald Thomson, the Australian anthropologist, at a dinner party. My heart raced. What a name for a novel! Then I realized that this was the bird that had wakened me time and again on the island where I had spent my last annual holidays. Something must be sold or pawned. I had to go back there.

Psalmist of the Dawn was written close to the dawn. Mainly on the island because that is where the birds call you early and urgently.

Islanders may fish before breakfast but they do not bathe at that heavenly hour. Visitors select the lagoon nearer the boarding houses for a pre-breakfast dip. Ned's Beach it was for me, because to reach Ned's you could run through the palm groves, the banyans, and the native bush where the little Yellow Bobs were already singing their morning chorus to the sun coming up out of the sea.

In the story all characters were thinly veiled. In a community of 150 humans—and an occasional new baby—it would be impossible not to use this material as personnel for a plot. Besides, there are no other people quite like them anywhere. So fresh, so frank, so friendly. One could catch their vernacular and get it down on the typewriter the same day.

Bravely I sent a copy to the island library and, though they were

ISLAND ROMANCE

Miss Mary Marlowe gives us a picture of Lord Howe Island that will set all her readers anxiously considering ways and means to go to that happy speck of basalt and coral in the wide Pacific, and stay there. No island can really be as delectable as this, fit, as it is, for the setting of a tale of a Prince and Sleeping Beauty.

The Prince is a Macquarie-street doctor, and the Princess, who is not too sleepy, is a singer in musical comedy, on holiday. The doctor makes his first acquaintance with the Lord Howe Islanders as the result of a shark attack at Coogee, and the amputation of a leg. His eyes have been failing, and the doctor thinks that a rest might restore them. So he goes to the island, and there meets Bryony Browne. The love story goes on romantically on the island, and after the doctor comes back and has an operation on his eyes, they marry and live happily ever afterwards. The 'psalmist of the dawn' is the yellow robin, which is the first bird awake and the last to go to roost. Those who want a real romance, without an ounce of that nasty, analytic modern sex business in it, should read Miss Marlowe's last novel.
Sunday Sun and Guardian,
16 September 1934

'*Most of the action takes place on this palm-crested speck in the Pacific, which is a romance in itself, and Miss Marlowe is to be complimented on the refreshing atmosphere she has created in her novel—there is about it a compelling touch of difference.*'
Woman's World, September 1934

'*As the first book in Australia or any other country to picture that curious little sub-civilisation, a tiny British commonwealth as distinct as Man or the Channel Islands, Lord Howe Island, it should be in the bookcase of every collector of Australiana. Apart from its historical value it has first-class fiction value . . .*'
The Australian Woman's Mirror, September 1935

'*The story is in keeping with the romantic atmosphere. It has a love story and a happy ending, and it is not a bit realistic.*'
The Sun, 2 August 1934

Psalmist of the Dawn *pleased many Australian critics.*

Coming ashore at Lord Howe Island after the voyage from Sydney. Mary spent five annual holidays in succession on the enchanting island and two of her novels, Psalmist of the Dawn *and* Island Calm, *are located there.*

self-conscious when the book came out, before long they were telling visitors to Lord Howe who they were in the story.

Island Calm was partly written on the island on another visit. By the grace of the God of authors Chichester, the airman, was there too, rebuilding the plane he had crashed in landing on the lagoon. It was simple to weave a story out of such fascinating material, and to tell a second tale of happy people. I had to rise at dawn to find time to write books about them. The Psalmist was my knocker-up. Close to the cottage where I was housed he had his snug nest and his little wife to twit her admiration of his song.

Meanwhile, when I was back in the office after those enchanting holidays—five annual holidays in succession on Lord Howe Island where the Psalmists knew me by sight at last—the work allotted to me was appallingly dull. When the reprint editor took ten months leave of absence to have his leg off, they made me the reprint editor. When the film editor was ill or on holidays I became the assistant film critic. The stage being now in its death throes, we acclimatized ourselves to appreciate its slayer, the cinema. Book reviews had been part of my regular work. Now I did them at a penny halfpenny a line, and no choice of selection as formerly.

What could be done to escape the dullness of routine and complete obscurity? Maybe I could break into radio? I volunteered to give six talks or interviews with prominent stage people. The first was 'Memories of Pavlova'. I could hardly speak for nervousness. A new medium is rather like a first night. Who doesn't suffer from the jitters at those? It was on station 2CH. I could scarcely speak my first sentence. Simultaneously, Mr Warren Penny, the studio's announcer, decided it was a good time to reorganize the record filing cabinets. Thanks to Mr Penny, but unknown to him, I found my radio voice. Had to. Listeners could not hear the rustlings and movements of Mr Penny, but if they did not hear the voice on the radio set there would be trouble. So I bawled my memories of Pavlova.

The months went by. Bleak and barren. Every Friday might be my last. Yet when five o'clock came and the day's end of dull jobs and meaningless work, I forgot it all. At home at the end of the street in a bedsitting room with a gas-ring, *Psalmist of the Dawn* was waiting for another chapter.

Our chairman, Sir Hugh Denison, had bought himself a radio station (2UE). I wrote, asking him for a session on it. He rang down: 'Come up.'

'I think you've been having a hard time,' he said when I took

Sporting shorts with a friend on Lord Howe Island. Behind the two women is Chichester's crashed plane.

the chair at the other side of his desk. 'Haven't seen any work under your name for a long while. Did they take it from you?'

'Umph.' It was easier to reply with closed lips.

'Did they reduce your salary?'

'Umph.'

'Why didn't you tell me?'

'It's editorial business. Employees don't bring their woes to chairmen.'

He was going to New Zealand the following day, he said, but he would have a word with his radio manager and he would give the question of my radio session favourable consideration. In the meantime he would raise my salary a pound a week.

The editor-in-chief was not very pleased to be told by the chairman to raise my salary. Nor was he elated that I had asked for a radio session. However, one day my phone rang. The chairman's radio manager was at the other end of the ether. Could I take a radio session for them in twenty minutes? Oh, on anything I could think of. There would be something in the morning paper. A taxi would be at the front door for me in five minutes.

Why the hurry?

'Because the woman who takes the session has forgotten she is on the air today. She's just phoned to say she can't be there in time.'

I took the session. On my nerves. Everything I have got in life has been through tenacity rather than talent.

The young woman was permitted to go on forgetting. The following week I was instructed to tell the radio public that they would at that time and on that station be listening to me in future. Whether they liked it or not, they had to listen to me—or twiddle the knob—for the next seven years.

The first year talks were along general lines, principally to advertise our papers in an easy-to-take manner. The remaining years were given over to impromptu interviews with the famous, the near-famous, and the had-been-famous.

There was the Chinese actress, Anna May Wong.

We were due on the air live in one minute. Anna rose from her seat and took a good look round the studio. 'Where's the spittoon?' she inquired.

The announcer who put us on the air noticed the disturbance through the plate glass windows of the control room. He hurried in to us. Could he do anything for Anna? Anna, the svelte, Anna the beautiful, Anna the mysterious, Anna, the inscrutable Chinawoman.

'I was looking for the spittoon,' said Anna. 'Don't bother. I'll manage.'

'Would my handkerchief do?' suggested the amiable announcer. 'Or a newspaper? We have a newspaper. We haven't got a spittoon.'

'No. Don't bother. I'll wait till after.'

She waited. The announcer fled back to put us on the air. It was a close shave.

Ella Shields came with me to the mike twice. That rich contralto makes the perfect radio voice. Burlington Bertie's shadow was at her shoulder. And Bertie is a fund of fun for Ella. But what I could not put over the air is more a piece of the woman herself—rank sentimentalist that she is.

Travelling the world with Ella, and set up in her theatre dressing room wherever she may be, is a portable gramophone with one precious record. She plays it whenever she feels homesick. Homesick for what? Ella is a product of the universe. Sometimes she thinks she is American (being born there helps that delusion). Sometimes she is feverishly British. Often—quite often—she is irresistibly Irish. Spasmodically—according to the enthusiasm of her audiences—she is a naturalized Australian, only waiting to take out her naturalization papers. A grandfather—some generations removed—came here with the First Fleet. Once Ella had me on the string to trace his movements.

In her dressing room Ella is all actress with the actress's romantic streak. On her little gramophone she plays the record which goes round the world with her. The record of a speech by a king who was never crowned. The 'Woman I Love' speech. Ella cries.

Bert Bailey was coaxed to the mike. He spoke of his Australian plays, most of them written by

Mary Marlowe, working journalist.

Mary Marlowe was given her own session on 2UE in 1934. She was the first person to introduce informal interviews to Sydney radio.

himself. Perhaps it was not in the broadcast that he said it. Maybe it was said one day in my own office. It was a trenchant remark—as most of his are, for he is a forthright man and hates sham.

'People talk a lot about the Great Australian Play and ask when it will be written. A plum for some literary genius some day. Well, the people who made *On Our Selection* don't make any boasts. They don't want to be considered literary. They are just theatre people. Of all the plays that have been written in Australia, of Australia and by Australians, *On Our Selection* has made the most money. And I'm not speaking in shillings.'

That is fact.

At the mike that day he told our listeners that I was his first Kate Rudd in *On Our Selection*, and his natural courtesy prompted him to add instantly: 'But you were just a youngster then.'

We took tea together afterwards and then he walked me to a seed shop and bought some plants for my garden.

'They should be onions, as a good Australian,' he said, 'but you always were romantic, Mary, so we'll get sweet alyssum and rose-coloured hibiscus that will bloom for you in and out of season.'

'And plumbago for a hedge,' I pleaded. 'It's hardy for an amateur gardener and the flowers are heavenly blue.'

Over a hundred others came to the mike to be plucked of their stories during my radio years. Not all theatre people, though they usually gave the best performances.

Among them were those Heavenly Twins in friendship, cricketer turned cartoonist Arthur Mailey and Jimmy Bancks, the creator of Ginger Meggs. Arthur told us how he sees people. No use being beautiful for Arthur. He would see Venus as a cartoon. Arthur is an amiable bloke and always looks cheerful. There is a whimsical joke at the back of his throat, waiting the opportunity to pop out. Frankly, I adore him.

Jimmy Bancks naturally found his best story in Ginger Meggs. When Jim was young and pretty poor he was a kind of Ginger himself. He knocked about with the boys. His sister made him an artist and her suggestions for cartoons put Jim on his way to fame and a few fortunes. You can always depend on Jim for a quid if you are running an office show for the copyboys. When I ran a baby show in the office for our own Sun Comforts Fund, it was Jim's quid for First and a sheepfaced Mr Bancks was overcome with shyness when he had to make the winning selection. Under his breath he said to me, during the passing parade: 'Would this one do? It seems a non-crier.'

On one occasion Mary Marlowe was forced to interview herself on the air for five minutes!

It was this way.

For her 'Woman's View of the News' Session (2UE, Tuesdays at 4 p.m., which features people of topical interest), Miss Marlowe had secured a visitor from Lord Howe Island. But he was recovering from severe illness, and when the opening announcement came, appeared on the verge of collapse.

Grasping the situation, Miss Marlowe, who is herself thoroughly conversant with Lord Howe Island (she has been there five times . . .), just went ahead. But she reversed proceedings, as it were—putting all the 'meat' into the questions and merely requiring the 'interviewed' to say 'Yes'.

At the end of five minutes he recovered, and the remainder of the broadcast proceeded to schedule!

Among the interviews Miss Marlowe enjoys most are those with stage celebrities, and no wonder! as she herself has been a leading lady in three Continents, in comedy, drama, Shakespeare and vaudeville.

Ella Shields, collected from the theatre 'between acts', created considerable excitement when she stepped from the taxi in full 'Burlington Bertie' costume—and still more when she literally dashed from the studio to the theatre to be in time for her next appearance.

The material for these interviews is rarely written out beforehand, although if the 'prospect' does show symptoms of being extremely 'mike shy', notes or a full interview are prepared.

One lady waxed so enthusiastic that she thumped the desk energetically—and continuously—to enforce her words, and said afterwards that she wondered at the sudden display of affection when Miss Marlowe grasped her hands. It didn't occur to her that too much vibration is anything but fitting treatment for a microphone!

The Telegraph, 26 June 1934

'WOMAN'S' NEW 2UE SESSIONS

Last week in this column we were telling you all about the new sessions for 'Woman' conducted every afternoon on 2GB.

This week we want to point out to listeners what they may look for in 'Woman's' sessions over 2UE.

On Monday and Wednesday mornings, at 10.45, Miss Mary Marlowe will conduct a session for us, and you may rely on this always being of great interest, for Miss Marlowe is not only an 'old hand' at the radio, but has had years and years of both theatrical and journalistic experience. Her charming personality always ensures her a host of followers. Chatting to us about her Monday session, Miss Marlowe says that she intends giving forecasts from the 'proofs' of the next issue of the paper, as well as general gossip, but on Wednesday morning she will be devoting her time more to details concerning all films covered in 'Woman', as well as giving intriguing little bits of gossip from English and American studios.

Woman, 11 March 1937

Mary Marlowe, broadcaster.

Gower Wilson—the indomitable Gower of Lord Howe Island, the man who could do anything with fish, fowl or bad weather, the born sailor, the genial comrade, the good mate at sea and on land—Gower came unwillingly to the mike. He knew I had used up his whole family for characters in *Psalmist of the Dawn* and himself as the Head Man, Power Horton—named so nobody could make a mistake—and he said that day that I had put a fish-hook in him and hauled him aboard.

Unwillingly he came, it is true, but he was a good sort and he knew I loved his island as he did. He had the story, the saga of Lord Howe. On the island he was forever telling it. I asked him just to talk to me and reply to my questions as he would in his own home when strangers came to stay.

I opened the session, told the folks a bit about Gower, and then all was sweet and ready for the Islander's own tale. It was an unforgettable moment. Gower put his hand to his brow, lent back against his chair and whispered, 'I can't.' Then he groaned.

For five minutes I had to talk about the island and its history. Then I began to ask Gower questions which he could answer in a single syllable. I knew the answers but somehow or other I had to draw him in. To aid this process I made some incorrect statements about the island. That brought him to with a jerk. We finished the broadcast in fine fettle. We had tea in the cafeteria afterwards and he even said he had enjoyed himself.

I never saw him again. Within a week he was on his way back to his island with his son who, having finished his apprenticeship in Sydney, was going home to build boats. His brother-in-law and four other islanders made up the crew of the new boat which Gower had had built in Sydney for the island fishing. They were never heard of again.

Beacon fires were lit on every peak on Lord Howe Island and the Pacific was raked for signs of them. Good sailors all, but the sea claimed them.

The Sun Junior

The greatest joy in newspaper work did not come through temporary triumphs in writing. Journalists know today's paper is tomorrow's meat-wrapper. Nor from the friendly association with famous people whom I admired, sometimes loved, always understood. Nor even from the day-to-day comradeship with newspaper staffs, though from machine-room staff to the roof I had splendid friendships. The greatest joy came through the boys. The copyboys. The little boys who trusted me. Boys who shared their ambitions and their triumphs with me. The *Sun Junior* boys.

It has been confessed that I wanted six sons. Suddenly I had a life interest in six boys. Six sons without the bother of bearing them, rearing them, or darning their socks. During the next five years the number grew to fifty-six.

While I was working back late one afternoon, six small boys burst into my office. Their eyes were shining. They looked very serious, determined, important. They had a good deal to say.

Their mothers knew them as John Harnetty, George Shaw, Alan Reid, Lionel (known as Bill) Hudson, Charles Nicol, and Jackie Nolan. Mervyn came later. It was a pity about Mervyn.

John Harnetty spluttered: 'We're going to start our own newspaper. Can we use your typewriter?'

'I've no doubt you can and probably you may.' If they were going to run a news-sheet they might as well learn something about grammar. The *Sun Junior* was born.

The first conference was held in my office. Staff was graded, editor chosen—Mervyn. Young Hudson was to be advertising manager. John was selected for leader writer, and he later also wrote our social column under the heading of 'Sarah's Suspicions'. George Shaw was special writer, Jackie Nolan and Charles Nicol general reporters, and Alan Reid was to handle international affairs—inside and outside the office. I was offered the post of business manager and 'charwoman'.

Lionel (Bill) Hudson as a cadet reporter.

I accepted. Nobody was to share in the profits—if any.

'We'll need money to run a newspaper.' My idea.

'We'll charge a penny a copy.' John's idea.

'You don't suppose any newspaper is run on its circulation, do you?' Sarcasm from me.

'We'll get advertising.' Bill's contribution.

'I know!' Jack was teeming with ideas. 'We'll have a lost-and-found column, an engagement column, a for sale column. We'll charge a penny a line.'

'Chicken feed!' Me, scoffing. 'Regular ads are what we need. Who's game to go up and word the general manager tomorrow? Offer him what space he can take.'

'I'll go up,' said Bill, the future wing-commander in the next war, 'and I'll offer him the back page to advertise the *Sun*.'

Me: 'He may consider the expense unnecessary. Quite a number of people here have heard of the *Sun*. But surely he could find use for staff notices as we have no staff newspaper? Try him on that.'

It was carried without dissent. We didn't call it a motion. We just agreed it was a good idea.

Bill saw the general manager next morning immediately after his conference. He came back with a contract. Nine shillings a week for the duration of the *Sun Junior*.

'I asked for ten bob. He beat me down to nine.' Bill explained.

The Sun Junior

YOU'VE GROWN UP NOW JUNIOR. HERE'S THE LATCH KEY

THIRD ANNUAL

BIRTHDAY

SEPT. NUMBER 1933

3ᵈ

Mary Marlowe was the power behind the copyboys' newspaper, the Sun Junior.

'He said it would learn me . . .'

'Did he?'

'Oh, well—teach me. Teach me something about the way advertising is run. If you take space by the year you don't pay as much as if you take it by the day. Newspapers charge a bit less to regular customers. Discount I think he called it. We have a long-term contract.'

'Now you kids get busy and write,' said John. 'And look out for libels. We can't afford them—yet.'

'We will later,' said Bill. 'We've got to be bright.'

George Shaw said: 'I'll take my lunch into the Botanical Gardens. I think I can get a story out of that.'

Alan said: 'I'd better look up the files and see what they're doing in Europe.' He came from Scotland.

Two young and healthy girl typists were roped in. They came quietly when the boys surrounded them. We bought a box of stencils and a tube of printing ink. The boys persuaded a girl in the Circulation Department to stay back in her lunch hour and run the sheets off on the office Roneo machine. So the production started. The first issue looked like the original papyrus, but everything has to start somewhere. It was sold in the building on Friday morning.

The only free copy of the first edition was secretly laid on the managing editor's desk. 'Where he can see it when he shoots back his cuffs,' explained Jack.

The managing editor met me in the corridor that afternoon. He had his copy in hand. He looked grim.

'What *is* this? Something concocted by newts? A disgrace!'

So long as he didn't say that to the boys, I could take it.

'The kids are just beginning. They'll do better.'

'You can't even read it.'

You couldn't. The ardent young typists had not pressed hard enough on the stencils.

'You're behind it, I hear. You ought to be ashamed of the thing. It hasn't even a cover.'

He went into his office. I went back to mine with moist eyes.

We would do better. The six eager little lads, the two typists and me. We knew we would do better. I could not tell them what the managing editor had said.

The following Friday the second issue was distributed. Without a cover. It was not much better to look at than the first.

On Monday the managing editor became a grandfather. At the end of the day he came to my desk, a copy of the *Junior* in his hand. He said: 'This is ridiculous. This thing can't go on without a cover. Get one of the artists to draw a design. Arthur Mailey will do it for you. Take it to Process and have a double column block made. I'll tell them not to charge for it. It can go on the House Account. I'll give you half a crown a week for paper for the cover. But you are not to talk about it. Here's a quid. Let me know when it runs out.'

Wonderful what a grandson can do to a man!

The *Sun Junior*'s first editor, Mervyn, was sacked. He had no immediate successor. The post lay fallow for two years. The paper came out quite well without an editor and no boy got above his station on the staff.

Arthur Mailey drew a startling cover—for love, naturally! We bought bright yellow poster paper from the office store. We found a girl with a stout heart and a terrific machine, and for the next five years Nell Pettitt was our printer, practically for the cost of the ink. She became so keen on the boys, so fired with their enthusiasm, that she would have let them put her in the machine if it would have made the ink any better.

Nell Pettitt churned out the third edition with cover. We put one on the managing editor's table. He asked for six extra copies and paid for them. These he sent, with a covering letter, to his editor friends—on the highest level—in other states. He asked them to notice what the boys in our office were doing. I know, because their replies, suitably enthusiastic, were handed to me for the *Junior* files.

As a literary organ we were stern taskmasters. There were a good many 'returns' each week and the boys had to take them. We were aiming for a standard. We kept a dictionary in our pocket. But we had our vernacular for ordinary conversation.

Three prizes each week were given for the best stories—three shillings, two and one. The weekly cost of production was one guinea. All labour was voluntary and nobody pinched a penny.

The boys gave their stories to me as early in the week as possible and they were sent down all together to the senior reporter chosen to judge them each week. The senior reporters took a bit of training to come quietly but we corralled them. When the judging was complete (in strict secrecy because no boy knew he had won a prize until the paper came out), the stories came back to me.

Twice yearly we published special numbers: Christmas and the *Junior* birthday numbers. All dividends went in cakes and fruit juices at the birthday party, and obedient mothers turned up trumps with homemade cakes.

For our most magnificent birthday number, in 1933, the office allowed us to have it printed. Bill Hudson interviewed the chairman on his past life for the first page and, when he had read it, the chairman sent me down two pounds to buy ice creams for the party.

We were an impertinent, and an entirely unofficial, organ but I was given to understand that the *Junior* was always read at the weekly board meetings. Not on Bible oath, mind you! But I was given to understand . . .

And the boys? First to get his cadetship was John Harnetty. He was a year younger than cadets are supposed to be but John was no ordinary boy. At fifteen he lent me Voltaire's *Candide*, which he had read. When he heard he was to be a cadet he rushed round

Paul Brickhill (on the left) before he started to churn out bestsellers.

to my desk to tell me and to phone his mother. When war came John went at once. He was a staff sergeant in the Middle East, saw a spot of Tobruk, came back for some New Guinea skirmishes, married an AAMC girl and went into radio.

Alan Reid, with Scotland in his voice, was the brightest star of our *Junior* debating club. We could always fill a page of the *Junior* with what Alan had said at the last debate. Because that was our wily way to bring the little fellows before the big fellows. Alan was the second to get his cadetship. He came to my telephone to ring his mother. Wasn't I lucky to have a phone out of the general scrum? Alan is a Canberra man today. He needs no introduction. He'll be a politician yet, if he doesn't look out. He has the voice for it.

George Shaw wrote with the pen of an idealist. He died at nineteen. Before he died he knew he had been given his cadetship.

Bill Hudson won his cadetship soon after being elected the *Junior*'s first real editor. As soon as war broke out he swapped the newsroom for a cockpit. He joined the RAAF, flying with the RAF over India and Burma.

Charlie Nicol became an expert Hansard writer and when last heard of was press relations officer to the minister for the army in Canberra.

Jackie Nolan went in for big business in a small way; he is always changing his venue but he has imagination. And a way with him. Occasionally he takes a job writing for newspapers.*

There were so many others who came into public notice. Peter Finch, who could talk magnificently at the debates but afterwards we never knew exactly what he had said. To the horror of the respectable aunts who reared him, I gave Peter his first three introductions by letter to theatrical managers. He had to leave home. If you have acting in your blood you have to keep going until you get a chance to act. Peter would have been a bad journalist. He is a pretty good actor. What the news editor said to me about those letters at the time is something nobody would print.

D'Arcy Niland wrote for the *Junior*. He had a flair for detective stories then. Paul Brickhill published with us and was later the editor, and it was not long before he won his cadetship. He got it while still writing for the lads' paper. Greater fame was achieved by *The Great Escape*, his book on adventures close to eternity in a German hell camp.

* He was still a young man when he drowned diving for pearls off his own lugger in Torres Strait.

Alan Reid before he went to Canberra.

The *Junior* boys were grand boys. They grew into good men. No shirkers. In the five years the *Sun Junior* ran, and in the later years when sporadic issues were brought out from time to time, to please some of the old boys and help some of the newcomers, we did not have one mongrel.

Now and again my first, and later dethroned, old English editor would pass my desk and he would note with a whimsical smile that we were stealing the Boss's time to bring out our own paper. He was a severe taskmaster in his day of authority but we were not his pigeon now. Many a time he said to me: 'You know, Mary, you should have had six sons.'

If he had only known!

Have it your own way

The modern trend of literature is to feed us with raw and mangy fragments of bad meat on rotten bones. The loose and semi-smart conversation of the day is peppered with facile 'bloodies' and 'lousies', mistaken by the mindless for good emphasis and pictorial effect.

I have washed blood and lice from the shattered bodies of soldiers. Men who came direct from the welter of blood and lice in France had the decency not to use such words before the women who were trying to patch up their wounds so that they might go back again.

Maybe it is the unknowing that are the unthinking. To be real is not necessarily to be raw. In restraint there is more strength than in crude eruption.

I have lived close to realities. Being hungry is real. Being friendless in strange countries sends you to seek beauty in arid places. Going deep into despair makes you understand better than anything else that the world still needs romance. I am forever trying to weave those golden threads through the grey warp of realities.

Romance has a way of turning up unexpectedly just when you think she is dead and will never come out of the grave.

One evening I was waiting in the foyer of the Sydney Town Hall for a woman to join me at a concert. The overture had already begun and I was in the foyer alone when I heard my name spoken.

My heart stopped beating and I felt as though I were choking. I knew the voice of the speaker. In a second David Cameron was by my side.

He held my hand as though he would save a piece of flotsam from a strong tide. His eyes were gentle. 'After all these years!'

There was that letter of mine—unanswered. I reminded him. He denied that he had received it but I was not convinced. The London post is infallible. I did not press the point.

'You don't look any different,' he said. That was not true but people say those things when they are fond of you.

'After the concert will you let me take you for some coffee?'

'Of course.'

My friend came up and I nodded to the outer vestibule. After the concert I would meet him there.

He was waiting in the shadow of the porch when the time came. I shook the woman off with difficulty. She clung to me but, on or under a tram, she had to go, so I shoved her on to one. She tried to back down from the tram when she found I was not following. I said: 'Oh, don't be a damned fool. Go on home.'

The steps of the Town Hall were clear when I got back to David. He slipped his arm through mine and guided me across the wide street to a coffee shop nearby. We ordered chocolate sundaes. They seemed appropriate—cool and sweet.

While we were waiting for them I remembered that Bob Davis of Munsey Publications had told me the perfect story completes a circle. Here it was. Destiny, the best plot-spinner of us all, had brought me back across the world to eat an ice-cream with David.

We talked with calm affection of the past and even a little of the future. The safe surface things. He spoke of his adventures at the war. I told of my experiences of the peace. He described his journeys round the world. I gave him a brief outline of mine.

When we reached the present he told me with pride of his son who was crazy to go to sea and be a deep-sea sailor. Imagine that! Just like my own David, my dream child, who might be, so I fantasized, on every new windjammer that put into Rose Bay. I lived in a house whose windows overlooked it.

Eagerly I listened to his tales of his David. I did not tell him about my six children. There must be certain reticences or the social system would crumble to dust.

We had an hour to remember. Then the cafe showed signs of closing and there was that last tram for me to catch. David took me to the corner and we waited for it, side by side. It was not long coming. It swaggered over the rails with the insolence of a juggernaut.

In that final moment while we waited for the tram David said: 'You never cared very much, did you?'

My heart turned over—so it seemed—but I was able to smile.

'Have it your own way.'

The tram was almost level with us and you do not argue with the inevitable.

The sight of a windjammer in the harbour only that afternoon had conjured up the thought that I might have had a son on her. Now all that was over. Clearly, I needed a change of scene.

Part Four

The Happy House

With a legacy of fifty pounds I bought a piece of land on a high hill overlooking Newport Beach and the Pacific [in 1933]. Forty feet wide, the land went down like a scarf to the sea.

For the next year I tried to entice builders to make me a small house that would be my home. I learned a thing or two about builders.

A builder takes your plan to make an estimate of costs. He retires with it into a monastery. He has no further communication with the outside world. Write, ring, telegraph him, but you will not contact him. Three, four, or five months later he gets in touch with you on a long distance phone and mutters abruptly: 'Cost you twice what you expected. Can't start until next year.'

I speak of conscientious builders. Others never reply. After many piteous pleas you may get your plan back by post.

This will test your tenaciousness. These men are your friends. They are putting you through the crucible. After half a dozen such experiences you will know whether you still want a house. I still wanted my house. Now I have got it my house owns me.

As hungry dogs search for food and old prospectors go panning for gold, I hunted builders. None wanted to erect a microscopic house on a hill, forty feet by the drop.

Every Sunday through that spring and summer, to ease that craving for my home, I would lie on the land, munching sandwiches, getting acquainted with the local cows—who were also munching on my estate—and telling myself, 'This is where the bathroom will be. The bedroom window will look out on this aspect. From the sitting room window I should be able to watch the birds in that tree. The south wind will blow through the windows here. When honeysuckle grows over the septic tank the perfume will blend with the daffodils on that hummock.'

So the dream went on. And the builders continued to retreat to their monasteries.

George rang me. That is, George the Tenth. Builders are usually called George.

'I have a motor car and nine children,' said George unexpectedly. 'We often have a picnic of a Sunday. Will you join us tomorrow and we'll make the picnic down your way? I must see the land before I can give an estimate. We'll call for you at nine tomorrow morning at your city address. Okay?'

'Okay with me,' said I.

Problem: what could I take to feed those nine children? Naturally I must throw my weight into that picnic. Result: immense watermelon and twenty-four bananas. George had said, 'Mum is a great cake-maker.' Not for me to compete with Mum.

When the car fetched up for me there was George, Mum, the baby, and a boy of twelve, included, said George, because he had a gift for blueprinting. The rest of the nine had been left at home.

We drove to the land and made a careful survey of the estate. 'One in ten,' said George, referring to the drop. 'Hard going but we'll make a good job of it. We'll mount the house on stone piers and put a tiled roof on it so you'll be weatherproof. We'll have malthoid under the tiles. Whatever you do never scrimp on your roof.'

Then we went down to the beach for our picnic. Between cakes and bananas George and I did things with a T square. We had become so matey by the close of the day that we decided to take a lottery ticket together, George putting in sixpence as his personal representation, and I paying the bulk as my share of the day's petrol.

We did not win. You can't expect too much luck in one gush. George had a house to build all on his own. For some years a long depression had forced him to work for other builders on small repairs. He was exultant. He would show me how a house should be built. I had a home in view and felt confident about George. No doubt about it, he was an enthusiastic creator. You need to be to have nine children.

George ran up a shed on the piece of land adjoining my lot, using my flooring for the purpose. Here he and his son, Young George, made their living quarters during the early stages of building the Happy House. They slept in hammocks made of hessian, nailed to poles. On a rough barbecue outside they cooked meals in a kerosene tin. Every week Mum sent down a stock of cakes.

On Sundays I spent the day on the estate. George listened to my suggestions patiently, offered to carry them out my way and then told me the correct way so that I should not blame him later if critical friends should point out the errors. He always won.

As the house grew we had meals in the kitchen, the front bedroom and finally in the sitting room. When we were in full strength— that is the nine Georges plus the painter plus the fencers and the electrician—we had meals in the kitchen and the front bedroom and the sitting room.

I felt my heart contract with a spasm of joy on that final Sunday when the meal was extra good and we all finished up with a fruit course and a glass of ale apiece. We drank a health to my little new home.

Can you wonder mine is a Happy House?

Now the builder has gone, at last I feel the house is mine. Twenty-four feet square, with an extra four-foot extension where the kitchen butts out at the back. My territory. My home. To own this I have suffocated in an office for years.

Forty feet by the drop! My land. Beyond the drop, stretching away to eternity, is the Pacific Ocean. Two high blunt cliffs, a long spit of basalt reef and a scimitar of sand cuddle the ocean into a wide bay. On the hillside between, my wee house is dead centre. It is like living in the sky.

Tonight I am a pioneer like my forefathers. They came from the old world to the new, land-hungry. They fought for the land through droughts and floods, bushfires, bad seasons and bank smashes. The elements won. The banks closed. Before I was born they had lost the last of the land.

I have been a long time catching up with my birthright.

The small house is built. One tree, a banksia, is nature's gift to the new landowner. The rest is up to me.

There are no near neighbours. No lights on the hill. All about the Happy House the land is wild.

I am alone in the house. Alone in the first home I have known since childhood.

Suddenly, close at hand, there is a creaking noise. My heart misses a beat. What is that little wind blowing through the new house? Stealthily, on my toes, I reach the hall. The front door has swung wide open.

Who owns this house? In my arrogance I had thought it was mine.

Who owns this house? Tonight it is the wind.

Neighbours and callers take pleasure in insulting the Happy House. Neighbour Luce calls it the 'Marmalade Jar'. Shining roof tiles rising

The Happy House overlooking Newport Beach. Mary bought the block of land on which the house was built with a legacy of fifty pounds.

pyramidally with a cute little chimneypot poking up at one side gave her that impression. She says the whole thing impresses her as sweet and tart.

Myrtle from the Opposite Hill inquires in her warm friendly drawl how the Doll's House is standing up to the sea winds. She rode her hired horse up to the gate one Sunday morning lately—a creature the very duplicate of Rosinante—and begged me to give her bread.

'Your house is so small she can hear you taking the lid off the bread-bin in the kitchen from the gate,' she said.

Gladiola Murphy has named it 'Eagle's Eyrie'—so high above the sea. My friend Bill speaks of it as the Pigeon Hole. Those who have not been to visit me refer to it as the Camp, the Hut, the Shack, the Shake-Down, Escape from Reality.

Mrs Four Eyes speaks of it as the 'Small House'. We call her Mrs Four Eyes because she uses field glasses to identify figures moving across the landscape. Through a small square cut in the lattice of her verandah she adjusts the glasses. People sometimes call her the Village Spy.

In a village such as ours there is little occupation for an old lady but to shop and cook, wash dishes and do the laundry on Monday. For such, taking a friendly interest in your neighbours is not uncommon. If you would criticize Mrs Four Eyes adversely, go and live in a village. Before long you will have your own pair of field glasses.

On the way to the Happy House I would often stop for a chat with Mrs Four Eyes. Once she praised the material in my suit. It was a gay tartan, broad black stripes on canary background.

'It's very old. I've had it for years and years,' I said deprecatingly.

Mrs Four Eyes picked up the hem. 'It's been a good bit of stuff.'

As I rather fancied it was still a good bit of stuff, I told Neighbour Luce, laughing over the incident.

Neighbour Luce is astute. 'I know why Mrs Four Eyes likes that suit. When you are going down the hill she does not need to pick up her glasses so she can identify you. She just says to herself, "That's the woman from the small house" and goes on shelling the peas.'

'Unless you build a stone wall across the land you'll wake up with a jolt some morning and find you have tumbled into the sea.'

That was Neighbour Walter cautioning me. Land-wise, loving the soil, a man who walked close to nature, Walter had something of the great Thor in his make-up. He knew the earth, how to dig it, grow things in it, save it from erosion.

Walter had been a private in the Australian Remounts through the Boer War and a corporal in France in the First World War. His brother, killed at Gallipoli, was a famous general. Neighbour Walter came out of both wars with the simple honour of having done his duty. Once his commanding officer called him from the ranks to present him to the General Officer Commanding the Anzac Corps, who knew his brother.

'With your background, Corporal, why are you not an officer?'

'Because, sir,' replied the forthright Walter, 'I have neither the brains nor the inclination.'

Great chunks of cut stone were lying at the bottom of the lot. These were the forlorn hopes of the last title-holder who had wanted to build a stone house on the land. Finance gave out and these chunks were sold to me with the lot.

Neighbour Walt was right. Erosion was evident after every rainstorm. But to build a wall required a man, a horse, and a steel rope. Walt found the man, a local. The local man found the horse. I found the steel rope.

The local man was the assistant to the plumber, the most important man in our village. He is Mr Fix-It for us all. And that doesn't just go for the plumbing.

The horse was on the payroll of the nearby quarry. His owner was persuaded to hire him to me on his day off to haul the stones into position up the rise.

The metropolis was raked until I uncovered a steel rope. Long-suffering friends were persuaded to bring it to the village in their car. 'Nasty greasy thing,' they said.

The three essentials having been assembled, work on the wall began on a Saturday morning. When I arrived some hours later work had stopped for refreshments. Twenty stones were in position and the horse was going home.

The horse had floundered in the soft clay. The horse's owner declared—and how glad I was he did—that he wouldn't have his animal's heart strained and that would be ten bob and call it a job. He'd had enough of my wall.

The working party dispersed until the following Saturday when another horse was engaged. This horse walked a straight line outside the fence, backwards and forwards, and, by some miracle past my understanding, the stones were hauled up to the correct position for the wall by the horse pulling on the steel rope. I was told the horse didn't mind this a bit.

The steel rope had then to be returned. It travelled in Neighbour

Luce's car until we reached town, where I hired a taxi to take it back to the bulk store. The cabdriver let me know his taxi was not accustomed to being hired for workmen's tools. I was late for work.

But it is a nice wall.

Visitors

Bill, my favourite cadet reporter, turned up at the Happy House with his first adult girlfriend the Sunday morning I was staining the kitchen floor. All movable furniture was out in the hall. Consequently the Happy House was not looking its best, but Bill had been impatient to see it. He imagined it would turn out to be the sort of dovecote he and Louise might borrow for a honeymoon. During the next couple of years he had the same idea with a number of different girls.

I had nursed and bullied Bill into journalism from a pup. When he came to the office, aged fourteen, he was handed on to me to be my special messenger boy. The moment I set eyes on his cheerful face, merry eyes and ready grin I thought, 'That is the youngest of the six sons I would like to have spawned.' He was later to command an RAF Mosquito Squadron flying over Burma. Don't tell me I'm not a good picker of sons.

Just now Bill was at the age where he 'gets it rather badly with eyes of a tender blue'. Louise's eyes were blue. Her family had money, a weekender-de-luxe a few beaches further on from ours, and a large car. In her entourage she brought her brother, her brother's girlfriend, and a spare young man to drive the car. They were all under twenty.

Floor-staining operations were suspended. I was distressed that everything was not in apple-pie order but Bill has the temperament to make any house a happy one and as well he was temporarily in love. At my place everything was cracker in his eyes. Louise was more critical. She had been through the love business before.

They made a tour of the house, including Slightly, the bathroom, which takes its name from the bath which was reduced because it was slightly damaged. By the method of two to a room at one time the inspection was possible.

Then we all strolled down the hill. Bill walked with one arm round Louise's shoulders and one round mine. Louise did not like that. Quite openly, she disengaged his arm from my shoulders. I had not met Louise before. Now I knew all about her.

The laughing, larky party went on its way.

In a few months this affair had fizzled out. Louise eventually married a foreign diplomat. I understand they are easier to manage than newspaper men.

Ella Shields was the first weekend guest at the Happy House. She was, literally, my star overnight.

Ella was thrilled at the idea of disappearing from the world. 'Nobody will know where Ella Shields is,' she said. 'It will be wonderful. I will simply vanish.' So she told nobody but her dresser, the members of the company, the publicity manager, the management, and the janitor at her block of flats.

Soon after midnight on Saturday we left the theatre in Ella's chauffeur-driven Cadillac. Ella lingered long enough at the stage door to sign a dozen autograph books submitted by her admiring public.

We reached the Happy House at 1.30 a.m. Guided by the chauffeur's arms, me ahead with a storm lantern, Ella gained the sanctuary of the cottage. I let her in, introduced her to her room and put on the kettle. The chauffeur faced a fifteen-mile journey back to town so I asked him to take a cup of tea with us. We had a matey threesome of tea and cakes and the chauffeur pushed off. Ella had disappeared from the world.

She slept like Sleeping Beauty. I slipped out on Sunday morning and ran to the village for a hurried dip in the surf and to pick up the newspapers. I knew Ella would like to see what the critics had said about her new show the previous night. She had varied her songs but finished up, as usual, with her favourite, 'Burlington Bertie from Bow'.

'Did the mosquitoes trouble you?' I asked when she woke up.

'No. They knew I was Ella Shields.'

For the simple country life, Ella had brought a large suitcase packed with two complete changes of slack suits. She spent the morning in navy slacks and a middy blouse embroidered in scarlet anchors, and passed the afternoon in a Mexican set printed with Red Indians.

She raced up and down the hills, taking the steepest grades for choice, loving the hard way. We paid an over-the-fence visit to Neighbour Ken, who works in the theatrical industry, accounts branch. He recognized our vanishing star. It pleased her to be identified in the Wilderness.

We romped on the beach, paddled, gathered shells. Ella looked up the hill and saw unfenced ground next to mine.

'How much land is there?'

'Five allotments, Ella.'

'I'm going to buy it all and build a little house right in the middle. See about it for me tomorrow, dear. I'd like to start building at once.'

On Monday morning we left for town by bus. Ella was bus-sick. She had not travelled in a bus for years. We got out at the first garage and travelled by taxi for the last ten miles.

'Thank you, darling. It's good we are friends,' she said as we parted at the theatre. 'Don't forget to find out today how soon I can buy that land and live a nice quiet country life for the rest of my days.' (Unfortunately the land was still in chancery and Ella could not buy it.)

Just before she vanished into the dark dilapitated theatre passage she called back to me: 'Always call the room I slept in the Ella Shields Room, won't you?'

Sport with Amaryllis and friends

'What can I give her to make her life happier?' Bill asked of Neighbour Winifred.

'A lady's light fork,' she told him. 'Ring up from the post office and order it. It will be delivered before she gets here at the weekend.'

On Saturday I arrived with Bill's latest girl. There was the new fork propped up behind the bathroom door. The Happy House is that kind of a cottage. The mythical tool shed, which is to take all the surplus out of the house, has not been built yet.

'You've been borrowing Winifred's garden fork, Bill?'

'No.'

'It's in the bathroom, you idiot.'

'That's yours.'

When he gives a present it is as simple as that. At Christmas he brought down a hammer and put it on a top shelf. He knew that I'd know he was the only person who had been to the cottage who knew I wanted a hammer.

That summer, when Bill was walking out with Amaryllis, he thought it would be idyllic to bring her to the Happy House and show her a pastoral scene.

'In return for a little slave labour you may bring anybody you like,' I told him.

Amaryllis came with a suitcase of clobber for the part. They roamed the countryside through Saturday's sunlight and, with arms interlocked, strolled in the moonlight.

Early on Sunday morning I brought them to earth. Bill was introduced to the greasetrap. He stripped to the hips for the job. Digging his toes into the hard earth, he straddled the tack.

Amaryllis was in the bathroom using up the last of the tank water for a plunge-bath. It was a hot, dry summer and the tank was at gasping point. I called out: 'You'll find an old painting frock on the peg behind the door. It will save your clothes. Your job is to paint the top of the tank.'

Amaryllis sagely decided, however, that the fewer clothes she wore the less paint she would get on them. Presently she was perched on top of the tank—a monstrous thousand-gallon tank—having been legged-up on Bill's shoulder. Her dark hair was swathed charmingly with a rose-pink scarf. For the rest, she had on a minute brassiere of fine maiden-blush crepe-de-Chine, and a pair of briefs to match. You could not tell which was Amaryllis and which was not. I passed up the old painting wrapper for her to sit on. In the morning heat that iron tank could act as a griller for her undercut.

Assiduously, Bill applied himself to the greasetrap. Amaryllis might have been a leaf in the breeze for all the notice he took of her. Once his head was down to masculine battle with mud and grease, he was not interested.

The milkman was. At the top of the path he saw the houri on the tank. In all the hours of his respectable, farm-bred youth and middle-aged life I doubt if he had ever seen anything like Amaryllis. He was pop-eyed and purple.

'Keepin' cool, miss?' he mumbled, anxious to be at ease with the company.

'I'm bloody hot,' said Amaryllis.

Amaryllis was impervious to his admiration and dumb astonishment. She had her mind on Bill. Bill had his mind on the greasetrap. As a study in human reaction to stimuli it was entrancing.

Some months later the idyll was broken. Bill joined the air force. Amaryllis, I suppose, decided that, should they marry then, she might be left with a baby. She was not the girl for that sort of thing.

Bill was now in the RAAF and he was in love again.

'May I ask her down for the weekend?' That was his way of telling me. 'Her pop thinks it's a bit cockeyed, you not knowing her. I franked you as the best chaperone on earth. He'll agree on that recommendation.' 'Pop' happened to be a prominent judge.

Well, I am the best chaperone on earth. I go to bed early and lock the door. Mine. I feed the lovers. The poor pets never need much. I don't ask them to wash up. I send them into the moonlight for walks. Encourage them to swim together in the world's most beautiful ocean. Serve them breakfast in bed. The same bed. One lover inside the sheets and one outside. They like that.

Phoebe came. The moon obliged. In her glow the lovers passed two glamorous evenings. They discovered they were the same age. What a miracle! They both liked lettuce. Amazing! Neither could endure Bernard Shaw. Cosy, wasn't it, to feel the same way towards

Mary in 1939.

Dear Dorothy Dix,

About a month ago I met a boy who is engaged to a girl in a hospital. He says he doesn't love her any more but won't tell her until she is well. In the meantime he wants me to go out with him. I don't think I should go with a boy who is engaged. Do you?

REPLY: *Emphatically you should not go about with this lad if he is engaged to somebody else. Supposing that should happen to you? Being a sneak-thief is the most horrible of treacheries. Make no mistake; this boy would drop you in the same way he wants to drop this invalid girl. He is no good. Be he handsome, rich, or amusing, he is still a most undesirable type of mankind. I urge you to break off your association with him.*

Dear Dorothy Dix,

Several months ago I became acquainted with a man who travels on the same bus as I do. He claims to like me very much but says it would be better if we didn't see each other any more. I am not sure that I love him but I do know I'd like to see him again.

REPLY: *This sounds very much as though the fellow-traveller is already married. Much better for you to catch a different bus and put all thoughts of love-making with the welcome stranger out of your mind. Don't pursue the man but take a hint from him and stay out of his way.*

Dear Dorothy Dix,

I am quite interested in a young man at my office, and would like to know how I can get to meet him. Although I pass him in the corridor he never says 'Hullo!' to me.

REPLY: *His silence indicates that he isn't in the least interested in you. If you flutter your eyelashes and look coy he will be even less interested and might, if he is an executive, get you sacked. You could say 'Good morning' as you pass him in the passage, but let it go at that, as you don't seem to know if he is married, engaged or divorced. Raves from girl employees are usually considered a nuisance by high executives.*

Few people were aware that the caring replies written to thousands of letters from the lovelorn and published in the Sydney daily newspaper, the Sun from the 1930s to 1957 under the name of Dorothy Dix were the work of Mary Marlowe, herself not lucky in love.

   The term 'Dorothy Dixer' is used today by politicians and journalists to describe a set-up question during question time in parliament. If a minister is keen to make a statement on a particular area, his staff will arrange for a back-bencher to ask a relevant question. The use of the term 'Dorothy Dixer' for such a question is based on a false premise. The letters to Dorothy Dix were real. Some Mary had to rewrite and condense but the gist of the original letter was always retained.

that old spoilsport? Phoebe did not believe in God. The Young Airman did. He felt he would be glad of that when he was up in the sky, fumbling through God's Own Territory.

On their second evening at the Happy House I was awakened at midnight by the rattle of falling iron in the garden. Possums again?

In the morning the Young Airman asked: 'Did we disturb you last night? The moon was over the hill and it was too good to come inside. We talked by the gate. We made plans. We are going to read the same books and discuss them in our letters.'

'And then what happened? Did you throw the lid of the rubbish bin at her?'

The Young Airman grinned. 'Did you hear? Sorry. We didn't know we were leaning against the tin because the moon was down. When I kissed her goodnight the lid fell off.'

Bill came to the cottage for another weekend with Phoebe before he left for flying training in Southern Rhodesia. They had known each other two weeks and were still a bit self-conscious. But he was not going off to Rhodesia without being sure of her.

They spent the day making love in the eucalyptus forest and on the beach. He had done all this before with the last girl and the one before last but, he told me, 'Phoebe is the real thing.'

The essence of their affair was almost a vow for education. She was to read deeply and educate herself to be worthy of him. He was to read still more deeply so that he would be always one lap ahead of her.

In the morning when she and I were alone she made a strange confession. 'Bill is inclined to be religious,' she said, 'in the way he looks at things. I do not believe in God. I think of Jesus Christ as another sort of Hitler. Somebody wanting to do good but always misunderstood. But when I am with Bill I almost could believe in God.'

As he clicked the gate of the Happy House for the last time before he went off to the war, Bill said with a grin: 'Look after Phoebe. I'll look after me.'

They were engaged. He had known her a month. He always thought that was long enough to know a woman before you asked her to marry you.

Phoebe came to work in my department at the newspaper. She had been at the job for three hours when Bill's ship sailed for Africa. Phoebe was overawed by the newspaper and most deferential to me as her immediate boss. At noon she came to my door to inquire should she go to lunch. That was the identical moment when Amaryllis turned up. Buoyant, breezy, in her high-pitched voice she said: 'I have a watch for Bill. How can I get in touch with him?'

Both girls were facing me. Amaryllis was half a yard in front of Phoebe and neither of them knew about the other. With undue severity and a managerial nod I sent Phoebe to her lunch. Then I dealt with Amaryllis but it was a sticky moment.

No rain for months. Sweltering sunshine and high wind to vary it. Unless you lived under the shower it was difficult to pick a cool spot that Christmas. Only the small Australian native possum which came to the Happy House could find a way to beat the heat.

I discovered him one midday on top of the rainwater tank. This fits up against the eaves, hard onto the house at the back. He was stretched full length, panting, a weary little vagrant, his back pressed against the wood, the eaves giving him shelter. In good slum vernacular, he was 'done in'. He did not care a hoot whether I saw him or not but his instinct for survival told him he was safe up there from the dog that barked on the other side of the road.

I put a shallow dish of water and some breadcrumbs on top of the tank. Poss looked from me to the food and repeated this several times before he crept out and tried the fare. In something between a hiss and a purr he told me it was not bad. I left him to it, knowing a wild creature likes to eat alone.

Poss stayed with me through the heat wave. He exercised on the roof tiles at night. We didn't sleep, either of us. He would skid down to the ground by means of the tank sometime during the dark and forage amongst the gum trees for his savouries. By day when the dogs were abroad he slept under the eaves with complete composure. A tradesman calling might try to jockey him out of his perch but Poss would merely blink bright eyes at him. Set the toughest butcher face to face with a trusting migrant such as Poss, and you can positively see the heart melt in his breast. He was a showpiece on my tank.

Sunrises, there and here

The Young Airman's letters from North Africa were, on the whole, light-hearted. He wrote as though he were still in the sky, as his heart was:

> Coming back from a raid on Cyrenaica . . . I'd been flying in cloud over the sea since midnight except when I ripped in over the coast and bombed. Near dawn I forsook the compass and used a pinking wisp of cloud to steer on. It was still murky behind me. The sun came up, new and wobbly like a newborn baby. I was wondering whether it would topple over when: 'For Heaven's sake, Bill, watch the course. You'll be taking us to Turkey.' It was my observer telling me that I was a few degrees off course.
>
> Then there are the dawn bombing raids. They are cruel. It's warm in the aircraft togged up in flying kit, but the poor Germans can be seen running like hell to their slit trenches barefooted and pulling on pants. They grovel in the cold sands of the desert while we unload our presents but I'm afraid few of the other pilots think aesthetically about these sunrises. Pity!

Then, after a long silence, the letters started coming from a restless Young Airman in Ceylon. Not enough action. He was soon bored with lazy mornings at the Colombo Swimming Club and holidays in Hambantota. He had two new sweethearts—one in the Australian army hospital there and another in his quarters near the airfield.

> Also in my bungalow are married blokes with kids at home, married who are keen for kids at home and single blokes who wished they were married with kids at home. But the arrival in our bungalow of a young lioness caused a furore that no new baby could have inspired. It has brought a new atmosphere into the place . . . grown men gambolling about the floor, more playful than the cub, sliding it across the polished wood on cushions and just watching it admiringly as it rips mosquito nets to shreds.

Dear Dorothy Dix,
My husband insists that his secretary must be attractive, with
intelligence and personality. He says these assets are important, since
she must meet people and conduct business for him. I am not a
jealous woman but I admit I am uneasy when he works with a pretty
young girl.

REPLY: *You are a jealous woman, and a silly one. Of course your
husband is right. What you should take care of is his home—making
it desirable to spend his leisure hours in, and with a cosy wife who
trusts him. These days in the business world all secretaries have to be
alert, well dressed, properly educated, with pleasant and agreeable
manners so that you and other wives can enjoy comfortable homes
and money to spend on themselves. For most women secretaries the
boss is just the man who pays their salaries. If your husband is the
kind of man who runs after women he won't stop at his secretary.*

Dear Dorothy Dix,
I have been married several years and have reason to believe that my
husband is unfaithful to me. Should I let him know I suspect him?
Can a woman overcome jealousy?

REPLY: *Some natures can't overcome jealousy but they torture
themselves and everybody near them. If you only suspect your
husband, shush yourself. If you are sure he is unfaithful then you
must weigh in the balance whether it is better to part with him
forever and be lonely and miserable for the remainder of your life, or
to be forgiving and try to win him back to you. Jealousy is nothing
but an inferiority complex.*

Dear Dorothy Dix,
I am a housewife with two small children and we are a happy family.
My husband comes home late from work and I am almost in tears
from being lonesome. His business takes him away for two weeks a
year and I almost go out of my mind while he is away. The children
keep me busy but I still can't be happy while my husband is gone.

REPLY: *What a nuisance you must be to your husband who, I take it,
has to provide the living for you and his children! It is time you grew
up. Count your blessings while you have them, because it is almost
certain that your busy, bread-earning husband must be getting very
fed up with this childish nonsense. Take a strong tonic. Hysteria is a
dreadful thing in a woman, and nothing would estrange a steady-
going husband as soon as this.*

Spindle, my pup, and the cub are playmates. No baby having its first bath ever had an audience like the one that watches the two having their afternoon play. The dog, just two-thirds the size of the lioness, always wins on points. He is smarter and out-boxes the cub. We scream at their antics. The lioness feints and stalks and uses all her cunning but she can't cope with Spindle's speed.

The lioness is three months old. She is the squadron's mascot. We are going to keep her until she eats somebody.

She slept on the mat beside my bed the other night. I trod on her when I rolled out in the dark to be on tap for a dawn show—an anti-submarine patrol . . .

Strangely, Bill's letter was in my mind one summer Sunday morning not long after I had read it. I was looking out to sea through my bedroom window. The village below was still snoozing and nothing moved on the landscape except the birds. For the first time, it seemed, since the war in the Pacific began, the sky was clear of aircraft.

Suddenly a double stream of foam ruffled the water. Something was moving swiftly, steadily, purposefully across the bay, heading south.

A sinister thought pricked me into unrest. Submarine?

Was that a cheeky Nip moving from cover to cover the quick way? There was nothing and nobody to stop him.

Should something be done about this? The double furrow moving rapidly might be a motorboat. But it might not. There was not the usual jerk of a motorboat. Suppose something serious were to happen? Life lost? Could I forgive myself?

The grocer's truck turned the curve of the road as I reached it.

'What would *you* do?'

'Phone the police.'

The opposite house boasts a telephone. The police were polite and calm. They took my address.

Twenty minutes later a fat, hearty sergeant knocked at the front door. He came inside and admired the view.

'Where did you see what you saw?'

'Coming straight across the bay from beyond the north cliff towards the south.'

'Garden Island wants you to ring. I have a car outside in case they want you to go there. Here's the number. I'll wait and admire the view.'

My heart did a flop. This was serious. Called as a witness by the navy! And what was that sound? Already! The anti-submarine bombers zooming up through the sky and crossing our bay. I had started something.

Again to the neighbour's telephone. 'I won't take your threepence for this call,' said my neighbour. 'I'm sharing on this.'

'When you have anything to report, ring us direct,' said the Garden Island staff officer. 'Don't waste time ringing the police. Thanks for your warning. We have already acted upon it.'

The big bombers overhead convinced me of that.

'Now where can we contact you for the next twenty-four hours?' asked the staff officer. 'The telephone number, please. And after that? The telephone number, please?'

The efficiency of the navy frightened me. Would they throw me in the brig if the damned thing turned out to be a motorboat?

All day the skies above the village were rumpled with aircraft overhead. I felt terrible. The country must have been put to great expense by my telephone call. 'Scaremonger, you,' I told myself. 'Don't indulge in that sort of tripe again.' Depressed, I turned in early and slept fitfully.

About midnight the telegraph wires hummed. A burring sound like starlings on the wires. 'Those little devils here! That will be a nuisance for the garden.' And again I fell into uneasy sleep.

Not starlings.

In the early bus to town next morning, over the shoulder of the man with the newspaper in the seat ahead I read: 'SYDNEY SHELLED FROM SUBMARINES LAST NIGHT.'

Bushfire

'The bush round your cottage is on fire. Take out some more insurance at once.'

The message came over the telephone one hot windy Saturday morning while I was in the office. I rang the subeditors.

'No, we have no news of fires through so far, but it's bushfire weather.'

Worse! It was nearly noon, when insurance offices close on Saturdays.

Already I held two policies, one for the house and one for the furniture, each with a different company. I rang the company that had insured the house. The man there said the company didn't increase insurance without inspection but that they would give me another hundred pounds on my property if there was anything else I could throw in.

'Right! Throw in the furniture and the fence.'

They were thrown in and a cover note would await me just on noon if I would call and pick it up. I called. I picked it up.

Chance then took me past the other insurance office. I went in and asked for another hundred pounds insurance on my furniture.

'It has probably deteriorated since you first insured with us. What else have you got to make the policy larger?'

'A house,' I said. 'The house the furniture is in.'

'That will do. I'll give you a cover note.'

I did not mention that I was now using two insurance companies for these safety measures. Why should I? Firms make their own arrangements. So, with two cover notes in my handbag, I went down by bus to the village feeling very clever indeed.

When the village came in sight I needed to feel smart. The hillside was a charred ruin. Not a tree with a leaf on it was left. The telegraph wires were down for miles and some of the telegraph posts had fallen with the trees. The ground on three sides of my cottage, right up

Dear Dorothy Dix,
I am seventeen, in love with a boy of the same age. He is away for the summer and he asked me to wait until he comes back. I have done that but now my girl friends are going away for two weeks and they want me to go with them. The boy wants me to stay at home. What's your advice?

REPLY: *Staying at home seems rather purposeless if you are denying yourself a pleasant holiday with your girl friends. If the lad is not to see you during your holiday period, why should he play dog-in-the-manger? It doesn't make sense. If he can't trust you to have a bit of freedom, he will turn out to be a bad husband. 'Beware, my lord, of jealousy . . .' said Shakespeare and you can look up the rest of that quotation in* Othello.

Dear Dorothy Dix,
Two months ago I married and now I find my husband is still in love with his ex-fiancee. He wants a divorce, but I am expecting a baby and I refuse to give in to him. I have pleaded with him to stay with me until the baby is born, but he refuses.

REPLY: *That is about the most dastardly thing I have ever heard of. Refuse the divorce until you have had the baby. The child might bring a change of heart to him. For the child's sake I urge you not to allow scenes to happen in your domestic climate. The child will be a nervous wreck at birth if you do. Try to be kind to your husband and don't enter into arguments with him. You are both going through an emotional time, and only your quiet demeanour will help keep the unsavoury matter in abeyance, which you should have during your present condition.*

Dear Dorothy Dix,
We are a group of school girls. A girl whom none of us likes makes a pest of herself by always tagging on to us. She doesn't mix with our set and we can't get rid of her.

REPLY: *It happens in the best regulated schools. Each group of girls so troubled has to find its own remedy, according to the nature of the interloper. But school girls can be very cruel and I hope you will give the lonely tagger-on every chance to win your approval. It is really ghastly to be lonely in a crowd. I detect, maybe, a hint of snobbishness in your reference to 'our set'. Could I be right? I hope not, because there is nothing more abominable in youth than that. It would place you as not well-bred.*

to the fences, was black. The ridge that embraces our hill was black. All this havoc broke on me by degrees because the air was thick with drifting smoke.

My neighbours, Win and Walt, had seen the fire come over the ridge and descend upon them—a blazing fury—and, helped by some kindly folks who live nearby, they dragged their furniture out onto the middle of the road. The fire leapt the road, consuming the furniture as it went. Yet their house was saved by tank water, good hoses, and some wonderful helpers.

Up from the beach came a squad of lifesavers and several picnic parties. They set to work to quell the fire with nothing more than wet branches from still-living trees. The milkman came up, the grocer, our good friend the plumber and some other local stalwarts. There was no fire brigade in our district so manpower was vital.

I walked across the charred ground to my home. It sat there in all that blackness like a piece of amber on a black velvet cushion. Not a whisker of the garden had been burnt. Not a blade of grass inside the fence had been scorched.

Down in the hollow below our homes little birds were flying low and crying havoc! They had been hunted out of their hill-fastnesses by the flames. Nearby, fowls and sea-birds were lying—dead from suffocation.

On a neighbouring lawn a koala and a jew lizard shared a sanctuary. On top of Win's dunny a mother possum sheltered her baby with her body as smoke plumed past. The flames had blinded her and her eyelids were gummed together. She could not see her hostess but she took her on trust. For days she drank from the saucer of milk which Win put close to her on top of the dunny.

When that kindly contact was well established Win, with her nurse's training and instinct to heal, bathed the mother possum's eyes with warm boracic until she could see again.

When I went back to town on Monday morning after the fire the two insurances were in my pocket. I rang the bank manager to tell him I was coming to see him in my lunch hour to collect my house policy, which he held against the mortgage. I explained that the insurance company had asked for it to make the new rating.

'What have you been doing?' he asked suspiciously.

I told him. There was a minute's silence at his end of the line. Then, apparently, he came out of his coma.

'You'd better come and see me at once,' he said and rang off. I didn't wait for the lunch hour.

He treated me gently, as a doctor would treat an invalid. 'My poor little friend,' he said. 'Don't you even know that you can't insure the same thing with two different companies at the same time? It's illegal. If your house and furniture had been burnt to ashes on Saturday neither insurance company would have paid you a bean.'

Failed to return

That Boxing Day (1944) the garden had been exacting. It was 4 p.m. when I called it a day. As I was climbing the home-made steps to the upper reaches of the estate, a cooee came sounding down the slopes from the front gate.

'Your news editor wants you to ring him. They won't give me a message,' called my neighbour. The office calling on my holiday? Surely they could wait until tomorrow.

When the news editor's voice came through it sounded a shade uneven. 'Thought I'd better let you know Bill is missing.'

I can remember opening my mouth so that it would be easier to breathe while the news editor went on talking. 'I'm ringing to tell you this so that you won't get a shock tomorrow when you come in. Somebody is bound to rush at you with the news. His brother-in-law has just called and asked us to help get news. We're doing all we can. I've cabled London and India and asked our correspondents there to do everything possible. We will also have the London *Daily Mail* behind us in tracing him.'

'Was the word "missing"?'

'Yes. The cable to his people said he was on an operational flight over Burma and failed to return.'

'You're sure the word was only "missing"?'

'Yes. Missing.'

Then I repeated aloud the phrase that had instantly sprung into my mind, into my heart: 'He'll be all right.'

On the eve of VE Day the Young Airman's father rang me at the office. For five months we had no news of his son. Nothing but speculation and the doubtful word of a Japanese prisoner-of-war that a wing-commander and his navigator had been taken prisoners when their plane came down in flames near the Irrawaddy River.

When I took up the receiver a half-suffocated voice came through: 'Billy is safe. I've had the official telegram.'

Early in the morning on VE Day, the newspaper's special correspondent in Calcutta sent a cable which was published under a four-column banner headline: '*Sun* Reporter Left Jap Prison to Rule Rangoon.' This was the cable:

Calcutta—Tuesday: Former *Sun* Reporter, RAAF Wing-Commander L. V. (Bill) Hudson of Kingsford, Sydney, emerged from Rangoon Gaol to rule the city for four days before the arrival of the British. The willpower that enabled him to survive the privations and indignities of a Japanese prison without mental scars carried him through his short but perilous reign as Rangoon's uncrowned king.

Hudson took control of the prisoners—about 200 British and 300 Indian and Chinese—and negotiated on behalf of His Majesty's Government with the remaining Burmese authorities. His authoritative air and brilliant initiative convinced the Burmese Defence Army that Hudson commanded a considerable force within the gaol and they handed over weapons at his command. They pushed rifles and other weapons through the bars of the gaol to the unarmed men inside. Then Hudson assumed control and declared martial law in Rangoon. He had a faded Union Jack, which had served for prison funerals, hoisted on the gaol roof at dawn on April 30, and sent a Sepoy to slip through the Jap lines to the British 14th Army. On the gaol roof he had had painted 'Japs Gone, British Here' and, when the RAF bombed the gaol, 'Extract Digit'. He put fellow prisoners to work on the airfield, and cleared a 1000-yard runway, writing a message on it in lime: 'Land on This.'

Now Bill Hudson is in Calcutta, complete with an impressive beard and a scarred knee—a memento of his crash in Japanese occupied territory last December. The Japs starved him in an effort to make him talk and then sent him to the Rangoon gaol into solitary confinement for two months for the same purpose.

At the end of that day I received a cable from Bill in Calcutta hospital which read: 'Your prayers have been answered Mary. It was an incredible experience.' Later on I received a letter which explained this cable:

Government House, Darjeeling
May 24, 1945

My Mary,
My mind has cleared up and I am sitting up taking notice. I want to start doing things again, so the first thing is to write to you.

Mary was at the airport to greet the emaciated Young Airman on his return from the war.

The last days in the clouds have worked wonders. I'm afraid I wasn't worth a bumper at the end of all the fuss. I hadn't slept for weeks and this was the first time it had happened to me. O gosh. I think they call it living on your nerves or something. It turned me from a very thoughtful young prisoner into a tormented and bad-tempered, mind-in-a-mess wretch. Everybody was very kind and so here I am almost sane again.

Today is Thursday. On Sunday I leave the clouds along with His Ex and his lady*, Pat (power behind the throne) Jarrett and the rest of the party to return to the plains and all that. Then will follow Bombay and a boat and Australia and a family party. God give me strength. Your prayers were really good for me, Mary. I used to lie back on my bed board in the cell with my head on my boot and feel them. They made me strong to take it all. Sometimes I saw you going alone into a big cathedral or something. You knelt down and prayed for me and there were only a few other people there. I know I should not say all this now. It's hardly fair. But it was so clear. The strange thing was that I felt that you were the only person really praying for me. I could not feel that anybody else I knew was capable . . .

The full story of those dramatic days was told in the Happy House. This did not happen until Bill had spent many weeks in service hospitals and rest-camps.

He went alone to the cottage with the magnificent scheme of writing a book in four days. On the fourth day he thumbed a ride to town and went to the races at Randwick.

When I went down to the cottage for the weekend I found the first four chapters of the book, typed and scattered on the couch. There were never any more.**

* Lord and Lady Casey.
** The book was completed forty-one years later. It was called *The Rats of Rangoon*.

The gentle lady

When the Japanese surrendered Bill was in Concord Military Hospital. With some fellow bed patients he went by ambulance to attend the VJ ceremony at the Cenotaph.

The following week he was back in the newspaper world and quickly got himself accredited as a war correspondent. Within days he was in jungle greens and on his way to Labuan Island, off Borneo, in a Catalina flying boat. His assignment: to fly into Japan with the RAAF and cover the Allied occupation.

Soon he was writing: 'I have known a girl here for a week. We met at a party in an air force tent—both there reluctantly. There is a rule that nurses and physiotherapists have to go out in fours and she was persuaded to go along to make up the number. I had just flown in from Singapore and was busy writing a story about the release of the Changi prisoners. She's a physio and is on her way back to Sydney on the *Wanganella*. She will call on you.' That was all.

A Gentle Lady called at the office. 'Do you know about me?' She was a shy, slight person wearing the khaki uniform of the Australian Army Women's Medical Service.

We stole the Boss's time and went out to have tea. 'I don't know much about you but Bill always sends his friends to me if he is not in town to entertain them. I think he imagines I show them around the composing room.' We talked of paddy fields in Borneo and the Dyak she had massaged. I had not imagined anybody could get a Dyak to that state of submission. This told me there was hidden strength and spiritual force in her.

At the moment she was based at Concord Hospital but expected a transfer north any day. She dreaded that might happen before Bill returned to Sydney. Neither the office nor anybody else knew Bill was coming back to Sydney just then but she seemed sure about it.

'I hoped for a week with him here. It will be terrible if I have to go north without seeing him before he goes on to Japan.'

Then I knew.

A week later Bill sauntered into my office, flung his kit-bag on the floor and perched on the typewriter table.

'I'm back.'

'Emphatically. Duty or . . .'

'May I use your telephone? Duty, naturally. I have to report things I couldn't cable.'

'There's no press censorship now, I'm told.'

'Don't you believe it.'

On my desk he spilt the contents of a small linen bag. Diamonds. He had picked them up at Bandjermasin for a pair of shorts and two tins of bully beef.

'Isn't she a honey?'

'Who?'

'This diamond. This is the one for the ring. I'll give it to her tonight.'

'You've known her one week. Wait a month. Nobody can be sure on a week's acquaintance.'

'What a quaint word! Oh, you must go to Borneo some time.'

'You're impressionable.'

'You bet! But she's what I want in a woman. She's honest.'

They gave him a week's leave. Next day he swung into my office, swept the desk clear of literary impedimenta, and sat on it. A second time he spilt out the diamond.

'Know anyone who'll make that into an engagement ring in a hurry?'

I did.

'I'm going to be married tomorrow or the day after.'

'The girl has parents I believe.'

'She has. I asked her father last night. He was a bit shaken but Mother is all for me.'

'You'd better bring her here today. How was I to know it was as serious as this?'

'You should have known. She said you made her do all the talking.'

'But we only talked about Dyaks and how elephants stamp down paddy fields. Not about you.'

'You're usually more astute. But I'll get her.'

He was back with her in half an hour. He left her with me while he went to ask the editor for two weeks leave. Two weeks. Tokyo to follow, without wife. She was brave when she heard that verdict.

'You have bought the wedding ring, Bill?' I asked.

'God, no! We need a wedding ring, darling, don't we?'

The Gentle Lady agreed.

'Get on the phone to your fellow. You must get us a wedding ring, Mary.'

I phoned. The engagement ring was not likely to be ready before the wedding, but there would be a wedding ring.

There were still plans to make, the main one being where to spend the honeymoon. It was Christmas time. Hotels, ships, aeroplanes were all booked to the limit. The Young Airman had a plan up his sleeve. Probably he had never been particularly serious about the others.

'If all fails, can we, Mary?'

'The cottage. Of course.'

So the Happy House became their honeymoon home.

Old lace

The Honiton lace handkerchief was falling to pieces. Threads, finer than spiders' webs, patterns of roses and pointed leaves were disintegrating. Edges were ravelling. It was dying.

The handkerchief had been a wedding piece of my great grand-mother. She had carried it, neatly held between her curled fingers, on her way to the altar. From that happy union she had produced a family of sturdy men, farmers by day, politicians by night, and my grandmother, Lady O'Shanassy.

Grandmother carried the same handkerchief at her wedding and produced fourteen children thereafter. She gave the men of her family to Australia. Her husband to make the laws and establish the water schemes that bear his name in Victoria. Her sons to work the land, her daughters to marry men who worked the land. She used the handkerchief at the opera in London, and in Italy, when she had gone abroad with her husband, and an Italian artist had painted her, life-size, with the Honiton in her hand.

When Her Ladyship died her daughters placed the Honiton lace handkerchief temporarily over her face. If there are libraries in Heaven she will take in the columns in the encyclopaedias allotted to Sir John's career at a glance. She knows all about that because she helped him through it all. Even the formal records descend from lofty pinnacles to admit that, 'when lacking capital and confronted by scab in his flock, he abandoned his small station near Western Port, but soon established a thriving business, mainly through his wife's energy, which became the source of a substantial fortune'.

But I think Her Ladyship would linger with pride on the final sentence in one such tome, the tailpiece to her beloved husband's indomitable career. 'From first to last his political work was marked with great parliamentary capacity, and entirely untainted by any suspicion of self-seeking.'

When the last of Grandmother's children was buried the handkerchief came to me. I like to think a little of her spirit passed on to me because I am the only woman among her descendants who has worked for a living. As I went my way, taking continents in my stride, undaunted by the world, as I was unaware of what the world can do to women alone, the handkerchief went with me.

With me it began a vagabond life. It went on the stage and it played many parts. One night it was a three-cornered cap worn over powdered hair in a play of the Beau Brummel period. A jewel—stage paste—caught it below the chin. Another night it was a cravat. It served its turn as widow's coif, hat drape, modesty piece for an over-daring décolletage in a modern gown. A Medici collar, a Juliet cowl. Sometimes it was simply a beautiful handkerchief one flirted in a minuet.

Everybody who knew about lace paid it compliments. What an exquisite thing, they said in several keys.

Stage days over, it highlighted a street gown, the one I wore when I first went to seek a newspaper appointment. It descended to brighten a house gown of black crepe de Chine. It had been washed in spirits, in tea, in coffee and at last in plain soapy water.

Stitch by stitch it died. Mended by my inexpert fingers, frayed and cobbled to the last, the time came when it cried to me for decent burial. Not a rubbish heap. A dignified end worthy of the beautiful ladies who had worn it before me.

Under the lavender bush, close by a young rosemary sprig, I made its funeral pyre. It has gone back to the earth it came from. It came to life with the sap of the flax. It has gone back to the earth in ashes.

Such should be the end of all old things that have been beautiful.

Are you worthwhile?

The following summer, while they were waiting for their baby to be born, Bill and his Gentle Lady swam in the ocean below the Happy House. I was afraid the little creature would be born in the sea. The Gentle Lady's father was also concerned. 'What are they up to, those two? I don't want to be grandfather to a mermaid.'

The child cheated them of a scheduled swim by arriving a day early. A girl. They called her Jane. I called her Jacky.

She was only weeks old when she came to the Happy House. They parked her on the couch while they went off to play golf. Bill reassured me. 'She's well behaved. Won't be any trouble. She sleeps between drinks.'

'If she wakes up and cries I'll phone the doctor.'

'If she wakes up that will be your chance to get to know her.'

After that the little creature came often to the Happy House. Best of all she liked to snooze on the wide couch in the sitting room, a soft little pillow under her head, a continent of room to kick around.

'She seems to know this place,' her father would say.

'She should,' her mother would agree.

'She'll sleep all the time,' her father would inevitably say when they left her with me. 'And don't pick her up.' Jacky did not sleep all the time or even much of it. She had to find out about me. The black-browed sprite would lie on her back on her couch in her spiritual home and raise her eyebrows, summing up the woman before her, and seeming to ask:

'Are you worthwhile?'

It was a curious feeling to be left alone in my house with a child. Girls had not interested this woman with the six phantom sons yet here was this wisp of womanhood raising her eyebrows and silently asking: 'Are you worthwhile?'

It was a searching question. I began to think a great deal about it. By all means I wanted her to feel I was worthwhile.

Some months passed. I went away for a holiday. When I came back, a day perfect for golf, found the sprite and me once more alone in the house. Was it my fancy that those raised eyebrows were once again putting me through the old test? But this time the words were different. So I read them in the silent baby's eyes.

'Who owns this house? You or me?'

'Would you turn me out of my home?' I said indignantly.

She moved her head from side to side. A woman's negative. Or was it half a negative? Her eyebrows went up and she smiled. Perhaps she was thinking, 'I can wait.' But she was profoundly dignified about it.

Then the day came when, as we were alone together in the house once more, the creature's eyebrows went up again. Emphatically a question.

'Are you asking me what I've done about it? Well, Jacky, I hope you'll decide that I am worthwhile. It would be a great relief to me if you do. Now, this is a secret between you and me. I've been to see the lawyer. So, if you can wait—if you really wait—the house will be yours.'

Jacky's eyebrows came down. She was tired of staring at me anyhow. She shut her eyes and went to sleep. I had to stay beside her until she woke up because her little fingers had closed around my thumb.